Innocent victims . . .

"Stay down!" Houril shouted, spotting two faint puffs of smoke gushing from the small craft's underbelly. He could hear McTeague's cries and finally discerned the one key word in his warning. *Missiles*. Acting on a rush of adrenalin charging through him, Houril took hold of his wife and dragged her several yards to his right, then sprawled across her, using his body as a shield. Moments later the two Secret Service agents had reached them and likewise flung themselves in the line of fire, providing an additional buffer as the two rockets thundered onto the clearing, exploding on impact and spraying a shower of dirt, stone, and charred shrapnel as they bored deep craters in the earth on either side of the once idyllic picnic site.

DEADLY SIGHTS

DEADLY SIGHTS

DEADLY SIGHTS

Ron L. Gerard

PaperJacks LTD.

TORONTO   NEW YORK

PaperJacks

DEADLY SIGHTS

PaperJacks LTD.

330 STEELCASE RD. E., MARKHAM. ONT. L3R 2M1
210 FIFTH AVE., NEW YORK. N.Y. 10010

PaperJacks edition published July 1987

This is a work of fiction in its entirety. Any resemblance to actual people, places or events is purely coincidental.

ISBN: 0-7701-0662-5

DEADLY SIGHTS

One

A wet Michigan winter gave way to a spring of abundant growth. The low-level foliage of Hiawatha National Forest was a riot of green, from the deep, dark hues of lush evergreens to the more vibrant, airy ferns that jostled in a breeze rolling inland from Lake Superior. Wildlife roamed freely beneath the canopy of tall trees that filtered the midday sun, mottling the forest floor with patches of shade and brilliant shafts of light where moths and other winged insects flitted about in vast profusion. A mother doe cautiously led her fawns down a dirt path leading to a stream that lapped noisily over a bed of rocks and moss-laden tree stumps. Overhead, chattering squirrels engaged in acrobatic feats of wonder, scampering from tree to tree, flinging themselves with graceful ease and rustling branches in their merry wake. There were birds in the trees, too, lending their own distinctive accompaniment to the forest's organic symphony.

President Richard Houril had hiked these scenic spaces in his youth, and as he sat in a nearby clearing taking it all in, dormant memories surfaced anew, bringing a wide, tight-lipped smile to his face. He'd been a Boy Scout back then, tromping about here with an almost grim determination, hell-bent on using the outing to garner as many merit badges as possible. Any appreciation of the beauty and harmony had been incidental. Now he was keenly aware of nature's hand, in awe of its power and eye-pleasing wonder. It was enough merely to take it all in, but Houril's photographic leanings demanded a certain appeasement, and when he spied a ground squirrel rearing on its hind legs atop a boulder some fifty yards away, he quietly raised his camera and deftly switched lenses from wide-angle to telephoto, giving himself a well-framed shot of the small rodent with a stand of pines behind him, well lit by the mid-afternoon sun. As the camera clicked, the squirrel cocked its head and looked Houril's way.

"Say cheese, little fella," Houril whispered, camera pressed against his face as he snapped off another shot, the last on his roll of film. Lowering the camera, he glanced over at his wife. Cecile, graying hair tucked beneath a bandanna, sat cross-legged before a checkered picnic cloth, spreading boysenberry preserves across a wheat cracker. She smiled back and held the cracker out. Houril leaned over, taking a bite.

"Ah, now this is a vacation." He finished unwinding the film and pried it out of the camera, slipping it into a small plastic container. "The Sierra Club could do a whole calendar just here."

"And you've already taken twice as many shots as they'd need," Cecile teased, finishing the cracker. Houril made a face at her, set the camera aside, and joined her on the grass. They'd just finished their lunch and he nibbled at a last crumb of homemade brownie from his plate, much to the chagrin of the ants that had been making their way toward it.

"Washington's a million miles away, it seems," Houril mused as he leaned forward, opening the lid to their picnic basket. "I can't believe I tried to tell myself I didn't need to get away."

"It took enough lobbying to get you here, Mr. President."

"Please, you can call me 'sir.'"

Cecile grabbed a twig from the grass and tossed it at her husband. "I hope you aren't rummaging for dessert, honey. I'm starved."

"You won't want to eat this." Houril pulled a jewelry case from the basket and set it on Cecile's lap.

"What on earth?" She picked the case up, pried open the lid, gasped with wonder. "Oh, Richard, I can't believe it! Oh, it's beautiful!"

They were pearls, a long strand of them, natural, with a pinkish luster. Cecile held them in the light, looking at them closely, running them through her fingers, delighting in their smooth texture.

"Happy anniversary, Cessie," Houril told her, his grin whiter than the pearls. "I love you."

"I love you, Richard." She leaned forward and kissed him, on the lips, then the cheek. "Sir," she added, whispering in his ear, moving closer to nibble the soft lobe.

Houril drew her into his arms, easing her down onto the grass. He looked into her dark brown eyes, hungry with desire. With the back of his hand he gently stroked her cheek, curled a strand of her hair around his fingers. "God, I wish to hell I had you alone...."

But they were far from alone.

Standing vigil beneath the shade of a poplar less than fifty feet away, Secret Service agents Seamus McTeague and Ken Seth took turns watching the First Couple and the surrounding wilderness. McTeague was tall, a slight reddish tinge to his hair, and a quiet intent in his pale green eyes. Through the woods he could see deer poised next to the bubbling creek, heads bent low to take in the clear water. Between him and the deer was another man, half hidden in a bed of waist-high ferns, an automatic rifle in his hands. McTeague knew there were at least four other armed men in the woods, trying to remain as inconspicuous as possible as they kept their senses alert for suspicious activity.

Seth was half a head shorter than McTeague, watching Richard and Cecile Houril with a coy sneer spread across his face. As the President kissed his wife again and stroked her hair, Seth smirked, "Gee, where's my violin?"

"Let's not be jealous, Kenny."

"Yeah, right. No way I wanna be in that guy's shoes." Seth craned his neck to track the flight of a blue jay from the poplar into the woods. "Poor bastard nearly got blown outta bed back in Maryland. It'd take more than a trip to the country to shake that off if it was me."

"That's why he's President and you're just a bodyguard."

"Mebbe so," Seth chuckled quietly. "Yeah, mebbe so."

The bomb had been a slab of deadly C-4 plastic that had mysteriously found itself smuggled into the President's East Coast retreat on Chesapeake Bay the previous weekend. Houril had had plans to get out on his houseboat for a couple of days of fishing and relaxation, but when the bomb had been discovered at the boathouse the day he was set to board, it had been determined that he should avoid the area until a more thorough investigation could be made into security arrangements around the bay. His heart set on getting away from the White House, Houril had mentioned Michigan's Upper Peninsula as a substitute getaway, and after a flurry of last-second activity a portion of the Hiawatha National Forest had been cordoned off for the week. Security measures had included a press blackout to keep the location secret. As a counterstory, Press Secretary Wyatt Howard had seen to it that word leaked out concerning the President's desire to spend the week in seclusion at an undisclosed health spa in southwestern Indiana, where he was supposedly being treated for the recurrence of an old back injury. Houril hadn't been thrilled with the prospects of deceiving the public, but he had been convinced that until more could be learned about how the bomb had managed to be placed at his boathouse in Maryland it would be in his best interests to opt for paranoia and let as few people as possible know of his whereabouts.

The First Couple was staying at a ranger's cabin near a section of the park least trafficked by the public and therefore the least apt to draw attention by the presence of not only a contingent of Secret Service agents, but also a small force of National Guardsmen and S.W.A.T.-trained sharpshooters. While the Hourils picnicked in the clearing, the Guardsmen were positioned near the cabin, where their transport truck was parked between a monstrous pile of neatly stacked firewood and an equally imposing split-trunked sycamore whose uppermost branches shaded the cabin all but three hours of the day. There was a sense of idleness among the troops, and several men had gone so far as to shed their helmets and lean back strategically across the front hood of the truck to catch a stray beam of sunlight on their faces.

"Ten-hut!"

Lieutenant Kit Garland strode into view, catching the men off guard. As soldiers scrambled to haphazard states of attention, he beelined to the men by the truck, a flash of rage in his narrowed eyes, his jaw taut.

"We aren't here to work on our tans!" he spat angrily, grabbing a loose helmet and jabbing it into the midsection of the man it belonged to. "You boys want a little color, I'll give you twenty lashes, got it?"

"Yes, sir!" the men barked in unison, eyes fixed straight before them.

"You're here to protect the President, and I damned well expect you to act like it!"

"Yes, sir!"

On the other side of the forest, more than two hundred yards from the clearing where Houril lazed with his wife, a group of hikers forged their way along a well-trod path, their steps muffled by a bed of pine needles strewn across the dirt. There were six of them: two married couples, a young child with wide eyes, and a deeply tanned docent wearing the khaki colors and insignia patch of the National Park Service.

Reaching a trailhead, the group paused momentarily and the child was led off by her mother to a coarse wooden outhouse set just off the path. From this point, three separate trails led off in different directions. One of them was barricaded with a running length of barbed wire posted with a sign declaring the route off limits. One of the men wanted to know why.

"We're doing some reseeding and redirecting the path," the docent lied as she hitched up her knee-high socks and tightened the laces on her hiking boots. She knew that the area beyond the barricade was crawling with G-men and members of the National Guard charged with vigilance over the most powerful man in the world. She also knew that one of her co-workers was supposed to be posted near the trailhead, ready to ward off any stray hikers venturing into the area without a guide. When the mother returned from the outhouse with her child, the docent asked if she had come across a park employee in the rest room. The mother shook her head, staggering slightly when her daughter suddenly pulled her to one side in an attempt to get a closer look at a fat toad hopping through the underbrush.

"Well, I think we'll head north, so you folks can get a look at the waterfalls," the docent said as she scanned the area around the trailhead one last time. Still no sign of the co-worker. Making a mental note to inquire about her when they reached the ranger's station near Cricket Falls, the woman wiped a bead of sweat from her brow with a red bandanna, placed it back in her rear pocket, and once more headed up the small group of hikers, leading them up a slight incline and around a bend that took them in the opposite direction to the President's picnic site.

Once the group had left the trailhead, there was a low rustling in the brush, caused by more than the digressions of a toad or some other small creatures. Men in camouflage, faces streaked with dark grease to ward off the sun's glare, crawled on their bellies through the protective covering of ferns and other foliage, pausing near a section of the barbed wire as their leader slowly, carefully squeezed heavy-duty clippers against the wire until it gave way. Then, one by one, the men crept through the created opening. There were at least a dozen of them, all silent, all dressed to blend with their surroundings, all armed with lightweight automatic and semiautomatic weapons. Behind them they left the twisted, sprawled body of a woman park employee, hidden deep in the brush behind the outhouse, a thin garrote still wrapped tightly around her neck.

The government sharpshooters were posted at the higher elevations, strategically placed to provide a perimeter of visual coverage taking in nearly a square-mile area surrounding the ranger's cabin serving as vacation quarters for Houril and his wife. There were four nests, each manned by two men, one relying on binoculars to scan the park grounds, while the other was constantly at the ready behind a mounted Parker-Hale M-82 rifle with a Mark-700 Star-Tron scope that would allow him to focus clearly on any potential target within range of the weapon's significant firing power.

"All clear to the north," the spotter in the nest atop Krebbs Hill reported, still peering through his binoculars as he held a walkie-talkie to his lips. "There's a group of hikers heading up the crest trail to Whitefish Falls, but they have clearance and I can make out a docent with them."

"Yeah, she's a beaut, too," the rifleman said, swinging his gun toward the hikers and focusing through the Star-Tron scope. "Look at her thighs, would you? Jesus, I'd hate to get my head stuck between those. One squeeze and I'm a dead man."

"What a way to go," the spotter cracked, lowering his binocs along with the walkie-talkie, setting down the latter in favor of a cigarette he'd left burning on a nearby rock.

The spotters, along with the Guardsmen and the Secret Service agents, were linked in terms of communication with a makeshift command post set up near the northwest corner of the cordoned-off area. The quarters were simple enough — one fair-sized vinyl tent and two smaller pups next to a parked Dodge pickup, where a dispatch radio was set up on the lowered tailgate and manned by a lean young man whose wire-rimmed glasses darkened themselves whenever he'd turn away from the set to face the other two men with him.

"So far, so good," he called out, prying away his headset and tending to an itch inside his ear.

Jack Demarrest was leaning against the pickup, skimming over a copy of the Marquette *Daily News*, which was filled with front-page news of the bomb scare in Maryland and the change in Houril's vacation plans. Demarrest was relieved to read that the Marquette paper, published less than fifty miles away from where he was now standing, contained no hint of the President's presence in the area, and, in fact, ran a few paragraphs about Houril's old back injury and speculation about the course of treatment he might be pursuing at the clinic he was supposedly visiting in Indiana. This was the fourth President Demarrest had served as part of the Secret Service's First Family Protection detail, and he wanted to make sure that Houril, like the others, survived his term of office. It was far from an easy task. During the four years that George Britland had been Chief of State prior to his defeat by Houril in last fall's election, there had been two assassination attempts thwarted during their execution and easily ten times that number sniffed out and quelled before they were able to advance beyond the planning stages. Dating back to the tragedy in Dallas that had claimed John Kennedy, the Secret Service had operated on the premise that wherever the President went he was a marked man, and today's precautions, seemingly excessive to the uninitiated, were actually routine.

Demarrest folded the paper and set it aside, then crossed the well-tracked ground to a card table set up near the large tent. Fellow agent Joe Karsen was pouring coffee from a Thermos as he sat before various maps and charts spread across the table. Karsen gestured to an empty Styrofoam cup, and when Demarrest nodded, he filled it with coffee.

"Don't see any problem letting them hike over to the lake later," Karsen said as he passed the cup to Demarrest, then pointed to the maps. "We can just shift everyone across the board and they'll have a human moat. Snake would be lucky to get close to 'em without us knowing about it."

"Good," Demarrest told him, glancing over the map.

There was a crackle of static on the radio behind the two men. Jack glanced back at the dispatcher, waited for him to finish talking with whomever was on the other end of the call.

"No big deal," the man in the wire rims assured Demarrest. "Just spotted some ranger up on Helms Peak in a landscaping truck. Checking seedlings, from the looks of it."

Jack frowned. "I don't remember anyone being charted for work up there." He looked over the charts in front of Karsen, finding those spelling out work orders for park personnel for each day that the President planned to be in the area. He found a listing for activities of the landscaping crew and double-checked the assignments. "Closest I see anyone down here for is the east end of the lake."

"Hell, it's not that far from there to the peak," Karsen interjected. "I wouldn't worry about it."

Jack sipped his coffee, still staring at the charts. Something about the report didn't sit right with him, but he didn't have time to nurture his concern over the landscaper, because his senses alerted him to yet another cause for worry. He glanced up at the vibrant blue sky, squinting against the sun's glare.

"Hear something?" Karsen asked him.

Jack grabbed a pair of binoculars from a case slung across the back of Karsen's chair and panned across the treetops as he fidgeted with the focusing ring. A little less than a quarter-mile away, he saw a speck in the air, far too large for a bird, but equally too small and quiet for a plane. Whatever it was, it was drifting with eerie grace just above the woods, heading on a direct course toward the presidential retreat.

"What is it?" Karsen queried again, now standing up, looking in the same direction as Demarrest.

"Some kind of ultralight," Jack guessed, lowering his binoculars. "And it's not ours. Put out a code seven." His voice was calm, but edged with an unmistakable urgency. He turned to the dispatcher to spread the alarm. "Air intrusion at two o'clock!"

Even before he heard the commotion at the command post, the man in the brush knew the ultralight was airborne, bound for its elusive target. The whole operation had been plotted out to the second, with all assassins given synchronized stopwatches to time their moves, eliminating the need for radio communication that might have tipped their hand to the small army standing between them and the success of their mission. As he crouched behind the profusion of thick, waxy leaves shielding him from view, the man slowly raised his 9-mm Beretta pistol and drew bead on Joe Karsen, who was unclipping a walkie-talkie from his belt. The Secret Service agent raised the communicator to his mouth, but before he could utter so much as a word, the man in the brush squeezed his trigger. The Beretta's silencer muffled the shots but did little to deter their deadly course. Karsen dropped the walkie-talkie and sagged visibly, blood already seeping through the fine weave of his suit. He tried to check his fall by reaching for the card table, but with his heart nicked and spine shattered, death came quickly and he toppled heavily across the maps and charts, spilling coffee and tipping the table over as gravity dragged him to the dirt.

The man in the brush veered his gun slightly to the right and emptied the last few shots at the crouched figure of Jack Demarrest, who had ducked behind the pickup and pulled out his gun, misjudging the direction of the gunfire so that he left himself wide open. One bullet shattered the window of the truck's cabin and two more ripped into Demarrest. The agent dropped his gun, bleeding at the wrist, and twisted to one side in pain as another shot tore through his chest.

Discarding his Beretta in favor of an Uzi submachine

gun, the grim assassin broke from cover, followed by ten others, dressed like him in combat fatigues and wearing elaborate headbands made of tooled leather studded with a maze of electronic circuitry. To a man they were all swarthy-skinned, with dark eyes and similar lean, wiry builds. With sweeping precision they swept across the compound, taking out the dispatcher with a spray of gunfire that also shattered the radio propped on the pickup's tailgate.

As the guerrillas rushed past him, Jack Demarrest lay still on the ground, bleeding from his wounds. His gun had fallen a few feet away, and when he felt certain that he'd been given up for dead, he slowly opened one eye and with equal caution snaked his uninjured arm across the dirt, closing in on the weapon. Before he could reach it, however, he was surprised from behind. One of the intruders strode past him, grabbing the revolver, while a comrade crouched over Demarrest, slipping a thin cord around his neck. Jack recovered his senses quick enough to reach up and get a few fingers between the garrote and his neck, but he was already weak from his wounds and was unable to put up more than a token resistance to the man trying to strangle him. He could feel his windpipe being crushed by the force of the cord and his vision clouded with a reddish-purple haze. The last thing he remembered was an unfamiliar voice shouting something at the strangler, who promptly let go of the garrote and let Jack drop to the ground. His own gun barked loudly, four times in quick succession. Each shot was fired at point-blank range into his already ravaged chest. Demarrest twitched from the impact of the bullets, then lay still in the dirt; the garrote was loose around his neck, but it had left deep, red marks where the cord had been pulled tightly.

There was more shouting. Then the guerrillas abandoned the ambushed command post and charged back into the forest, heading in the same direction as the low-flying ultralight that raced by overhead.

Custom-made of lightweight, durable components and powered by a specially encased motor that gave off only a minimal amount of noise, the ultralight was the perfect vehicle for the task to which it was assigned. Flying low enough to have avoided radar contact on its approach to the National Forest, the aircraft was also surprisingly agile and maneuverable. The lone rider jockeying the craft from within an almost form-fitting bulletproof shell had no problem banking from side to side or dipping below the treeline at regular intervals and successfully penetrating the security perimeter so painstakingly set out by the Secret Service and allied agencies. Now that he had been spotted, the pilot brought the ultralight up high, ignoring the faint, almost discernible jolts he felt as snipers' bullets glanced off the Teflon mesh of his shell. His full concentration was on the steering controls and the guidance compass that would allow him to match the established coordinates giving the position where he could expect to bear down on his ultimate target, the President of the United States. He knew there was little chance of him surviving his part in the assassination attempt, but he looked forward to his role and the glory of dying on his self-envisioned field of battle. Before he left this world to meet his Maker in the next, he would line the President in his sights and trigger the release of his lethal cargo, two compact, high-powered Rycho-38 missiles housed in a twin-barreled rocket launcher mounted on the underside of his dwarf aircraft.

A few more intermittent bursts of ground fire skimmed off the shell and plexiglass of the pilot's windshield, the last one managing to create a weblike network of cracks in the panel, partly obscuring his view over the blunted nose of the ultralight. He grinned, noting the readings on his instrument panel, and banked the ultralight sharply to one side, then leveled off so that, no more than a hundred yards ahead of him, he could see the clearing where Houril and his wife were just beginning to realize that more than ants were out to spoil their picnic.

The sharpshooters atop Krebbs Hill had the best crack at the ultralight, catching it in their sights just as it was coming off its bank. The spotter hoisted a Parker-Hale similar to the one used by his partner but lacking mounts. He assumed a half-prone firing position and looked through a conventional scope up at the approaching aircraft.

"Damn it, go down!" he shouted with frustration as his shots glanced ineffectively off their target.

"Looks like it's carrying some sort of missile payload," the other sniper said, peering through the Star-Tron scope.

"Take it out!" the spotter shouted. "Take the bastard out!"

Both men were staring intently at the aerial intruder when a fierce blast of ground fire strafed their nest. Dead on their feet, the sharpshooters squeezed off a pair of errant shots as they slumped to the ground and the ultra-light's shadow swooped over them. A trio of guerrillas in combat fatigues charged the rest of the way up the slope from where they had cut loose with their gunfire. They quickly took the two Parker-Hale rifles off the dead men, then left the nest and continued down the other side of Krebbs Hill, using their confiscated weapons once they had emptied their Uzis into the woods trying to thin out the ranks of government gunmen using trees for cover in their attempt to hold a strong line of defense against the assault on the presidential compound.

For Richard Houril, it seemed to happen in a quick, almost surreal blur of images and sensations. First he'd heard the clatter of gunfire far off in the woods, then a few scattered cries. He'd been lying beside his wife, and as he bolted upright he motioned for her to stay put and went so far as to pin her to the grass with his arms. Out of the corner of his eye, he next detected motion and turned to see Seamus McTeague and Ken Seth running across the clearing toward him and Cecile. McTeague was looking at the President, shouting something Houril couldn't hear amid all the growing commotion, but Seth's eyes were turned upward, looking past the First Couple and above the stand of pines. Houril turned his head just as the ultralight came into view, clearing the leafy canopy like a trout breaking the surface of a calm lake, then dipping sharply until it had straightened its course so that it was heading straight for him and his wife.

"Richard, what in the name —"

"Stay down!" Houril shouted, spotting two faint puffs of smoke gushing from the small craft's underbelly. He could hear McTeague's cries and finally discerned the one key word in his warning. Missiles. Acting on a rush of adrenaline charging through him, Houril took hold of his wife and dragged her several yards to his right, then sprawled across her, using his body as a shield. Moments later the two Secret Service agents had reached them and likewise flung themselves in the line of fire, providing an additional buffer as the two rockets thundered onto the clearing, exploding on impact and spraying a shower of dirt, stone, and charred shrapnel as they bored deep craters in the earth on either side of the once idyllic picnic site.

Under orders from Lieutenant Garland, all but four of the National Guardsmen had been dispatched into the woods at the first sounds of trouble, and a number of those soldiers were already trading shots with the enemy, sending the forest wildlife fleeing in a maddened haste toward the clearing or else deeper into the forest. Two of the men left behind stayed near the cabin while Garland advanced toward the picnic site along with a private who was carrying an Olin Stingshot, a hefty rocket launcher intended primarily for antitank fire. However, when Garland spotted the sleek ultralight a split-second after it had released its missiles, he'd quickly pointed out the aircraft to his private and commanded him to fire at it.

The bulky weapon had a limited firing range, and after the private had dropped to one knee and propped the Stingshot on his shoulder, he had to restrain his finger on the firing mechanism until he was sure that the ultralight had come to within a thousand feet of him. He was at a further disadvantage because the aircraft's movement was incredibly swifter than that of a tank, thereby restricting the Stingshot's accuracy. Once he had a bead on the ultralight, the private smoothly followed its flight, then swept the front tip of the weapon forward, anticipating the vessel's course as he fired.

"Yes!" Garland exulted when he saw the ultralight suddenly disintegrate in midflight, taking a direct hit from the Stingshot. Reduced to a blazing fireball, the wreckage of the aircraft was carried along by the momentum of its flight, showering the woods with flaming shrapnel. A series of small fires immediately began to spread across the forest floor, giving off thick clouds of smoke.

"All right, now let's take care of their ground force!" Garland shouted, giving the private a complimentary jab to the shoulder before leading him into the woods and toward the confrontation between opposing forces. "Make sure and save one of the bastards for questioning!"

The President strained against the weight bearing down on him, feeling warm blood trickling down his neck and wondering if it was his. He whispered his wife's name and she looked up fearfully at him from the grass. "Are you okay?" he asked her, and he was answered by a trembling nod. She didn't look well, though. There was a glimmer of wild terror in her gaze, which was not focused on Houril but on Secret Service agent Ken Seth, who lay atop her husband, a section of his skull ripped away by shrapnel from the missiles. It was Seth's blood and brains that Houril felt as he struggled to crawl out from under the dead man's body. Seamus McTeague was bloodied as well, but his wounds were only superficial and he was able to stand up and help both Houril and the First Lady to their feet, all the while taking care to keep his body between them and that part of the woods where gunplay still raged. Two of the National Guardsmen trampled across the grassy clearing to provide additional support.

"Let's get them to the cabin!" McTeague shouted.

Flanked by McTeague and the two soldiers, Houril put an arm around his wife and led her past the smoldering craters to the cabin, where two more soldiers were still stationed. One of them opened a side door to let Houril and Cecile slip inside. The others stayed outside, staking out defensive positions, determined to hold the last line of protection against whomever it was trying to add Houril to a list of American Presidents felled before they could complete their term of office.

Half of the guerrilla force was gunned down deep in the woods while trying to steal past the government forces alerted by the initial assault upon the command post. There were heavy casualties among the National Guardsmen and Secret Service, but they heavily outnumbered the assassins and bettered their position in the tradeoff. By the time the surviving eight gunmen in headbands had forged through the forest and into the clearing, they had a force of two dozen hot on their trail, not to mention those guarding the ranger's cabin. Caught up in a crossfire, seven of the interlopers crumpled to the grass in a matter of seconds, leaving a lone survivor standing in the field. He fired a last burst from his Uzi, then dropped from view, hugging the earth as the wild grass rose around him.

The gunfire abruptly ceased, leaving in its wake an eerie silence punctuated only by the crackling of the small fires started by the downed ultralight. Birds and small beasts added their nervous chatter soon after, and the government forces crunched the ground under their feet as they cautiously emerged from the forest, weapons held tightly, ready to fire anew at the enemy if any of them dared buck the odds.

"You're surrounded!" Lieutenant Garland called out to the unseen assailant. "Stand up, hands over your head!"

There was no response from the clearing where the man had dropped.

"You have ten seconds!" Garland warned him, signaling for his men to fan out and surround the area where the man had last been seen. "Ten . . . nine . . . eight . . ."

Slowly the intruder rose to his feet and put his hands in the air. He was shaking visibly and looked to the ground, avoiding Garland's stern gaze as the lieutenant advanced toward him, an M-16 cradled in his arms.

"Just who the fuck are you?" Garland demanded. When the man didn't respond, he shifted his grip on his rifle, pointing the barrel at the guerrilla's chest. "I asked you a question."

The man in the headband glanced up and licked his lips, as if preparing to speak. Then, without warning, his head suddenly and inexplicably exploded. Garland reeled back, stunned, and watched the headless torso remain standing a long, gruesome moment before toppling to the grass. The other soldiers looked around, dumb-founded. The lieutenant was about to demand to know who'd blown their prisoner's head off when, all around the clearing and off in the woods, a series of sporadic explosions caught him off guard. He instinctively dropped to the ground, as did most of the other men. Less than twenty yards away, he saw a body where one of the explosions had just occurred. It was another one of the would-be assassins, now headless and missing much of his upper torso as well.

The landscaping truck was still parked atop Helms Peak, but the man mistaken for a ranger was no longer out checking seedlings. He was in the vehicle, taking advantage of his unobstructed few of the distant clearing where Garland's men and the Secret Service were trying to make sense of the explosive decapitation of the entire assassination squad. Through high-powered binoculars, the man in the truck could see the confusion and it gave him a vague sense of solace. With the President safely secreted away inside the cabin, their mission had failed, but at least those men who had died in the effort wouldn't be able to betray those who had masterminded the operation.

Rowdy Trent was the man's name. Unlike the dead men below, his skin was dark, not by birth, but from constant exposure to the sun. His large frame strained tightly against the ranger's uniform he'd taken from the man who now lay dead in the back of the truck. In his lap was a strange box, looking like some cross between a remote-control device and an electronic calculator. Capable of detonating charges of C-4 plastic from distances of nearly one mile, the gadget had served its purpose well. Trent set it aside on the other seat and started up the truck's ignition. He still had a few obstacles to wrangle past before he could be clear of the park and on his way to report the unfortunate results of today's encounter. There would be hell to pay for the failure, but he wasn't going to take a fall for what had happened. After all, he had insisted all along that the attempt had been thrown together too quickly. The men had needed more training; the terrain was less familiar than what they hoped for; it was too soon after the bomb scare on Chesapeake Bay — there were plenty of reasons that should have been taken into account. He'd damned well make sure everyone remembered that he'd brought them all up when he'd first gotten the order to haul the men to Michigan. If there was any justice in the world, they'd own up to their errors in judgment and would put Trent another few notches higher up the totem pole. He was tired of being a glorified errand boy, the one who carried out other people's orders. He'd tell them that if next time they'd let *him* call the shots, he'd be able to deliver.

"Yeah, next time," he muttered, gunning the ignition and driving toward the dirt road that led down from the peak. In the distance he could already hear the wails of the first ambulances . . . .

An hour later there were still men scouring the woods in search of more bodies. A dozen paramedic vans had wound their way through the park to the clearing, and eight of those had already left with the most seriously wounded. A few of the other casualties had been whisked away in the President's helicopter for fear that they might not survive the longer, more arduous drive to the hospital. A second chopper had set down in the clearing, dispatching more troops to help in combing the terrain on the chance that there might be additional assailants either lying in wait or else trying to elude capture. And, of course, the press had caught scent of the blood and the Park Service had called in more people to man all entrances to the forest and hold back the media tide as well as they could.

The dead were laid out in neat rows at the edge of the clearing, ready for transfer into the paramedic vans once the wounded had been tended to. A priest had been called onto the scene and he walked alongside the bodies, whispering prayers for the entire group before going from corpse to corpse, lifting blankets or unzipping body bags to sprinkle holy water on bluing faces and apply ointment to the accompaniment of Extreme Unction. Off to one side were the assailants, easily discernible from the other fatalities by the blood soaking through their coverings where their heads should have been.

"I don't fucking believe it," Lieutenant Garland muttered as he eyed the slain guerrillas. He was standing with Seamus McTeague and one of the injured Guardsmen near one of the vans, where paramedics treated their superficial wounds. "Fingerprints surgically removed, heads blown off so we can't get mug shots. A neat trick, however the hell they did it."

"I got a good look at that first guy," the Guardsman said. "I'm pretty sure he was Cuban or Puerto Rican."

"Yeah? I had him pegged for an Arab," Garland said. "What about you, McTeague?"

McTeague had only been half listening and he shook his head, still looking out at the grim tableau. A group of men had just broken clear of the woods, carrying three stretchers. As they drew closer, the Secret Service agent cringed involuntarily, recognizing fellow agents Karsen and Jack Demarrest, as well as the radio dispatcher from the command post. All three victims lay still on the stretchers, which were set down near the bodies of the dead. McTeague waited for a paramedic to finish bandaging his wounded forearm, then walked away from the van, intercepting one of the men who had brought back the latest casualties.

"Those guys, are they going to be all right?" he asked.

"No way," the other man responded, shaking his head. "Poor shits didn't stand a chance. Excuse me, but I need to wash off . . . ."

McTeague let the man by, then stood staring at the

bodies of Karsen and Demarrest. He'd worked with Karsen for two years; Demarrest he'd known since they'd first joined the First Family detail more than a dozen years ago. He and Jack had been through a lot of times together, more good than bad, always living with the prospect of having to put their lives on the line. And now Jack's number had come up, along with that of Karsen and God only knew how many others. It hardly seemed possible. The past few hours felt like a dream, a very bad dream he couldn't wait to wake up from. But he knew it was all too real, and that as one of the living he still had a job to do. As he saw the presidential chopper floating back down onto a makeshift pad near the ranger's cabin, he started off for it. Houril and his wife were still waiting in the cabin, coming to grips with the nightmare their vacation had turned into. On the way, he veered over and stopped by the bodies of the dead, watching as the priest knelt over Jack Demarrest, making a haphazard sign of the cross and turning a page in his prayer book. He sprinkled holy water on Jack's face and started in on the last rites, barely looking at the recipient of his mumbled blessing.

Seamus McTeague was looking, however, and he let out an involuntary gasp. The priest, shaken from his ritualistic reverie, also glanced down at Jack and opened his mouth in an expression of awe, whispering, "Mother of God . . ."

Jack Demarrest blinked again.

Two

A tuxedoed band was giving last year's Top Forty the elevator Muzak treatment, making tunes by Whitney Houston and Prince sound like they'd been custom-composed by Lawrence Welk for the gathered Washington socialites at the Heritage Place's Gold Room. It was black tie all the way, old money rubbing up against the nouveau riche in the name of a good cause, cystic fibrosis research, and a chance to write off four or five figures' worth of income while scoring points with the powers that be under the new Houril Administration.

Jane Britland had been in Washington for five years and around politicians most of her life, but she still felt a certain unease at the predatory grace with which people attended functions like this. As she stood in line near the bar, watching the buzzing throng around her, hearing the band lend its homogenized schmaltz to the gaiety, her lips toyed with a smile that was one moment ironic, the next fluttering between condescension and embarrass-ment. She could imagine most of the people around them laughing and joking their way through the afternoon, putting on a good show for all concerned, then breaking off into pairs for the limo ride home and putting on their truer faces while they compared notes, analyzed their tête-à-têtes of the past few hours as if they were moves in some strange new variation of chess devised by Emily Post and Prince Machiavelli.

"Afternoon, Ms. Britland," the bartender greeted her. "What can I get you?"

"Ginger ale, please."

The tender winked and went to it. Jane plucked a maraschino cherry from the garnish tray and twiddled with its stem, turning it once for each month she counted off since her last drink. The stem broke on six turns, but she'd been dry for a few months longer than that. It hadn't been easy, particularly around the time of her husband's murder and her brief involvement with J. T. Aames, but she'd fought back the urges and felt stronger for it, strong enough to face the additional challenge of coming back here to the nations's capital, where her four years in the public eye as daughter of then-President George Britland had sent her life on the downward spiral that had inevitably ended up in the bottom of a bottle.

"Ah, Jane, dear, how good to see you!" a shrill voice beckoned from behind. Jane turned to see a woman flitting toward her in a garish fashion statement heavy on the chiffon with a plunging neckline, the better to showcase a diamond-crusted pendant that dipped low toward her bosom.

"Hello ..." Jane couldn't place the woman and did a poor job of bluffing recognition.

"Faye Tedrow," the older woman introduced herself, a whiff of New England aristocracy in her voice and bearing. "My husband ran your father's re-election campaign in the seaboard states."

"Oh, yes. Of course. Nice to see you again." Jane took

her drink from the bartender, flashing him a quick smile before turning back to the woman in chiffon. "My father was certainly grateful for the work your husband put in for him."

"Damned shame he lost, if I must say so. He was a fine President." Faye's eyes were on Jane's drink, as if counting the bubbles to make sure it wasn't champagne. "Tell me, Jane, how has it been for you, living out of the limelight?"

"Fine, thank you. I prefer it that way."

"Of course you do, my dear. All that pressure, living in a fish bowl. It's a wonder anyone can survive it in one piece." Faye fondled her pendant absently, the way a genie might fondle an amulet to replenish his powers without tipping off those trying to divine the secret to his magic. "But isn't it ironic that you're working for the press now, after all the hell they put you through?"

"Maybe a little," Jane confessed, having asked herself the same question countless times before. "It gives me a chance to write, though."

"With the *Post*, aren't you?"

Jane shook her head. "The *Sentinel*."

"Of course. How silly of me!" Faye tilted her head back and laughed, three short bleats, then continued the motion until her gaze had drifted to the bartender. "Another one of those wonderful gin fizzes, young man."

Jane made a move to escape to a nearby group, but Faye was back to her before she'd taken a second step. "You took over for Ellie Pandross on the society beat, right?"

"Yes, that's right." Jane smiled stiffly, sipped her drink.

"It must get to be awfully tedious, keeping track of all these people putting on airs all the time." Faye was watching the crowd, straight-faced, no hint of irony in her voice. Jane traded glances with the bartender, who rolled his eyes as he garnished Faye's fizz. As he was handing the drink to her, the band abruptly stopped playing, leaving several dozen dancers in the lurch.

"My heavens!" Faye sipped her drink, seemed to stretch her neck trying to get a better look at the bandstand, where the various players clutched their instruments uncertainly, like parts of a massive windup toy waiting to be wound up before they would slip back into their musical grooves. Jane was watching, too, and she recognized the man taking over the podium from the bandleader as Tony Frankovitch, press secretary to President Houril.

Frankovitch was a tall, gangly man with a gaunt face that looked even more haggard than usual. He fidgeted with the podium mike, waiting for the throng to quiet down. The undercurrent of whispers and murmuring showed little sign of abating, though. "Ladies and gentlemen, may I please have your attention?" His voice was a strained monotone. He pulled a thin stack of note cards from his pocket and referred to them as he launched into his address.

"At approximately twelve forty-five Central Time this afternoon, there was an assassination attempt on the President and First Lady while they were vacationing at Hiawatha National Forest in Michigan's Upper Peninsula."

The brief silence Frankovitch had secured gave way to a renewed outburst of exclamations. Reporters on hand for the benefit led the swell of movement toward the podium. Ignoring a spurt of questions shouted his way, the press secretary leaned closer to the microphone and raised his voice. "Neither the President nor the First Lady suffered any apparent injuries, but there were extensive casualties among Secret Service agents and military personnel guarding the area."

Jane flinched at the mention of casualties, spilling ginger ale onto her hand. She set the drink aside, still trembling, and wiped herself with a bar napkin, barely hearing the rest of Frankovitch's comments.

"The identities of the assailants are not known at this time, but there were at least a dozen men involved, none of whom survived the defensive retaliation of our forces." The secretary put his notes away and glanced out at the mob crowding around the bandstand. "That's all the information we have at present. There will be a press conference at the White House in an hour. We hope to have more details at that time."

"Is there any link between this attempt and the earlier bomb incident?" one reporter cried out.

Another, talking over his colleague, asked, "Is there any evidence the attack was in response to President Houril's recent change in Middle East policy, especially with regards to —"

"Sorry, no questions," Frankovitch insisted, abandoning the podium and striding quickly through a doorway behind the bandstand.

"How perfectly dreadful!" Faye gasped before draining her fizz to blunt the impact. "What a world we live in!"

Jane left the socialite to her theatrics and hurried from the ballroom, taking deep breaths to slow her heart. One way or another she was going to track down Tony Frankovitch before he left Heritage Place and ask him for more details about the Secret Service casualties. She wanted to know the fate of Jack Demarrest.

Three

There hadn't been time to summon back the helicopters that had earlier taken casualties to the hospital, so, at Houril's insistence, the presidential chopper had been pressed into service, flying Jack Demarrest from the isolated park while two paramedics huddled on either side of his stretcher, drawing on nearly their full repertoire of resuscitation techniques in a relentless effort to nurture along that frightfully thin line between life and the death that Demarrest had thus far cheated. They'd swathed the deep, wicked gash in his neck from the garrote and had given him an emergency tracheotomy so that they could get oxygen to his lungs. His bullet wounds had been dressed as well, but there was nothing they could do about the internal bleeding until Demarrest was in an operating room. Both his pulse and blood pressure were dangerously low, and except for that brief span of seconds during which his blinking had alerted McTeague that he was alive, Jack had been unconscious since he'd been found with Karsen and the dispatcher back at the command post.

Marquette City Hospital was a madhouse of activity even before the helicopter arrived. Reporters trying to glean fresh information had besieged the building an hour earlier, and their numbers increased when it was learned that Hiawatha National Forest had been declared off limits to the public and press alike while the manhunt for other suspects took place. Houril had been forewarned of the situation, and after Demarrest was taken from the chopper, he made only a short appearance in the doorway of the passenger compartment, waving out to a coterie of photographers on the helipad anxious for a shot they could wire back to their papers as sure evidence that he had indeed survived the assault in the woods.

Seamus McTeague asked for, and received, permission to be part of the Secret Service force that would stay behind at the hospital, and began his vigil in a waiting room down the hall from the operating wing. However, there were close to a dozen other people in that room, relying for diversion on a television set mounted high up near the ceiling. Pat Sajak was trading quips with "Wheel of Fortune" contestants, and McTeague couldn't handle either the onscreen inanity or the rapt attention it was getting. He left the waiting room and took a doorway outside to a terrace overlooking the city. Marquette, though the largest city in the Upper Peninsula, was still small by most standards, with a population of little more than twenty thousand. The downtown area had a few high rises and busy streets, but McTeague could see, less than a mile away, the sprawl of wilderness that made up most of this part of the state. It struck him as odd that here, in such a quiet, out-of-the-way part of the globe, the course of history had nearly been altered more significantly than by any number of political maneuverings taking place in capitals throughout the world. And there was still a chance that the repercussions of the attack would have an impact every bit as dramatic as if Houril had been killed. Once the identity of the assassins could be established, fingers would be pointed and the cries for retribution would be loud and persistent. In many ways McTeague knew that the crisis was far, far from over.

Normally, McTeague found his pipe to be a calming tool, what with the slow, meticulous ritual of cleaning the bowl, packing in a fresh thumbful of tobacco, and tamping it just right so that he could get a steady draw, but as he lit up out on the terrace, the smoke seemed excessively harsh and bitter, perhaps reminding him too much of the smell of the burning ultralight back in the forest or the cordite aroma left in the wake of gunfire. He finally put the pipe out and slipped it back in his pocket, returning inside and contenting himself with pacing the corridors near the operating room where his close friend had been taken nearly an hour before.

Inside the operating room, a team of three surgeons was at work on Demarrest, each one a specialist attending a different life-threatening wound with the help of assistants and a team of nurses. The anesthesiologist stood off to one side, monitoring Jack's condition in response to the injections he'd received to ensure that he remained unconscious throughout the operations. Everyone in the room was dressed in green, with bluish caps on their heads and surgical masks across their lower faces, giving them a uniform appearance, like insect drones united in their service to the queen.

While one surgeon worked intently at sealing a puncture in Jack's lung, the doctor next to him concentrated on using forceps to retrieve a flattened slug buried in muscle tissue near an already-stitched area where the patient's spleen had been removed as the source of the internal bleeding. A nurse held out a flat metallic pan, where nine other bullets already lay in bloody pools. The latest slug to be removed clanged ominously against the pan as the second surgeon let go of it so that he could turn his attention back to yet another of the deadly projectiles.

"What about this one near his spine?" he murmured, pointing out a bullet fragment with the tip of his scalpel. The doctor next to him finished with Jack's lung, then shifted his gaze to see where the other man was pointing.

"Too risky," he said. "Harv, what do you think?"

Harv was the third surgeon, working on the damage Jack had sustained in his throat. He didn't bother to give the wound in question more than a cursory glance before replying, "He'll be lucky to pull through as it is. Let's not stack the deck against him any more."

One of the nurses was off near the far wall, weighing reddened swabs on a scale calibrated to measure blood loss. "He's still down," she reported to the others as she hurried to a nearby supply stand, where units of blood had been readied for just such an emergency. She took one of the plastic bags and brought it over to the operating table, replacing the pint bag that had already been transfused into Jack's body through an intravenous needle.

"If we pull this guy through," the first surgeon said as he waited for a nurse to clean blood from his clear gloves, "I think we ought to take a crack at Humpty Dumpty . . ."

Four

"Well, that makes it official."

The short, squat young man snapped off his ham radio and pushed himself away from the table it rested on. He was sitting on a swivel chair with casters, allowing him to swing about without undue effort and face the other three men in the room, all older than he, looking his way expectantly.

"President's definitely okay," he said, confirming Rowdy Trent's earlier disclosure. "His old lady, too."

Trent shrugged. "What else is new?"

The other two men were Jake Morrison and Hal Dewez. Both in their mid-fifties, they shared other similarities in appearance as well. Stocky builds, large eyes under thick brows. But despite their similarities, in temperament they were almost direct opposites, as if they were part of a play in which each acted the alter ego of the other. Morrison wore a Brooks Brothers suit, gray herringbone, over a silk shirt, and carried about him an air of quiet authority. His eyes were pale, almost bored in their expression as he reacted to the official word that their mission had failed. By contrast, Hal Dewez paced excitedly in his combat fatigues, brown eyes sparking with furor. Without warning he lashed out with the back of his hand, swiping at a Rolodex on top of a file cabinet next to him. They were in a windowless underground bunker, and the plastic container shattered loudly against the reinforced concrete walls, sending its file cards fluttering to the floor like doomed white moths.

"We trained those bastards for eight weeks!" he railed at Trent. "Eight fucking weeks!"

Trent held his ground, refusing to look away from Dewez. However, the resolve he'd been trying to muster on the way back from Michigan left him. He said nothing, letting the sullen sneer of his face speak for him.

The dispatcher, post-adolescent baby fat still layering his face and arms, scrambled from his chair and crouched over the fallen cards, looking them over intently as he picked them up, hopeful that this ploy would keep him clear of Dewez's wrath and yet still in the room, where he could see what might happen next. Like several of the other young recruits in the employ of Dewez and Morrison, he was eager to please, to learn, to earn his way up the ranks of the organization.

"Don't go blowing a gasket, Hal," Morrison told his partner calmly. When the dispatcher had gathered up the stray cards, Morrison took them and motioned for the youth to throw the broken Rolodex in the trash on his way out of the bunker. The dispatcher, whose name was Billy, did as he was told, hiding his disappointment. Once he was gone, Dewez faced off with Morrison.

"We're out two million bucks because those fucking olive-eaters couldn't storm a goddamned picnic, and you want me to play calm?"

"You weren't there, man!" Trent snapped, finding his

voice. "They were up against a friggin' army. Shit! Custer had better odds."

"Balls!"

Trent turned to Morrison. "At least the headbands took care of 'em. We didn't blow our cover."

"Thank God for small favors, I guess." Morrison tugged idly on the lapels on his suit, then flicked a bit of lint off his sleeve as he told Rowdy, "Why don't you go make sure Billy doesn't go running around here like the town crier?"

"Yeah, okay, but I just want you to know that it ain't my fault this whole thing backfired." Rowdy was on a roll, reciting his practiced spiel. "I said all along we should have waited for him to play into our hands instead of going out after him. I —"

"No one's blaming you, Rowdy, all right?" Morrison put a hand on Trent's shoulder, eyed him avuncularly. "In retrospect it looks like maybe we should have heard you out."

Trent softened, unprepared for such stroking. A flush of embarrassment crept through his tanned face as he stood dumbly before his superiors, once more at a loss for words. Morrison flicked him a lazy salute and Trent returned the gesture with more fervor, then strode purposefully out of the room.

Left alone, Morrison and Dewez were silent a few moments. Morrison tapped the file cards into a neat stack and skimmed through a desk drawer for a rubber band to wrap around them. Besides the radio setup, desk, and file cabinet, there were a pair of home computers in a corner and a Naugahyde sofa along one wall beneath a corkboard filled with a messy collage of notes, clippings, and other information. The other three walls were lined with maps, more than twenty in all, each one matted on cork so it could be stuck with pins as the need arose.

Dewez was the first to break their silence, lighting up a cigarette and talking through its smoke.

"Ten years we been putzing around on nickel-dime shit," he muttered bitterly. "This year was gonna be different, right? Join the heavyweights. What a laugh!" He looked at Morrison as he tapped ash onto the floor. "Or maybe you think Hoummari's gonna pay us anyway . . ."

"No, she won't pay," Morrison conceded. "But we have other clients besides Hoummari. I suggest we quit whining and move on."

Dewez took a long draw on his cigarette, then dropped it on the cement floor and crushed it under the heel of his combat boot. When Morrison strolled to the nearest wall and started looking over the maps, Dewez joined him, temper in check. "Look, it ain't every day I lose out on that kinda scratch. But you're right. Fuck it! Let's scare up something else."

"Our Syrian friends will be crossing the border tonight, won't they?" Morrison asked.

"Yeah. It's all set for two A.M., no problem."

"And we have the course ready for them?"

Dewez nodded. "What's the terms?"

"They'll pay half up front, half when they get the gas."

"Two hundred grand all told, right?"

"That's right."

Dewez started on another cigarette, blew a smoke ring and watched it slowly grow, then fade, under the glow of the overhead lights. "How much of that gas do you figure we can get our hands on, anyway?"

"Depends," Morrison said. "If we can pull the raid off without a hitch, I'd say plenty. As much as we can carry, most likely."

"How much do the Syrians want?"

Morrison looked hard at his partner, trying to figure out what he was getting at. It wasn't difficult. "Well, Hal,

I think we just might be able to satisfy the Syrians and still have enough left to cut a deal with Hoummari."

Dewez grinned. "I was hoping you were gonna say that ..."

Five

Jane strode through the commotion of the D.C. *Sentinel* newsroom, bypassing her cubicle and acknowledging fellow staffers with vague nods on her way to the office of J. V. Pierce, the paper's longtime editor in chief. Even before knocking on his closed door, Jane could hear him bellowing through the frosted glass about the latest technical foul-ups on the *Sentinel's* newly installed computer system, once again threatening to throw the whole fleet of overrated hardware out the tenth-floor window and revert back to the good old days of manual Underwoods and lead-set printing.

"What's your problem?" he growled at Jane after calling her into his office. Bald and potbellied, Pierce relished his roots in what he considered to be the journalistic heyday of his youth, when he'd peddled newspapers on street corners during the Depression prior to getting in on the ground floor at *Life* and working his way up that magazine's staff ranks until its initial folding in 1972, at which time he'd jumped over to the *Sentinel* with a promise that he'd give the *Post* a damned good run for the circulation sweepstakes in Washington. He lorded over his paper like an overzealous father, demanding unquestioned loyalty and dedication above and beyond the call of duty from his employees, with whom, on principle, he would never express satisfaction.

"It's about what's happened up in Michigan," Jane began tactfully, knowing she had wandered onto thin ice the moment she'd entered the room, given Pierce's foul mood.

"What about it?"

"I've got a slant on the story no one else can touch," she told him. "Let me off society so I can run with it and I'll guarantee you page-one copy."

Pierce pried off his bifocals and fogged them inside his mouth before rubbing them clean with the end of his tie. He looked up at Jane with his weak eyes, snorting derisively through his nose. "You think I was maybe born yesterday?"

"Beg pardon?"

"What you really want is an excuse to go check up on that Secret Service agent..."

"Demarrest," Jane corrected, "Jack Demarrest." She hadn't like Pierce from the moment she'd met him two months ago, and although she'd done an admirable job of controlling her distaste for him, it had been an irritating task and she was losing patience with the need to kowtow to him.

"Demarrest," Pierce repeated. "That's right. He's the one you were 'involved' with last winter, isn't he?" He saw that Jane was ready to say something, but he cut her off with a wave of his pudgy hand. "It was in one of our own columns, for Chrissakes! I do read this rag before I put it out, you know."

"Yes, I know," Jane retorted, feeling her last few reins of resistance straining inside her. She was determined to go to Michigan, regardless of what Pierce said, and that determination cut the reins. She stopped shifting from foot to foot as she stood before Pierce's desk and leaned forward, putting their equally forceful gazes on the same level plane. "Look, can I go there as part of this paper or not?"

Pierce eased back in his seat and chuckled as if he found her outburst amusing. "My, my, she can't even say *please?*"

"Mr. Pierce, I asked you a question."

"And I'll give you an answer, young lady," Pierce shot back. "Even if I thought you could handle an assignment like you're proposing, I already have this whole fucking story covered from more angles than we'll have space for. Savvy? My best men are already on it."

"Your best *men?*"

"Spare me the Gloria Steinem routine, okay? You know what I meant."

"No," Jane retorted. "Maybe you had better explain it to me."

Pierce sighed, looking away from Jane and leaning far enough to one side to liberate an inch-thick cigar from a humidor next to a paperweight in the shape of a mini- ature typewriter. "You've been on this paper only two months, Ms. Britland. You want to go page one, you'll work your way up to it like everyone else had to." All this was said with his eyes on his cigar and the tiny shears he used to clip its tip. When he finally looked up at Jane, he'd composed himself into a state of menacing serenity, Dr. Calm ready to turn into Mr. Storm at the slightest provocation. "I put you on staff as a favor to your old man," he told her matter-of-factly. "Don't press it, okay?"

The editor lit his cigar and reached for some news copy in a wire basket next to his telephone. As far as he was concerned, his discussion with Jane was over. Jane decided the feeling was mutual and she started for the door. Before letting herself out, she turned back and waited in the doorway until he felt compelled once more to acknowledge her presence.

"Why don't you file that favor up your ashtray, Mr. Pierce," she told him. "I resign."

Without waiting for his response, she left the office and slammed the door shut behind her. On the way to her cubicle, she stopped off at the teletype machine and helped herself to one of the empty ream boxes. At her desk she began packing her things into the box, already feeling a sense of relief at the decision she'd made.

"Told the man off, you did," Tracy Comstock called across to her from the city desk, keeping her voice to a low whisper that was half lost in the clatter of the teletype and the ringing of phones. "Congratulations! I hope I get the nerve to do the same thing before he fires me."

Jane thanked the other woman as she hurriedly emptied her desk, pausing only long enough to put a call through to Dulles International Airport and cradle the phone between her chin and shoulder so she could keep working while she talked. When an airline representative answered the phone and asked what she could do for Jane, Jane requested departure times for the next few flights from Washington to Michigan's Upper Peninsula.

Six

Jack Demarrest dreamed he was walking down a dark street just after nightfall, no one around, no lights in the tall buildings that surrounded him. He looked up, saw stars in what little sky he could see past the tops of the skyscrapers, where branches stemmed out, full of leaves, as if the buildings were in fact gigantic trees. As he was looking up, head tilted back as far as it would go, something burst from the shadows, making a sound like fluttering wings. Before he could react, Jack felt hands around his exposed neck, trying to choke him. He began to struggle, swinging his arms backward so his elbows would slam into his attacker. But there was no one behind him. The hands around his neck were not connected to the arms of an assailant; they had a life of their own, like the wings of some hideous moth that had lighted upon him with foul intent. He was about to reach up to pry the hands away when he heard more fluttering from a darkened doorway beside him. More hands flew out at him, grabbing his wrists and ankles, dragging him to the street. He landed softly and realized the street was paved with moss, wet with dew. The hands were overpowering and somehow they were carnivorous, because he began to feel a sharp, stabbing pain in his neck, as if the hands that were strangling him were also trying to bite through his flesh, as if to get at his Adam's apple. He wanted to shout but the pressure against his throat was too intense. He could only stare up past the leafy canopy of the buildings, where the stars twinkled indifferently.

When he awoke, the tightness in his throat persisted. He saw that he was in the recoverey room of a hospital, hooked up to several suspended bottles by way of tubes running into his veins. There was some sort of mask over his face, with a tube of its own running down into his throat. He could hear the sounds of several machines surrounding him on the bed. One beeped dully, the other wheezed faintly in time with his own breathing. A plastic curtain surrounded him, blocking his view of the rest of the room, where he could hear other equipment, the hum of air conditioning, and the soft voices of nurses trying to appease other patients, who groaned with sounds of pain that vaguely reminded him of his brother weeping quietly on the way to the hospital the night he'd broken his arm falling from a tree.

A spate of questions began running through his head, but he was too exhausted to dwell on them, and for much of the next hour he drifted in and out of sleep. A Filipino nurse came in several times, checking his pulse and blood pressure and changing one of the bottles he was connected to. She smiled at him when she saw that he was awake and patted him on the forearm, telling him something he couldn't comprehend in his drowsy state. She was gone by the time he felt clear-headed enough to respond, so he lay silently in bed, trying to make sense of things. Thinking back, he recalled spotting the ultralight and the first phase of the guerrilla assault, but beyond the point where he remembered the hot sting of gunfire plowing into him things went black, save for a few words of whispered Latin that he couldn't recall hearing since his youth as an altar boy.

When the nurse returned again, it was with two orderlies, who carefully rolled his bed from the recovery ward and down a hallway to an elevator. As they went up to another floor, the nurse assured him he was out of immediate danger now and was being transferred to a regular hospital room. There was more he wanted to know, but with the tube down his throat and intravenous needles in both arms and hands, he had limited movement with which to get the nurse's attention. Fortunately, when he was left in his new room, alone, the nurse turned on the television set in the corner, and at the top of the hour there were several news stories concerning the attempted assassination. There were helicopter shots of the park, maps of the region, and footage at the hospital, all displayed over the news anchor's account of what had happened. Jack felt a surge of pride at news that the President and First Lady had emerged from the assault unscathed, but the elation was quickly balanced by a sense of frustration and anger upon learning that the identity of the perpetrators had yet to be established. Mention of the casualties included names of the slain Secret Service agents, and Jack mourned the death of his friend Joe Karsen and the other men he'd known through his years on the force. He found solace when he didn't hear Seamus McTeague's name among those of the dead. Then, as if in answer to his thoughts about his longtime colleague, Jack saw McTeague entering the room along with a short, elderly doctor wearing a close-cropped white beard and dark, owlish horn-rimmed glasses. The two men were whispering to each other, barely within Jack's earshot.

"He's very weak, so don't stay long," the doctor was telling Seamus, who nodded, then looked to Jack, forcing a grin.

"Hey, sport. Sandbagging it, huh?"

Jack managed to grin back around his mouthpiece and raised one hand enough to flip McTeague the finger, wincing as he did so because the needle in his hand scraped a nerve.

"Hi, Jack. I'm Dr. Glover," the bearded man told him as he switched off the television set and looked over the clipboard at the foot of Jack's bed. "I'm one of the mob that put you back together. It was touch-and-go there for a while, but you're going to make it, no problem."

Glover's confidence was assuring but not specific enough for Jack. Enduring the needle pain in his hand, he raised his arm so he could point to the apparatus strapped across his mouth.

"You'll be on the respirator a few days," the doctor told him. "You had a punctured lung and your throat's in bad shape. The paramedics had to do a trocar tracheotomy, so you might have problems talking when you're off the respirator."

Jack lowered his hand and eased back in bed, realizing how much of his breathing was being done for him by the machine, which had been wheeled along with him into the room. A second realization came over him when he tried to use his feet for leverage while he shifted in bed. He craned his neck slightly, looking down and seeing his legs and feet beneath the covers, resembling white hills and peaks on a cotton landscape. Despite his efforts, they remained equally immobile as fixed bumps on the earth.

"I'm sorry, Jack, but you still have a bullet pressed against your spine." Dr. Glover set down the clipboard. "It's blocking nerve impulses to your legs."

Jack continued to stare at his uncooperative limbs,

stunned by the news. McTeague looked to the doctor. "You're saying he's paralyzed?"

"From the waist down, I'm afraid so," Glover said. He looked at Jack. "At some point down the line we *might* be able to go back and extract the bullet. There's a chance that would reverse the paralysis."

Jack stared at the blank screen of the television for a lingering moment, coming to terms with the prognosis. There was a lot more he wanted to know, but one question struck him as the most pressing at the moment. He weakly raised his hand again, gesturing for something to write with. Glover unclipped a pen from his coat pocket and gave it to Jack along with a piece of scrap paper from the clipboard. Demarrest had enough strength to scrawl four wobbly letters.

"Odds?" the physician read. "What — that you'll be able to walk again?"

Jack nodded.

"I'd be lying if I told you I knew. It's too soon to say. At this point I think it'd be best if we took it one step at a time. We just snuck you away from death's door. I think that's a good start."

Anger, denial, helplessness. Jack felt all three emotions grappling for control of his thoughts. *Fuck this shit! I'll go back to sleep and wake up a healthy man. It's just the drugs; they pump you with so many different things there's bound to be temporary side effects. No way I'm going to end up like Uncle Bill, stuck in a wheelchair, hiding toothpick legs under a wool blanket. No, not me. Not Jack Demarrest.*

The pen broke in Jack's hand and he dropped the two pieces. Dr. Glover foresaw Jack's next move and leaned forward, pinning his patient to the bed as he shouted for McTeague to get a nurse. Jack struggled, but he was too weak to overpower the surgeon. The nurse came back in with McTeague, answered Glover's command for a sedative by tracking down a syringe loaded with Valium. Jack closed his eyes as he felt the needle's sting. Even before the drug took effect, he stopped struggling. *Why bother?* he thought.

Seven

The green Dakota hills were dotted with grazing cattle. In the valley between two of the larger gradations was an old dairy farm, consisting of a modest-looking ranch house that appeared to be a good fifty years newer than the ramshackle barn resting dully on a slight knoll, surrounded by smaller rundown buildings yearning for fresh paint and the nurturing of a good fix-it man. Horsemen were out in the fields, watching over the herd as it loitered in place. Most of the cows were working their cuds in time to the swishing of their tails, but a few of the beasts contented themselves with lounging in the shade of scattered elms that looked as if they had strayed from a thick woods located just beyond the next rise. It was a timeless setting, and save for an antenna atop the farmhouse and power lines running above a nearby two-lane road, this might have been a turn-of-the-century locale, lorded over by hard-working cowboys who one day would become the inspiration for a cigarette company's ad campaign.

But the ranch hands were far more than mere Marlboro

men. When a long, two-tanker delivery truck lumbered down the country road toward the farm, one of the cowboys watched it carefully before leaning to one side and reaching into his saddlebags. There, rather than rope, tobacco, or some other ware of the range, were an Uzi submachine gun and, next to it, a walkie-talkie. The horseman plucked up the walkie-talkie, activating the call mode as he turned his gaze back to the delivery truck, which was stenciled with the logo for a Canadian dairy outlet.

"The milkman cometh. . ."

His call went through to the main gate of the ranch, where Rowdy Trent and Billy were clearing away clots of tumbleweed that had become caught in the fence during the previous night. Billy was unarmed, but Rowdy wore a tooled-leather holster with the butt of a .357 Magnum sticking out like the head of a snake. Trent pulled down one last tumbleweed and let Billy put it in a trash bag while he swaggered to a spot near the gate where he had a clear view of the truck's driver.

"Rollover Seven," the driver said as he leaned his head out the window. "Electric Rodeo."

Trent smirked as he unlocked the gate and swung it open on a small wheel that left a curved track in the dirt. "What ever happened to 'Open saysame'?" he chided the driver.

The man in the truck had shoulder-length brown hair and a Neanderthal jawline. He glared at Rowdy as he drove in. "Ain't *my* idea to play around with fucking code words," he grumbled. "I got enough things to worry about without I gotta make like Man from U.N.C.L.E. whenever I come here."

"I don't see you bitchin' when they pay you."

"Yeah, yeah."

The driver circled around to the back of the old barn, where another pair of ranch hands was already opening the half-rotted wooden gates leading to an area apparently built beneath the barn, inside the knoll itself. The wooden doors proved to be purely decorative, because the two men next had to contend with a more formidable barrier, steel-plated and locked by a computerized system requiring yet another code. The steel doors pulled apart on rollers like horizontal jaws and the driver eased his vehicle into a huge underground cavity roughly the size of a small airplane hangar and made of sectioned concrete panels. Several passageways led out from the main chamber, linking all the surface structures from below the earth.

The driver climbed down from the truck's cab as the gate doors closed behind him and the ranch hands, who immediately clambered aboard one of the vehicle's tanks with tool kits. As they began working on the bolts that held the tank seams in place, they were joined by four other workers coming out from one of the tunnels along with Dewez and Jake Morrison.

"Right on schedule," Dewez said, shaking the bearded driver's hand. "No problems?"

"Nah. Border was a piece of cake."

"Good, good," Morrison said, eyes on the milk truck. With six men working on the tank, it wasn't long before the seam was cracked and, with a serpentine hiss, the two halves were parted, revealing an inner cavity where six men huddled. They were, like the guerrillas who had died in Michigan, dark in complexion, wearing loose-fitting clothes. One by one they stepped down to the floor of the chamber, moving awkwardly due to the stiffness of their joints after the long ride in such tight quarters. As the new arrivals stretched, Dewez and Morrison walked over to one of them, a young man who was stretching his torso and taking long, deep breaths.

"Sorry we couldn't bring you in first class, Argvai," Morrison told the man.

"We know the need for caution." Argvai's English was fluent but choppy, thick with the accent of his homeland.

He waved to indicate the five men beside him, as well as another six Syrians being liberated from the second delivery tank. "These are our best men. I hand-picked them."

"Look like a Mediterranean Dirty Dozen, all right," Dewez cracked, looking the men over. Some of the Syrians returned his gaze with looks of hostility, while others glanced away.

"Six months they trained at our private camps," Argvai boasted. "They are at one with the cause, ready to shed blood in the war against our enemies."

"If they're as good as you say, the blood they shed won't be their own," Dewez said. "You won't mind if we run them through a bit of our own training?"

"Whatever is best for the cause," Argvai replied, reaching into the folds of his shirt for an envelope. "And I have the first payment we agreed on."

Morrison took the envelope and peered at the currency inside it. Hundreds and fifties, almost an inch thick. He cast a sidelong glance at his partner. Dewez was eyeing the money, too. Both men smiled.

Eight

The television was off in the waiting room, where two women sat near a potted plant, one reading, while the other stabbed at strands of colored wool with knitting needles, making a pair of pink booties. When Seamus McTeague walked in, fidgeting with his pipe, the knitting woman coughed to get his attention and pointed out a no-smoking sign posted on the wall. McTeague apologized and pocketed the pipe in favor of a month-old magazine left on one of the empty chairs. He was flipping through pages when a familiar woman stepped out of the corridor elevator and smiled at the sight of him.

"Seamus!" Jane said, entering the room. They embraced briefly, platonically.

"It's been a while, Jane," McTeague told her. "I didn't expect to see you here."

"I came as soon as I could. How's Jack?"

McTeague sighed as they broke their embrace. "He's been through the wringer."

"Can I see him?"

"He's getting a sponge bath and having his sheets changed," McTeague told her. "How'd you get off work to come here, anyway? Or are you here on assignment?"

Jane shook her head. "I quit."

"Jane ..."

"It was a dead end, Seamus. I wasn't up to oinking with the 'good old boys' to get ahead."

A belt beeper whined to life at McTeague's waist. He turned it off, telling Jane, "I have to go make a quick call. Good seeing you, Jane, but I still say that job was a step in the right direction, all things considered."

Jane eyed McTeague with a flash of anger. "I've kept my act clean all year, I'll have you know."

"And I'm glad to hear it, believe me." The bell for the elevator rang outside the room and McTeague called out for someone to hold the car. He smiled back at Jane. "Listen, give my regards to your sister and the rest of the family, okay?"

"Will do, Seamus. Good seeing you, too."

McTeague left Jane in the room. She noticed the two women staring at her and stared back. The woman with the book retreated back to her reading, but the knitting woman was less easily intimidated. "You're someone famous, aren't you?" Before Jane could reply, the woman tapped her head with one of the knitting needles as if it were a magic wand meant to jog her memory. "Yes! You're that daughter of President Britland, right?"

"Former President," Jane corrected. "Yes, that's me."

"And that man — he was with the Secret Service?"

"He still is."

Jane excused herself and sought out the nursing station across the hall. As she waited for someone to help her, she could hear the two women behind her whispering as if they thought she couldn't hear them.

"She's the one with all the problems," the knitting woman confided. "You know, the drinking, her husband being murdered and all. Cost her father the election with all that bad publicity, if you ask me."

"I didn't," the other woman retorted.

Jane was no stranger to such gossip and insinuation. All through her father's unsuccessful campaign there had been an undercurrent of rumors and innuendos regarding her problems, and George Britland's outspoken defense of Jane had only exacerbated the issue. Of course, her husband's murder had occurred after the elections and wasn't a factor, but it had provided more fuel for gossip columnists looking for new angles after Jane had successfully undergone treatment at a Maryland substance-abuse clinic. In recent months, as her prominence in the media had dwindled following Britland's departure from office, Jane had found it easier to come to grips with public exposure, but there were some wounds she doubted that she would ever get over, especially when she encountered people intent on dwelling on her past.

Jack was off the respirator, two days ahead of schedule, but his throat still felt raw and ragged, bound in gauze so tightly it hurt when he swallowed. He sat up in bed, wary of his precarious balance, ashamed at having to be washed by the nurse, a woman older than he with coarse hair pulled back into an antiquated bun. She reminded him not to talk any more than he had to because his larynx was still inflamed. Gently she sponged his lower back, carefully avoiding scars left both by surgery and exit wounds from the gunfire in the woods. He was only half listening to her. The prospects for his future preoccupied him, pitting him in an ongoing battle between self-pity and determination. A part of him raged at the thought that the men responsible for his condition were already dead and beyond his reach, as he'd been toying for some time with an irrational fantasy in which he turned on the man who tried to strangle him and closed his bare hands around that man's neck, choking the life from him and in the process revitalizing himself to the point where he could walk away, avenged.

Caught up in his reverie, Jack hardly noticed when the nurse stepped away from him to rinse the sponge. Moments later, he felt a woman's hands on his shoulders, gently kneading the taut muscles around his upper spine. He reflexively pulled himself away, startled by the touch. Because of his neck wounds he could barely turn his head.

"Hello, Jack."

It was Jane, standing in place of the nurse, watching him with a frail smile. She leaned forward and kissed Jack gently on the lips and cheek. When she pulled away, he was still staring at her, stunned.

"Come on," she teased. "You can do better than that."

One of Jack's hands had been cleared of intravenous needles and he used it to reach out to Jane, stroking her chin. He noticed her eyes on his neck and whispered hoarsely. "Hard for me to talk."

"That's okay," she told him. "Go ahead, lie back."

She helped him down and pulled up a seat next to the bed.

"You didn't have to come."

"Baloney," Jane said. "You were there for me when I needed someone, remember? Now I have a chance to return the favor."

They shared a quiet moment, holding hands, oblivious to the drone of a television set across the hallway and the murmur of orderlies wheeling supplies past his room. It had been more than four months since they'd seen each other; although they'd written and spoken on the phone several times, maintaining a relationship of ongoing uncertainty, always hedging toward, and then retreating from, the commitments of something more than just a close friendship. There had been talk of getting together for a weekend in June, flying to his brother's guesthouse outside Chicago, where they'd shared a long week of intimacy at the beginning of the year. Now they had been brought together under forced circumstances, and there were unspoken questions shared in their silence.

Dr. Glover walked in with a small plastic contraption. "Ah, already flirting with the ladies, Jack? That's a good sign." He looked at Jane, eyes sparking with recognition. "Jane Britland! What a surprise!"

"Hello, Doctor . . ."

"Glover," the surgeon introduced himself. "How's your father like being out of the White House?"

"He's too restless to retire," Jane told him. "Houril just brought him in as an advisor on this whole assassination situation."

"A terrible thing," Glover said with a shake of his head. "But we managed to salvage one of the casualties, at least. Jack, how's the breathing?"

Jack wavered his hand in a so-so gesture and took in some air. The surgeon gave him the plastic device, which consisted primarily of a breathing tube connected to three clear plastic shafts holding Ping-Pong balls. "Come on. All balls in the air for at least three second."

Jane watched as Jack took the instrument and placed the tube to his lips. He exhaled, barely stirring the balls.

"You can do better than that," Glover encouraged.

Jack tried again, but his breathing was even weaker. He lowered the contraption to his lap and shook his head. Jane felt a chill run along her spine and she looked away from Jack and the surgeon, fighting back a sudden rush of tears.

Nine

Government agencies were renowned for their territorial imperatives, and both infighting and a lack of cooperation between various outfits had often been cited as a cause of excessive inefficiency and wasted manpower spent on duplicated work, particularly in the areas of intelligence work and crime-fighting. President Houril was painfully aware of this sorry state of affairs, and within hours of his return to Washington following the debacle in Michigan, he had called together the heads of virtually every law-enforcement and intelligence group at his disposal, demanding that they put aside their petty differences and unite in the formation of a special task force that would deal exclusively with an investigation into the attempted assassination. The CIA was expected to work hand in hand with the FBI, Interpol in accord with the State Department, the National Security Agency with the Secret Service — everyone bound by a spirit of cooperation and a duty to see that the masterminds behind the guerrilla assault were brought to justice. Even with J. Edgar Hoover

long in his grave, the biggest protest had been set forth
by the Federal Bureau of Investigation, normally the agency with priority in the handling of domestic terrorism
activities. Director Stan Bartholomew was additionally
no great friend of Houril's, and when the President put
his foot down and threatened reprisals if the Bureau didn't
fall in line, Bartholomew washed his hands of the issue
by putting several of his subordinates in charge of FBI
involvement with the task force.

Seamus McTeague was among those members of the
Secret Service assigned to the assassination detail, and
following the phone call from Washington confirming his
appointment, he was back at Hiawatha National Forest,
flashing his credentials to state troopers guarding the area
and passing innumerable plainclothes agents on his way
to the clearing where the last moments of the confrontation
had taken place. There was an odd, surreal feeling to
the tableau, with men in suits wandering the field like
some strange herd, lingering near scars left by missiles
and flagged locations marking where the dead had fallen.
In the charred section of woods where the ultralight had
landed, McTeague came across a crew of men in one-
piece outfits wearing plastic gloves as they tagged bits
of debris.

"Making any headway?" McTeague inquired.

One of the investigators shook his head as he labeled
one of the larger pieces of wreckage and carefully wrapped
it for placement in a cart already half filled with other
evidence. "All this shit's supposed to have identifying
marks, you know? Serial numbers, manufacturing stamps,
whatever. But no dice. All we got here's a heap of untrace-
able junk. You ever try to put together a blank jigsaw
puzzle?"

McTeague shook his head. "I have a hard enough time
on the ones with pictures."

He left the crew to their work and crossed over to

an outdoor headquarters set up next to the ranger's cabin. It looked similar to the command post farther into the woods where the assualt had taken place, with perhaps more equipment. A stocky man with a shaved head sat at a card table, reading over a report as he hand-rolled a cigarette on the tabletop.

"Well, well. Tony Bex," McTeague called out. "I thought I might run into you here."

"Hey, McTeague! How's it hanging?" They shook hands after Bex flicked a few stray bits of tobacco from his fingers.

"I'm fine, thanks. How's the Bureau treating you?"

"Took me away from the desk and put me on this, so I can't complain. Be nice to spend some time without having to see Bartholomew." Bex pointed to a folding chair propped up next to the table. "Take a load off."

McTeague unfolded the chair and sat down, taking out his pipe. Both men lit up as McTeague glanced out at the agents still prowling the woods. "They're not too optimistic out there."

"Can't blame 'em, can you?" Bex licked his fingertips and snuffed out his match before crushing it under heel in the dirt. "Funny thing is, we got crackpots lining up to take credit. Libyans, Cubans, PLO, Jihad — you name it."

"And they're all lying, of course."

Bex nodded, blew smoke out his nose. "If whoever did this wanted credit, they would have left a calling card. You were here. Who's your money on?"

McTeague had been thinking about it often the past two days. He speculated, "There was a lot of planning behind it, especially when you figure Houril came here on less than forty-eight hours' notice. No press leaks either, except for the bogus ones about Indiana."

"Inside job?"

"Don't sound so surprised, Tony."

"Shit!" Bex rolled the cigarette between his fingers to even the burn before taking another puff. He squinted through smoke at McTeague. "Okay, you got all the answers. Hit me with a motive."

"You got a week?" McTeague scoffed. "Be serious! You start counting skeletons in Washington closets and you're going to run out of fingers real quick. Hell, there's people right here with motives for wanting Houril dead."

"Yeah, maybe so. Of course, these days it might not have anything to do with Houril personally. We got guys passing secrets for chump's change. Somebody offers some poor shit five figures to squeal the man's travel plans, he's thinking more about buying Porsches than being some kinda Benedict Arnold." Bex smoked his cigarette down and stomped it out, making a face. "I got a feeling this is gonna turn out being one ugly mess. . . ."

Ten

Hal Dewez had skimmed a few fifties from the Syrians' first payment and spent the night in Bismarck, baiting dancers at a strip joint with change until his sweet talk turned up a lady willing to suit the appetite Dewez hadn't been able to satisfy with draft beer and a pastrami-dip platter. Checking into a blighted motel at the edge of town, they'd taken a room and locked themselves in, paying to have adult films flashed on the rental set as they drank tequila, smoked some quality Thai stick, and did their best to mimic the sexual excesses depicted on the tube. It was past three in the morning when Dewez passed out, drunk and sated, raw between the legs, lost in dreams inspired by visions of his face burrowed between spread thighs, licking the gap in his playmate's crotchless panties.

Eight hours later he was roused by the thumping of an angry fist on the motel door.

"Hey! You in there?" the manager hollered. When he didn't get an answer, he used his master key to open the door, flooding light into the room. Dewez groaned and shielded his eyes from the blinding glare. His head was throbbing with the ghosts of tequila past and his stomach ached from a certain unpleasantness between the booze and the pastrami.

"Jesus! Look at this mess!" the manager snapped, remaining in the doorway so that Dewez could see him only in silhouette, a big man carrying a flashlight the size of a billy club. "It's already an hour past checkout time, pal. You just rented out for another night. Sorry to bother you."

The door closed, returning Dewez to the cloistered darkness. He slowly gathered his wits, saw strange marks on his belly in the glow of TV test patterns. A message, scrawled with lipstick:

I earned it, asshole.

"Whaaaa?" Dewez sat up, holding his head, looking around the room. No sign of the woman. His pants on the floor, not where he left them, wallet lying nearby. Even before he grabbed it he knew the money was gone. Nearly two hundred bucks.

"Sumbitchincunt!"

Dewez pulled on his pants and shirt, stabbed his feet into snakeskin boots, and left behind the torn sheets and broken bedframe. The sunlight was brutal and he had to cup one hand over his brow to fend off the rays hitting his bloodshot eyes. The motel office door swung open and the manager stepped out, patting the flashlight in his meaty palm.

"Not goin' somewhere, are you?" he drawled, taking a step toward Dewez. "You're down for another night. Gotta pay that in advance."

"Go fuck yourself," Dewez muttered as he strode through the dust to his Bronco Jeep. The manager caught up with him before he could get his key in the ignition.

"What'd you say?"

Dewez leaned over, pulling a Browning automatic from under his seat and pointing it at the other man's face. "I said I think I'll pay with my credit card here," he taunted. "How big a tip you want?"

The manager backed away, eyes on the small tunnel inside the gun. Dewez shifted gears and pulled out of the parking lot, backtracking to the strip joint on the other side of town. It was closed, but he kicked at the door until someone answered. Like the motel manager, the janitor who answered was ready to give Dewez a hard time until he found the export end of the Browning half buried in the folds of his beer gut.

"I'm lookin' for one of your girls," Dewez said. He gave a brief description and the janitor bobbed his head, said she'd just come by to pick up her things on the way to the bus depot. It seemed she had to go all of a sudden to visit a sick aunt out of state.

Dewez left his gun in the Bronco and was more discreet at the Greyhound terminal, finding out that the woman who'd written on his belly was now halfway to Pierre. He took out his initial frustration on the depot vending machine when it didn't give him cream with his coffee, then drove back to the cattle ranch, looking forward to a chance to vent his spleen on the Syrians. Rowdy had already taken the group into the woods at the far end of the ranch property, where a military training camp had been built adjacent to an old hunting lodge. When Dewez caught up with them, the Syrians were on the obstacle course, crawling through a muddy trench covered by twisted coils of barbed wire. Trent was watching over them from the far end of the course, squatting next to a mounted Bren machine gun.

"Look like you been through hell and back," Trent said, looking Dewez over. "When you didn't show up this morning, Morrison had me go ahead and take these guys out for —"

"I know all that, shitface!" Dewez took up position

behind the machine gun and waved Rowdy away. "Go keep an eye on 'em from the side while I find out what kinda backbone they make in Damascus."

Rowdy was about to say something but thought better of it and wandered off as Dewez fit an ammo clip into the Bren and fired a burst to get the Syrians' attention. They'd cleared the trenches and were now a few dozen yards downhill, standing near a dry creek bed. "Okay, Argvai!" he shouted. "Tell your girl friends I'm an enemy gunner and they gotta take me out or their mommas are gonna get humped by a pack of camels!"

Argvai stared coldly at Dewez, then gave his men a liberal translation of Dewez's command. As the Syrians bounded into the creek bed and started crawling up, Dewez squeezed the trigger, spraying hot lead above their muddied burnooses. When he lowered the gunfire and started taking nicks and gouges out of the rocks and dirt around them, the men veered their course from side to side to avoid being hit.

"Zigzag more, damn it, or I'll stitch your asses but good!" Dewez snarled above the Bren's roar. He reached to his side, readying another clip so he could reload with minimal delay. In doing so, he tipped the gun enough to send a volley ripping into the side of a Syrian who had lost his footing and slumped awkwardly into the silt. The other men abruptly stopped their advance toward Dewez and rushed to their injured comrade, who twisted in the dirt, clutching at his wounds. Before they could reach him, however, they were driven back by a stream of well-placed shots from the machine gun nest.

"Leave him and finish the fucking course!" Dewez demanded.

The Syrians glowered up at Dewez, needing no translators this time. One of them spat a curse at the American gunner and grabbed a rock the size of a softball. He was about to hurl it at Dewez when Argvai intercepted him and knocked the rock away, then angrily berated the man in his native tongue. He directed a few more well-chosen words to the rest of the men, who reluctantly resumed their scramble up the incline. Dewez continued gunning at them, but took care to make sure his shots fell wide. "This is going to be life-and-death when it comes to the real thing," he warned them. "You towelheads want a vacation, join Club Med!"

Eleven

While Dewez had been paying the price of indulging his libido, Morrison had flown east on business, arriving in Washington and taking a cab to the Diplomat Hotel, where he had not only booked a room but had also made reservations for lunch at the establishment's posh dining room. He showered and shaved before changing into a charcoal suit, then stopped off at the Diplomat's bar to unwind from the flight with a sampling of cognac and a five-dollar cigar. Thus fortified, he presented himself to the maître d', confirming his lunch reservations and waiting for the arrival of his guest, who turned out to be a woman every bit as exotic and mysterious as Dewez's playmate from the strip joint had been coarse and forward in terms of flaunting her allure.

Koura Hoummari was a tall woman with skin the color of almonds, her short, dark hair teased and held in place through the miracle of mousse. There was a lively glitter in both her deep green eyes and the row of sequins running down the side of her black satin dress. She held a slender hand out to Morrison and he clasped it gently, bowing slightly from the waist.

"A pleasure to see you, as always," he told her.

"I doubt that you could possibly mean it, but thank you all the same." Though born in Lebanon, Hoummari had been educated in the States, and her flawless English was seasoned only slightly with a hint of her lineage.

"And I thank you for coming on such short notice." Morrison secured the maître d's attention and they were led to a private booth overlooking a plushly landscaped garden where there had once been train tracks and concrete. "Now, then," he began once their waiter had come by to drop off menus and take orders for drinks.

"I still don't see any reason for this meeting," Hoummari insisted, clasping her hands on the tabletop. "As I said on the phone, you failed, so we owe you nothing more."

"And we ask for nothing more," Morrison assured her, adding, "except, perhaps, for a chance to provide another service."

Hoummari was unimpressed. "You won't be able to get near the President now. We both know that."

"There's other ways to achieve your goals without taking out Houril. We both know that, too."

They fell silent a moment as the waiter returned with their drinks. Scotch on the rocks for Morrison, whiskey sour for Hoummari. They hadn't looked at their menus yet, so the waiter said he'd wait to take their orders.

"What's your point?" Hoummari asked once they were alone again.

"Why bother with our policies here when you could just take matters into your own hands?"

"We've had this discussion before, haven't we?" She ran a long, painted fingernail idly around the rim of her glass, collecting a growing dab of condensation on it. "You couldn't give us what we need for the bomb . . ."

"And we still can't. But, then, the bomb would leave

you with nothing but rubble to take over. Not very efficient, I would think." Morrison stirred his drink, letting his words sink in. "You'd have the whole world against you, too. Hell of a way to start out a new age."

There were pieces of skewered fruit dangling above Hoummari's drink. She picked up the skewer and pried off a slice of orange, nibbling at the rind, playing her own games with Morrison. "You have something else in mind?" she finally asked, raising her gaze to him.

Morrison reached into his suit coat and pulled out a newspaper clipping. He handed it to the woman. "This is from a couple days ago. With all the stink about what happened in Michigan, it got stuck in the back of the paper."

Hoummari frowned at the clipping and slid it back across the table. "I didn't bring my reading glasses."

"I know you have perfect vision, Koura."

"I also have perfect hearing," Hoummari countered. "Why don't you just tell me what it says?"

Morrison sighed, put the clipping away. "Our Congress just approved funds to update our chemical warfare stockpiles. We've already started phasing out supplies of nerve gas dating back to World War Two."

"Nerve gas?" Hoummari repeated. "Out of the question."

"Is it, really?" Morrison asked. "The Iraqis have used it against Iran. And what about the Soviets in Afghanistan? There's precedents, Koura. It's not out of the question at all."

Hoummari sipped her drink slowly, turning her eyes slightly to take in the view through the window across from them. "Tell me more," she whispered.

"The army wanted to have the old stockpiles destroyed on site rather than being transported to a central incinerator," Morrison explained, "but there was a lot of pressure put on from the states where the stuff is stored.

None of them wants to risk the consequences of any problems with the on-site burnings. So what's happening is they're shipping the weapons cross-country to a plant in Utah over the next five years."

"And . . ."

"The first shipment's next week," Morrison said. "We know the itinerary. It hasn't been widely publicized, so the security precautions aren't what they might have been otherwise. And make no mistake; just because the weapons are outdated doesn't mean they aren't potent. On the contrary."

Hoummari took another long sip, finishing her drink. She picked up the cherry still on the skewer and bit into it seductively as she picked up the menu, murmuring, "I think I'm ready to order now . . ."

Twelve

At the same time Jake Morrison had settled down for lunch and negotiations with Koura Hoummari, a man named Frank Tennleton had boarded a westbound flight from New York's LaGuardia Airport. His destination was Marquette. After a forty-minute stopover in Detroit, where he had met briefly at the airport lounge with a new writer pleading for an extension on the deadline for his first novel, Tennleton had continued on up to the Upper Peninsula, where his newest client awaited him. As in Detroit, he took the meeting in the lounge, sipping coffee as he talked while jumbo jets hauled themselves up from the tarmac out on the runway behind him. Tennleton was in his mid-seventies but looked much younger, wearing a stylish trenchcoat over his tailored clothes. During his fifty-four years in the publishing business, he'd worked with a wide range of writers, from highly esteemed novelists to crackshot hacks whose specialty was fast volume, and within the industry he was known as an editor's editor. Tough-minded yet diplomatic, charismatic with a conversational wit that served him well on the talk-show circuit the few times he'd penned his own works, Tennleton had a reputation for hands-on nurturing of those under contract to him, calling to mind the likes of Max Perkins and his stable of literary heavyweights who had dominated an earlier generation. While most other editors had to contend with any number of overlapping projects, Tennleton's prominence and seniority had earned him the enviable position of being able to concentrate solely on one book at any given time.

The next book he wanted to become involved with concerned the woman who sat across from him at the Marquette airport lounge, sipping juice as she discussed contract terms and her idea for the story she proposed to tell. Tennleton jotted down notes, clarified points, expressed his usual charm as all the necessary bases were covered. When this had all been attended to, he almost physically changed, from businessman to confidant. He set down his pen and smiled across the table at Jane.

"I have to say, this still comes as quite a surprise," he told her. "A few months ago you threw our offer back in our faces."

"Times change," Jane replied, smiling back. "I was a little paranoid back then. I didn't trust myself, much less anyone else."

"Of course."

"But so much for that. Do we have a deal?"

Tennleton cast a casual glance over the figures on his legal pad. It was a mere formality, as he'd already committed everything to memory. "We've covered all the basic terms. If we can shake on it, I'll have contracts drawn up and sent to your lawyer first thing Monday."

He handed her the pad, and as she looked the terms over, an emotionless voice on the public address system announced the pending departure of a flight bound for New York. "That's my plane," he told Jane.

Jane gave him the pad as they both stood up. "Deal," she said, holding out her hand.

"Good." Tennleton smiled again as they shook hands. "You've made the right choice, Jane. Trust me. Always best to be the first one out with your own story."

"Well, the tabloids already beat me on that front, but I know what you mean."

The p.a. message droned again as they walked together to the departure gate. "You can feel free to call me in New York at any time. Collect. It's important for you to realize I'm in your corner and not the adversary, okay?"

Jane laughed lightly. "That paranoia's mostly behind me now, Frank. I promise to keep in touch, but I think I want to sweat my way through the first draft without running to you for help. It'll be good for me."

"Fine. Whatever you think works best."

They reached his gate and Tennleton took out his boarding pass from his shirt pocket.

"I appreciate your coming out on such short notice."

"It was worth it for me," Tennleton told her, indicating the deal memo scrawled on the legal pad. "You've got a great story to tell. Go to it."

He winked and was ushered up the boarding ramp to the waiting jet. Jane remained behind, feeling a sense of both elation and fear. What had she gotten herself into? She'd acted on impulse and wondered if her instincts might have betrayed her. Moving near the terminal window, she stayed until Tennleton's plane had taxied out to the runway and raced down the airstrip, hurtling upward, eastward bound. Watching the plane vanish into the horizon, Jane faced up to the finality of her decision. Whatever it might take, she was determined to stick to it.

Before leaving the airport, Jane crossed the waiting area to a bank of pay phones lined across the wall between two rest rooms. One of the newer units operated off a phone credit card, and she used it to put a call through to Washington. Her father answered on the fifth ring.

"Hi, Daddy," she told him. "I've got some good news, but first I have a bone to pick with you . . ."

Thirteen

"A book?"

Jack's voice was still weak, but he mustered a tone of incredulity. He set aside the Ping-Pong contraption, having just finished his prescribed set of breathing exercises. A long sleep had bolstered his strength markedly since the last time Jane had seen him.

"Yes. Isn't it wonderful?" Jane moved closer to him in her chair, taking his hand. "I know it'll be a challenge, but I'm ready for it. I really am."

"I'm glad." Despite the sleep he still felt sluggish mentally, as if he were in a fog. Dr. Glover had attributed it to his continued need for the medication he was taking for the pain of his various wounds. He wanted to think that if he could just get over his dependency on drugs and the intravenous diet he was on, the rest of his problems would fall away. But even before the staff psychologist had come by his room earlier that morning with a few words of encouragement about dealing with denial and depression, Jack knew he was indulging himself in wishful thinking. It wasn't drugs or tubes fouling up his ability to walk, to get about. It was a bullet, and he could imagine it inside him, anthropomorphized into some living entity, like a troll with its arms around his spine, squeezing just hard enough to pinch a few crucial nerves. Bastard.

"The best part is I'll be able to schedule my own time," Jane was telling him, softly stroking his forearm. "I can be with you as much as I want."

Jack stiffened, pulled his arm away from Jane. "I don't want a nursemaid, damn it!" He looked away from her, fuming.

"I'm not talking about being a nursemaid. Jack, look at me." When he continued to stare out the window, Jane stood up, forcing herself into his field of vision. "Will you please look at me?"

"I can take care of myself!"

"I'm sure you can." Jane checked her own temper, kept her voice calm. She recognized the hurt and pain in his eyes, knew that feeling from her own stay in another hospital. Back then, her hostility had been reflexive more than sincere, and she'd known bouts of guilt after she'd lashed out at loved ones who'd come to visit and had said the wrong thing. *Be patient*, she told herself. *Be kind.* She told him, "Did it occur to you that maybe *I'm* the one who'll need looking after? Writing takes a lot of discipline; I could use a coach to make sure I put in my time at the typewriter, right?"

Jack saw through her, knew she was putting on the kid gloves. *I deserve it*, he thought, *flying off the handle like that*. This wasn't like him, carrying on like a spoiled brat. He reached out, took her hand back in his lap, and forced a wry smile. "You really know how to lay it on, lady."

"I was raised by a politician," she told him. "What do you expect?"

"Look, I'm sorry, okay?"

Jane nodded, reached out to brush a strand of hair that had flopped across his forehead at an angle. "Look,' she said, "we have a chance to be together. Why don't we make the best of it?"

"It's not that simple." Jack's throat was aching from what little talking he'd done. He pointed to the table by his bed and Jane handed him a Styrofoam cup with a straw in it. The water was cold, soothing. When he finished drinking and gave the cup back, he told Jane, "I don't know if it would work out."

"We'll never know unless we try." Jane went over to the window, opening the shades, giving them both a view of the clear afternoon sky. "Jack, think back to when you came and visited me at your brother's. Remember what fun we had? You were just checking up on me and you ended up staying all week." She turned back to him. "Jack, that was the most wonderful week of my life."

Jack frowned at her, waited until she returned to his bedside so he wouldn't have to raise his voice. "Then why did it have to end?" he wanted to know. "I was ready for more."

"I know," she said. "I didn't think I could make a commitment then. You knew all I'd been through. It just wasn't the right time."

"And now that I'm crippled and you're full of pity for me it's a good time, right?" The anger came from nowhere.

"Don't be like that, Jack."

"I can't help it. Let's be honest here, okay? Yes, we had a great time that week in Chicago, but it just wouldn't be the same now." He looked down at his immobile legs. "Can't you see that?"

"I love you, Jack Demarrest," Jane told him forcefully. "Can't you see that?"

Jack looked in her eyes, couldn't help but see the love there. *Why now?* he wondered, cursing the fog in his head. Here was the woman he loved, had propositioned twice, swearing her devotion for him, and all he could feel was an overwhelming fatigue and irritationality sweeping over him, creating a barrier between them. He wanted to tell her how much he cared — ached — for her, but his body was suddenly heavy, sinking deep into the foamy dimples of his mattress pad. "I'm tired," he heard himself telling her as the blackness crept over him.

Fourteen

Cal Winslow's contact lenses were bothering him, so he dipped his last bit of sushi into the hot mustard sauce before eating it. The spices brought tears to his eyes, lubricating the lenses and bringing him relief. He finished his sake and left money at the table on his way out of the restaurant. The hostess, a petite woman in a pink-flowered dress, smiled at Winslow, reminding them of their date that evening. He smiled back, promising to pick her up at eight. He was looking forward to some relaxation and diversion after the past few days. It had been hard enough lobbying for a position on the special task force dealing with the attempted assassination of President Houril. He'd had to call in favors owed him from two higher-ups at the Bureau, and even that manipulating barely got his foot in the door as a low-level functionary. On top of that there was this whole business with the army, requiring him to spend most of his free time yesterday and today making a series of secret rendezvous at points around the capital. He'd gotten only five hours of sleep the past three days, and he was damned glad that after one last dropoff he could go back to his apartment and crash for a few hours before getting ready for his date.

Hailing a taxi at the corner, Winslow rode silently down Washington side streets, yawning as the sake conspired with his fatigue to make him increasingly drowsy. He snapped out of the doldrums as the cab turned south on Ninth Street, heading toward the Smithsonian Mall. Grabbing a newspaper he'd bought back at the restaurant, Winslow opened the sports section and stared blankly at the standings, less concerned with how many games out of first place the Orioles were than with hiding his face from view until the taxi had passed both the FBI building and the Justice Department. The last thing he needed to contend with was being spotted by a colleague and having to share the cab rather than risk suspicion. It wasn't until they were heading through the tunnel running beneath the mall that he lowered the paper, in the same motion leaning forward to remove an envelope from his shirt pocket. He set the envelope on the floor and sat back up as they cleared the tunnel and took the highway across the Potomac to Arlington. When he reached the dropoff point, all he would have to do was nudge the envelope under the seat and his job was done. Of course, if he didn't see his contact when the cab dropped him off, he'd have to pick up the envelope and spend the next two hours following through on a contingency plan. He hoped to hell it wouldn't come to that. His body was begging for a little horizontal indulgence, the sooner the better.

Jake Morrison bought a pear from a corner produce stand and sat down on a curbside bench to eat it. A bus rolled to a stop alongside him several minutes later and hissed its doors open, but Morrison told the driver he was just resting and didn't need a ride. He coughed as the bus left a dark cloud of exhaust in its wake and tossed the rest of the pear into the gutter rather than bother with wiping the skin clean on his coat sleeve. He checked his watch. Five after three. Winslow was late.

Two minutes later a cab pulled over to the curb twenty yards ahead of the bench where Morrison sat. It was a quiet, residential area, with only a few kids playing on the sidewalk in front of an apartment complex down the block. As Winslow climbed out of the cab, Morrison ignored him and waved instead at the cabbie, who kept his engine idling. Morrison picked up his overnight bag and got inside the taxi, telling the driver to take him to Washington National Airport. As the cab pulled out into traffic, Morrison set his bag on the floor between the front and back seats. Before sitting back up, he reached under his seat and removed the envelope Winslow had left there. He opened the envelope and pulled out a few sheets of paper, each marked CLASSIFIED across its facing. Morrison smiled as he skimmed the documents.

"Well done," he whispered to himself.

Back in North Dakota, Hal Dewez sat on the stump of a felled tree and watched as the Syrians took turns crawling up a sheer rock facing, clawing at small niches for support.

"That's it, gang!" he cheered them on while tapping out a cigarette. "You might just shape up after all."

Rowdy Trent came into view, striding down an elm-lined path, carrying a leather case, which he set down next to Dewez and opened to reveal a portable cellular phone. "It's Morrison," Trent said, holding out the receiver.

"Hey, Jake!" Dewez drawled around his cigarette as he took the call. "How's things in Washington?"

"It's gone well," Morrison told him. "I'm at the airport.

Hoummari's interested and Winslow came through with the specifics on the gas shipment."

"Glad to hear it."

"The Syrians going to be ready by Monday?"

Dewez glanced up at the men scaling the small cliff. Argvai was the last one up, and as he caught his breath the man closest to him started the equally arduous climb back down. "They're as ready as they'll ever be, Jake."

"Good, good. If you have a pen, I'll give you the itinerary."

Dewez grabbed a pencil from the case and scrawled notes on a scratch pad as Morrison relayed the information Winslow had secured from his Pentagon contacts. "I was hoping they'd use that route. I know the perfect place to set things up. What kind of security they sending along with it?"

"No changes from what we anticipated."

"That's sweet. They won't know what the fuck hit 'em."

"Let's hope so. Look, my flight leaves in twenty minutes, so I should see you around sundown. How about dinner at the Hacienda?"

"You got it."

As Dewez hung up, Argvai walked over toward him, his face bathed in sweat. His eyebrows were arched inward, giving him an angry gaze. "We have done enough drills," he told Dewez impatiently. "It is not the reason we came here."

"You're right," Dewez replied with a grin.

Fifteen

They looked like the assembled members of a corporate
board of directors, gathered around a large oak desk to
plot their firm's course through the waters of commerce.
But the seven men gathered in this White House conference room were more than businessmen and their discussion had to do with more than matters of free enterprise. The dossiers on the table in front of each man
contained an exclusive report of all known data on the
attempted assassination in Michigan, condensed into a
succinct, readable format for quick evaluation. They had
all agreed on one key point — time was of the essence.
Those behind the forest assault were still at large, and
the trail that might lead to them was cold, getting colder
as each day passed, raising levels of frustration throughout
the ranks of the intelligence community. And no one felt
the anxiety more than the man who had been the principal
target of that attack.

"There has to be something more we can do, damn
it!" President Houril slammed his fist on the table, waving

the file with his other hand. "Come on, let's hash this out!"

Besides Houril, there was his predecessor at the White House, George Britland, thin, gray-haired, dark circles under his gray eyes, Quinton Daniels from the CIA, his suit rumpled, liver spots sprinkled across his craggy face, peering through bifocals at the report in search of anything that might link up with his knowledge of international intelligence activities. Interpol's Benson White was the youngest man present, but he still looked haggard, having read a Telexed version of the dossier while taking the Concorde from his organization's Paris headquarters during the early hours of the morning. Everett Kopp, who had briefly been Houril's adversary in the primaries a year before, now sat at the President's right-hand side as Secretary of State, calculating how to handle the crisis in terms of the global political arena. The two lowest-ranking members of the task force, Seamus McTeague and FBI agent Tony Bex, were ironically the most well-versed with the contents of the dossier, having been the ones most responsible for its preparation. It was Bex who broke the uneasy silence following the President's outburst.

"We could run on some wild guesses, but it'd eat up our manpower," he told Houril. "We spread ourselves too thin and we might be playing into their hands."

"He has a point, Dick," Daniels agreed, taking off his glasses long enough to rub his aching eyes.

Houril rose from his chair and went to the nearby window, parting the shades enough to get a look at the cheery Washington day outside and squint at the glare of the midday sun. "George," he said to Britland as he moved away from the window, "you had a couple incidents like this during your term. Are we covering all the bases?"

"As far as I can see, yes." Britland ran his thumbnail along the edges of the dossier, as if to emphasize the number of pages. "But remember those attempts on me were made by outsiders. Here we have to assume there's someone on the inside pulling strings, and that makes it a whole different ball game."

"Well, if we all agree that we smell a rat around here," Daniels proposed, "then I think our best bet is to lay a fucking trap and load it with as much cheese as possible."

"Metaphors aside," White added, "what are you getting at? We should stick the President out in public with a target taped to his suit and hope we can nab whoever might take a potshot at him?"

"No," Daniels shot back, "I'm not for anything like that. I say we just go on record as making more progress than we really are. Try to force their hand, flush the bastards out of the brush."

There was a lull, during which time the men whispered back and forth, scribbled notes in the margins of their reports. The Secretary of State finally raised his voice above the din. "I'm going before the press in an hour," he announced. "If we all agree, I'll follow Daniels's lead and throw out a bluff, see what happens with it."

Houril checked his watch. "Well, I can't keep Premier LaSalle on hold any longer. Look, if bluffing's the best we can do right now, we have to try it. Agreed?"

Around the table there were nods of affirmation, grunts of assent. Houril adjourned the meeting and excused himself, leaving the room hurriedly to make his next appointment. The others were slower to depart, breaking off into smaller groups for further discussion. Britland cornered McTeague, asked the Secret Service agent for a word in private. They left the room together, heading down the main hallway.

"Seamus, did you happen to run into my daughter when you were up in Michigan?"

"Yes, sir," McTeague told him. "She was up there to see Jack Demarrest."

"Yes, yes, I know." Britland grinned, but his expression was pained. "She quit the *Sentinel* to do it and gave me hell over the phone for having pulled strings to get her the job in the first place."

At the end of the hallway, Britland asked McTeague to wait a moment while he went to exchange greetings with Premier LaSalle, an old political ally and trusted confidant. Houril was there, too, and the three men conducted a short conversation while McTeague stood off to one side, watching a work crew disassemble the velvet-rope barriers used to keep tourists from straying into forbidden areas during guided walks through the White House. All tours of the presidential residence were being eliminated as one of many increased security precautions instigated in the aftermath of recent events.

When Britland rejoined McTeague, they left the White House and loitered a few moments near the rose garden.

"Now I hear Jane's signed a contract to write her memoirs," the former President said, shaking his head at the thought. "A wrong move on her part, if you ask me . . . of course, *she* didn't."

"I think she can handle it," McTeague said.

"For her sake I hope you're right." Britland leaned over to sniff one of the fragrant buds. McTeague's assurances hadn't been enough to appease Britland. "I'm worried about her," he went on, "off alone, dredging through her past. There's a lot of wounds she hasn't given time to heal."

"She won't be alone, sir," McTeague reminded him. "I understand she's going to be staying with Jack during his convalescence."

Britland spied his limousine waiting along the side drive and started toward it. McTeague followed him. "Don't get me wrong," the older man said. "Jack's as fine a man as I've ever known, but after what he's been through . . ."

"I think they'll end up helping each other, sir," McTeague said, opening the rear door to the limousine for Britland. "You shouldn't worry."

"Easier said than done." Britland slid into the back seat of the limo, glanced back at the agent. "I guess without a country to look after these days I've gone back to being an overprotective father."

McTeague closed the car door and stepped back to the curb, waving as Britland was driven away. Glancing around at the White House grounds, he marveled sadly at the presence of National Guardsmen at strategic points along the fence and around the periphery of the main building itself. It seemed almost impossible to him that there was a time when Presidents had mingled freely among their electorate without fear of taking their lives into their hands. Now, of necessity, the nation's leaders were insulated behind an almost suffocating wall of protection, and even that had occasion to prove inadequate in the face of those who sought to thwart the ballot box by using violence as a means of political change. *What a world*, he mused. And it was getting worse rather than better.

"Hey, sport," Tony Bex called out to McTeague, catching up with him from behind. "How about some Thai food and a few good jolts of *Singha*? My treat."

"Sounds good."

"Come on, I've got a ride waiting."

They headed down the walk to a plain brown sedan parked at the end of the driveway. The man behind the wheel leaned over and unlocked the doors so McTeague and Bex could get in.

"Sorry for the delay, but the meeting ran on longer than we figured," Bex apologized.

"No problem," Cal Winslow said, starting up the ignition. "You guys come up with anything?"

Bex shook his head. "Dead ends up the wazoo."

"That's too bad," Winslow said, his face a mask of neutrality.

Sixteen

A row of rustic, one-story cottages rested on the bluff overlooking Marquette Bay and the azure waters of Lake Superior. Pines rose from the fertile soil, lending their shade to the small vacation homes. It would be more than a month before all the cabins would be in use and the sounds of playing children would compete with the chatter of jaybirds and tree squirrels. There were cars parked in the driveways of only three of the lots, and the only signs of human activity were those of an elderly couple sitting on their front porch, the wife tossing bread crumbs to the lawn, while her husband sketched the birds drawn to the grass by the bits of crust. Both of them glanced up from their diversions when a blue Chevy van turned off the main road and started down their narrow street, which ran parallel to the shoreline, less than fifty yards from the water.

Jane pulled the van into the driveway of a cottage half-way down the block. She shut off the engine and beamed at the view, which seemed even more inviting when compared to the dozen or so other places she had looked at the same day she'd first come here. The van was a custom model, equipped with a hydraulic lift that enabled Jack to be lowered from the vehicle to the driveway without having to leave his wheelchair. He was thin, still weak from his stay in the hospital. A turtleneck sweater hid the scars on his neck, but he refused to wear a blanket over his legs. As Jane wheeled him off the lift platform and closed the doors to the van, Jack looked around. The older couple lived two houses down and he nodded slightly as they greeted his gaze with tentative smiles. The birds that had taken flight when the van had passed now settled back on the other lawn, pecking at the bread. Jack turned his attention to the cabin before him. Its paint was faded and some of the roof tiles were loose under a blanketing of pine needles, but the garden was well tended, alive with blooming flowers and the round shapes of ripening plums. A picket fence divided the property from neighboring parcels, extending from the road on to the backyard, where, past the rows of stately pines, Jack could see the diamond glitter of sunlight on the bay.

"Beautiful, isn't it?" Jane said brightly. "I couldn't believe my luck finding it."

Jack smiled blandly, tightening his fingers around the wheelchair armrests as Jane pushed him up a wooden ramp leading from the driveway to the cabin's front porch.

"The previous owner was a paraplegic, so everything's already set up," Jane told him, sorting through her keys for the one that worked the front door. The porch was in need of sweeping and Jack could see the tire imprints left by another wheelchair.

Inside, the cottage was neatly kept and sparsely furnished. Modifications designed for the handicapped blended subtly into the decor, painted to match the walls or otherwise given a face-lift to make them look less like extensions of a hospital environment. Jane guided Jack across the main room, with its overstuffed sofa and Franklin stove, to a doorway facing the kitchen and a screen door providing a view of the back patio. "See?" Jane said, pointing out the back door. "I can set up my typewriter out there. You could fish off the railing, read, whatever you want. . . ."

Her voice trailed off as Jack raised a hand to get her attention. When he spoke, his voice was still weak, raspy, requiring considerable exertion. "Bring it down a notch, okay?" he asked, doing a poor job of mixing tact with his annoyance. He realized as much and patted Jane's hand gently.

"I'm sorry," she replied, her face changing color with a flash of embarrassment. "Guess I'm going on like one of those overeager social workers I had at the rehab clinic."

Jack mustered a smile. "Bingo!" He kissed her hand. "Let's finish the tour."

"Sure."

She took him to one of the back rooms. An adjustable bed was set next to the window, allowing a view of the bay. There were handrails positioned along all four walls and inside the small bathroom next to the doorway.

"Like it?" Jane asked.

Sitting up as high as he could, Jack could barely see out the window from his chair. "Nice view," he murmured.

"I'll go get the luggage and be right back." Jane leaned down for a kiss. Their lips met but it was an awkward embrace. She forced her smile as she left the room. Alone, Jack lowered his hands to the rim grips of his wheelchair. He had enough strength in his arms to propel himself slowly across the room to the nearest hand railing. He ran his fingertips along the smooth, polished wood. After closing his eyes a few moments, summoning whatever vitality he thought might still lie within him, awaiting an outlet, he took hold of the railing. His knuckles whitened and he clenched his teeth as he leaned forward, trying to pull himself up from the chair. Without the use of his legs, however, he had no way of supporting himself, and halfway out of the chair he lost his balance. He landed hard on the oak floor, feeling a bolt of pain shoot along his shoulders and rib cage.

"Jack!"

He could hear Jane's voice out on the front porch and he swore to himself, beating a fist on the hardwood floor. He was only a few feet from the bed. Jane called his name out again as she rushed into the bedroom and leaned over him, holding out her hand. He slapped her hand away, shouting, "I don't need help, damn it!"

Jane recoiled from him, stunned by the intensity of his anger. She watched, agonizing over the need for self-restraint at the sight of Jack dragging himself across the floor. He was sweating profusely already, and when he took hold of the bedframe and began to pull himself up, his breathing came in short, pained bursts.

"Jack ..."

"Shut up!"

With Herculean effort, Jack was able to lift himself up and onto the bed. Falling back on the mattress, he gasped for breath, sweat sparkling on his brow and in his hair. He turned his head just enough to give Jane a look of angry triumph. Although his throat felt ravaged from his shouting, he still had enough voice left to murmur, "Just don't smother me, all right?"

Jane stared at Jack, confused. She said nothing, though, and set his tote bag on the table beside his bed before leaving the room. Alone once more, Jack looked out the window. And looked some more, as if out there were some elusive answer that might at long last reveal itself to him.

Seventeen

The train hurtled across bleak, barren terrain, far removed from the nearest concentration of Oregon citizenry. Since leaving Umatilla Army Depot up near the Washington border, the engine and its three cars had deliberately followed an obscure southern route, bypassing as many cities and asphalt thoroughfares as possible. Once out of Oregon, the train would cut through Nevada and across the least populated area of northern California before reaching its destination — an isolated, top-secret port north of Fort Bragg, where a freighter would pick up the deadly cargo of nerve agent CW-34 and tote it across the Pacific to Johnston Atoll, a spit of land southwest of Hawaii. There a newly constructed disposal plant would be put to use in destroying the long-unused stockpile of toxic gas that had first been formulated more than forty years ago.

The desert plain stretched out before and behind the train, baking in the midday heat. Mirages shimmered in the distance with their lying promises of water where there

was none. Here and there a swirl of hot wind invited
the sand to dance, pulled it up into a brief twister that
would jitterbug across the land, sending prairie dogs running to their holes. Overhead, a hawk circled lazily, wings
taut, not about to mistake the train for a sidewinder and
swoop down at it, talons extended. Had it done so, the
bird would have had more to contend with than the overwhelming size of the train. Aboard the three custom-made
transport cars trailing from the engine was a contingent
of National Guardsmen, two dozen in all, each armed
with an M-16 and standing guard over the carefully stored
racks of reinforced canisters containing the nerve gas.

Up ahead, several minutes away, was a rise of small
mountains, wavering slightly in the heat. Atop one of
the first peaks, Hal Dewez lay on his belly across an
escarpment of bald rock, peering through binoculars at
the distant train. He was in his combat fatigues, looking
like an army surplus version of an Indian sentry in an
old Western movie. He could see the gleam of sunlight
glance off the sides of the railcars, the thin stream of
dark clouds churned out by the laboring engine.

Right on schedule.

Rising to a crouch, Dewez advanced, crablike, to the
edge of the escarpment, giving himself a view of the gorge
through which the train would soon be passing. Down
below, half hidden by mountain shade, two of the Syrians
huddled near the railbed, backs turned to Dewez. He
had to put his fingers to his lips and whistle before one
of them glanced up and saw Dewez waving them away
from the tracks. The second Syrian quickly scooped a
last few handfuls of dirt over the area they'd been tampering with. Then both men scrambled down the pitched
incline of the railbed and vanished into the scattering
of rocks and mesquite lining the gorge basin.

Dewez retreated from the ledge. In a recessed area between two other outcroppings, Argvai and the other Syrians sat cross-legged in a tight half circle, eyes on one another as Argvai led them in whispered prayer. Dewez signaled to get their attention as he leaned over a large wooden crate and began pulling out full-face gas masks. "Show time, girls," he said, passing the first of the masks to Argvai.

The Syrians were all wearing the same sophisticated headbands as the assassination squad had sported during the assault in Michigan. One by one, they donned the masks over the bands and pried at the edges to make sure there were no gaps in the seal around their faces. One of the men, however, was having trouble getting his mask to fit and he was about to yank off his headband when Dewez spotted him and rushed over, waving a gun in the darker man's face.

"The headband stays on!" Dewez glanced at Argvai. "Tell him, damn it!"

The Syrian leader already had his mask on, so his voice was muffled as he turned to his companion and translated Dewez's command, pointing to the man's headband as he spoke. Undaunted, the other Syrian shouted back at Argvai, then glared menacingly at Dewez.

"He wants to know why," Argvai told Dewez.

"Because I ordered him to — that's why!"

"I don't think that's going to be good enough for him," Argvai replied.

Dewez noticed that the other Syrians had their eyes on him as well. In their gas masks they looked like mutant insects. Each man held an Uzi submachine gun. Dewez sensed mutiny. So close to their crucial moment and the Syrians were backing out. He couldn't — wouldn't — stand for it. He unclipped a remote transmitter from his belt and held it out before him, thumb on the switch.

"You shits want a one-way ticket to Allah, keep it up."

The Syrians knew the significance of the transmitter. There had already been one earlier flare-up concerning it and the men's need for the headbands. Dewez reiterated the bottom line. "I've already told you that if everyone does their part you'll all go home heroes. Nothing's changed. Now cut with the cold feet and get your buddy to shape up. Now!"

The man still holding his gas mask saw the others turn toward him. Argvai and two others chastised him in Arabic. He glumly patted his headband, keeping it in place as he pulled the gas mask over it.

"That's more like it," Dewez said. "Now get to your positions . . ."

Eighteen

The first bomb went off just as the train was rounding a bend leading into the gorge. Rent by the explosive force of charges set under the rails, a large section of track ripped loose, sending a spray of stone and wooden splinters from the rail ties into the air. The blast echoed loudly in the gorge, dislodging a few stray rocks and sending small landslides pouring down the mountain slopes. Sparks flew from the wheels of the train's engine as emergency brakes squealed from the exertion of trying to halt the rolling behemoth before it reached the obstruction. Already suspecting the worst, National Guardsmen appeared in full force throughout the train, scanning the gorge for a trace of those responsible for sabotaging the tracks.

From his position behind a cluster of boulders thirty yards from the train, Argvai waited until the train had almost stopped and some of the Guardsmen were about to leap down to the ground. Then he tightened his grip on the small plunger propped between his knees and pushed down with one sharp, forceful thrust.

· On both sides of the train, there was a rapid series of more explosions, less violent than the initial burst. Noxious clouds of a yellowish smoke swelled up from the ground, enveloping the entire train. Three Guardsmen who had been preparing to jump from the lower rungs of ladders welded to the railcars were jarred by the blasts and fell awkwardly, tumbling down the slope of the railbed. One of them was already dead; the other two were quickly overcome by the toxic cloud, which deterred the others from leaving the train. There was a steady, pained chorus of coughs and curses as the men struggled against the growing screen that blocked their view of the gorge. Some held their breath and tried to peer through the fouled barrier, while others slipped back inside the railcars and closed off doors and windows in hopes of keeping the cloud from penetrating.

The Syrians had staked out positions on both sides of the gorge and they carried out the ambush with well-rehearsed precision. Bursting from cover, they dashed toward the train, Uzis blazing, their masks shielding them from the disabling effects of the smoke. Gunfire was returned their way, but the Guardsmen were firing blindly and most of the shots fell wide, scarring dirt and rock. Several more men from the train dropped to the ground, eyes streaming tears and lungs burning. One of them managed to stay on his feet long enough to stagger through the fog and face his attackers, who promptly felled him with a deadly volley.

"Jesus mother-fucking Christ!" the engineer swore as he abandoned his controls and snatched up an axe on his way to the window. He was a tall, broad-shouldered man in faded denim coveralls, wearing a sweat-stained cap over his matted gray hair. Two months from retiring and he had to volunteer for this run just so he could pick up a little bonus money to help with his next alimony check. "What the fuck's going on?" he asked the other man in the engineer's cabin with him, a young, gangly man whose face was pale with terror.

"It's an ambush!" he wailed. "We're gonna die!"

"Shut up!" the engineer told him. "We got a fucking army backing us up, so nobody's gonna die, got it?"

The other man shook his head as he pulled himself away from the window. "They already shot down some of our guys! If they don't get us with guns, that gas'll kill us." He sniffed the air, already convulsing in the throes of shock. "There! Can't you smell it? We're gonna die! We're gonna die!"

The engineer shot out the back of his hand, catching his assistant across the face. The younger man reeled backward until his back slammed into the wall. Then he slumped down to the floor, weeping uncontrollably and repeating his mantra of doom. Axe in hand, the engineer turned back to the window and glanced out, waiting for the roiling cloud to shift so he could have a better view of the gorge. He was still staring out when a bullet shattered the window, taking out his right eye en route to his inner brain. Dead on his feet, the engineer toppled backward, landing in the lap of his fearful associate, confirming the bad news he'd been predicting all along.

Dewez was still halfway up the gorge, watching the ambush from the safety of a deep niche that kept him hidden in shadow. He was impressed with the Syrians, who had taken up posts surrounding the train from ground level, using rocks and boulders for protection as they took potshots at Guardsmen through the thinning smoke. From where he was he could count eight bodies sprawled about the railbed, and he guessed at least that many more

Guardsmen were lying dead beyond his view. Aside from one Syrian limping from a bullet wound, there seemed to be no casualties among the guerrillas.

Although Dewez remained above the battlefield largely out of concern for self-preservation, he also had a contribution to make to the master plan of the ambush. He and the Syrians had been flown into the area by helicopter, and the chopper was a quarter of a mile away, shielded under camouflage netting and watched over by pilot Rowdy Trent. When Dewez fired the flare gun he had with him, Trent would clear the netting and hoist the large Huey back into the air, flying into the gorge to help the Syrians and Dewez make their getaway. Of course, if something had gone wrong and the ambush were to have ended with the Syrians being cut down, Dewez would have forsaken the flare gun in favor of slinking back up from the gorge and reaching the chopper on foot. That option was not going to be necessary, Dewez decided as he continued to watch the one-sided battle below.

It was the second of the three cars that contained the canisters of nerve gas, packed tightly in cushioned racks and guarded by three men with M-16s. One of them also worked a shortwave radio, and he was making a desperate call for help as the sounds of gunfire thundered outside the railcar.

"May Day! May Day!" the soldier shouted into his microphone as he stabbed frantically at the bank of switches and dials in front of him. "We're under attack near Cabrillo Pass! Send reinforcements. Repeat, we're under —"

The railcar rocked violently as a new explosion jarred the main door off its hinges. The men inside lost their footing and were struggling for their balance when two Syrians forced their way in, taking out the Guardsmen with swift, well-aimed blasts that stayed clear of the canisters of gas. As the latest victims of the ambush dropped to the floor, one of the Syrians leaned back out the doorway to signal to his comrades. Argvai was the second man, and as he slowly approached the cargo he smiled beneath his gas mask. Now it was theirs.

When Dewez saw the Syrian's signal, he leaned out of his niche, aiming the flare gun upward. His shot arched beyond the top of the mountain before the projectile burst in a wide bloom of color. The gorge continued to echo with gunshots as he deftly sought out his footing on the way down to the ambush site, where the Syrians were advancing through the last shreds of smoke to finish off any Guardsmen who had not yet fallen. Even before he could smell the foul odor of the cloud, Dewez lowered his gas mask into place. He'd already clipped the flare gun to his belt and hauled out a submachine gun, which he put to use when he saw a Guardsman crawl up onto the roof of the last railcar with an automatic rifle. The soldier took three bullets across his midsection and toppled from the car, unleashing a wild shot into the sagebrush before he landed.

By the time Dewez reached ground level, the large Huey was banking into view, the drone of its rotors amplified by the rock walls of the defile. Dewez waved to Trent, guiding the chopper down to a clearing close to the middle railcar.

"Speed it up!" he shouted to Argvai as the Syrian carefully passed down the first of the heavy canisters to his comrades. Although no larger than a quart Thermos, the container was lined with three separate layers of dense metal alloys, making it extremely bulky to carry. Two men were required to transfer each of the canisters from the railcar to the waiting chopper.

Dewez kept staring at a stopwatch he'd pulled from

his pocket, monitoring the time that had elapsed since the initial explosion that had torn up the tracks. From information Cal Winslow had managed to wrest from his Pentagon sources, he knew of all the backup security measures for the transfer, and based on careful calculations, he knew, almost to the second, how soon military reinforcements could be expected to arrive on the scene following notification that something was amiss. They were running out of time.

"Okay, just two more!" Dewez raised his voice so he could be heard through his mask and over the loud drone of the Huey's rotors. Four of the canisters had already been transferred from the railcar to the chopper. As the last two were being pilfered from the train, Dewez started counting Syrians. He came up one short and counted again as the other men began piling into the Huey.

"There's one man missing," he told Argvai.

Both men remained on the ground and headed out in separate directions, scanning the ambush site. Oddly contorted corpses littered the ground around the train, but none of the victims was Syrian. Dewez checked his stopwatch and waved Argvai back to the chopper.

"He must have been shot up in the foothills," Argvai surmised.

"Great! Just great!"

"I can take some of my men and search. We will find —"

"No way!" Dewez pointed to the Huey's doors. "Let's go!"

Argvai reluctantly boarded the aircraft, crowding in with his comrades, who warily eyed the six canisters of gas lying in separate foam-lined crates like oversized metallic eggs. Dewez clambered aboard next and signaled for Trent to lift off. As the Huey slowly rose into the air, Dewez took out his remote transmitter and made several adjustments to the controls so that when he activated the detonator he wouldn't trigger explosions within the copter. Instead, only the headband of the missing Syrian exploded, revealing his positon down amid the sagebrush below, not far from the hiding place where he'd apparently been downed by rifle fire from the train.

Setting aside the transmitter Dewez yanked off his gas mask. The Syrians did likewise as he grinned at them, chortling, "You fuckers didn't do half bad."

The Huey had cleared the Oregon-Idaho border and was already halfway across the Rockies when government troops arrived at Cabrillo Pass in response to the truncated distress call from the ambushed train. A ground force fanned out around the site of the massacre, ready to contend with an enemy that might still be in the area. When it became clear that there was no sign of life, the troops went to the train and began the grim task of tending to the fatalities. Overhead a handful of small copters buzzed about the gorge, looking for clues to the identities of the attackers. Off in the distance jets could be heard, widening the search area.

Colonel Grant Stander was in charge of the ground operation, and after he had assessed the situation he went back to his Jeep to radio in an update. His normally bland features were pinched in an expression of rage and disgust.

"Bastards sure as hell knew what they were doing," he growled over the microphone as he eyed the ruptured tracks and bullet-riddled train. "Hit-and-run all the way. From the smell of it, they used some kind of phosphorus for a smoke screen after they got the train to stop. Wiped out everyone here and took their dead with 'em. There's no tire tracks anywhere that we can see and there's signs of rotor wash near the train, so my guess is they came and went in a chopper. I've got a search under way, but I don't think we're gonna run into 'em."

Another officer wandered over to the Jeep and gestured to get Stander's attention. The colonel finished his radio call and hung up the microphone.

"Sorry, Colonel."

"That's all right, Captain," Stander told the other man. "More bad news?"

"Afraid so. We inventoried the storage car," the captain said. "Looks like they made off with six canisters of nerve gas."

"Six?" Stander was dumbfounded. "Fuckin' massacre like this for six lousy canisters?"

The captain was an older man. He shook his head grimly. "Sorry, Colonel, but what's in those six containers could kill everyone in New York City. At least twice."

Stander's face turned even whiter. He looked past the other officer at the bodies being piled alongside one another at the edge of the railbed. "Shit!" he muttered.

Up in the foothills another soldier waved his arms to get the officers' attention. "Looks like one of 'em didn't get away after all."

"How's that, soldier?" Stander demanded.

The soldier glanced down at something hidden from the view of the officers. "Got a body up here without a head, Colonel."

Stander let out a slow breath and turned to the captain. They both knew the meaning of the soldier's discovery. "Double shit!" the colonel groaned.

Nineteen

Jack Demarrest grew weary of self-pity within a week of moving into the cottage in Marquette. There were only so many hours he could spend staring out the window at Lake Superior, bemoaning his condition. Jane had kept her distance much of the time, yet she always managed to be nearby when Jack felt desirous of her companionship. He was restricted to a soft diet while his throat healed, and Jane went through cookbooks looking for the most exotic fare Jack could handle. The extra effort paid off, as Jack quickly regained his appetite and began to fend off the drastic rate at which his weight had been dropping. His strength increased proportionately, and after securing approval from Jack's doctor, Jane came back to the cabin one afternoon with a set of adjustable dumbbells and flex grips. Following a prescribed workout schedule, Jack found the physical therapy something to focus on and look forward to. There was an undeniable elation that came from the exercising, but his mood would bottom out abruptly the few times he tried to move his legs, in most cases managing only to strain the muscles of his lower back. He finally decided not to concern himself with any delusions about miracle cures. He would work within his limitations and not let his hopes for a full recovery get the better of him. It was easier said than done, but he was determined to make the best of his situation. Today he'd even broken out in a fit of laughter, watching Jane trying to juggle an overloaded breakfast tray as she crossed his room, her head bowed forward so that she was propping up a glass of orange juice with her nose. She'd sneezed halfway to his bed, sending Jack's breakfast spilling across the floor. The laughter had been incredibly painful physically, but worth it for the effect it had had. Jane had been initially upset, but at the sight of Jack doubled over in mirth she'd begun laughing herself, helping to cut through some of the tension they'd both felt all week.

But that had been this morning, before either of them had looked at the newspaper. Now, with the late-afternoon sun slanting through his window, Jack was solemn once again. He had the paper on his lap, the front pages filled with news of the guerrilla assault on the delivery train in Oregon. The television was on as well, broadcasting updates on the story, including the just-revealed link between the heist of the nerve gas and the attempted assassination of President Houril. Jack squeezed the flex grips as he watched, first one hand and then the other, trying to work off a fierce sense of anxiety that had been growing inside him for the past two hours.

"In the latter incident, twenty-five National Guardsmen acting as bodyguards for the shipment were killed by an as yet undetermined number of attackers," a somber-faced news anchor intoned on the screen. Behind him was a map of Oregon, showing the site of the ambush. "No mention has been made as to the amount of gas, if any, taken in the raid, but other sources both in Oregon and Washington report that a portion of the shipment could not be accounted for when authorities arrived on the scene of the tragic ambush."

The anchorman switched to a field reporter at the Washington Institute of Technology, and as a ranking professor was interviewed regarding the lethal potency of the missing nerve gas, Jack leaned over, setting aside his flex grips in favor of the phone. He put a call through to Washington, managing to track down Seamus McTeague after several referrals.

"Jack, buddy, it's great to hear your voice."

"What there is of it," Jack said. His larynx was still tender but he was able to talk louder than a whisper now.

"How you holding up?"

"Getting antsy," Jack confessed.

"I'll bet. Cabin fever, huh? You have to give it time, you know. How's Jane?"

"Fine. She spoils me rotten." Leaning to one side in bed, Jack could see her out on the back porch, drumming her fingers on the frame of her typewriter. She glanced up at him and he smiled, waving to her.

"Well, I doubt that you called about the weather," McTeague told him. "What's up?"

"That's what I want to know," Jack said. "Let me in on this business in Oregon."

"Some damned mess, isn't it? The Bureau and CIA's handling it for the most part, but we've got this special task force so I'm privy to more than I would be otherwise."

"I figured as much. Making any headway?"

"I talked to Tony Bex yesterday and he said something about a lead up in Chicago. No details, but I got a feeling he's gonna come up with some link to that gas heist, too."

"What's the Service up to on this?"

"The expected," McTeague said. "Beefing up security around Houril, his wife, and kids. You know how it goes."

"I wish to hell I was there," Jack said.

"Yeah, well, we miss your ugly mug around here, too." They talked a little longer. Then Jack hung up the phone. He looked down at the newspaper, then up at the television. A Georgetown University political science teacher was speculating on the identities of the group responsible for the two recent instances of domestic terrorist activity. He was pointing fingers at Central America and the Soviet Union. Demarrest had his doubts about Russian involvement, and he didn't think any forces in Central America would have made such provocations without boasting about their responsibility. No, there had to be someone else behind it. He wished to hell he knew who it was, because the anxiety that had been gnawing at him all afternoon was becoming increasingly pronounced, and that anxiety had a name.

Revenge.

Twenty

Even the most disciplined of writers had a knack for diversion, and Jane was no exception. The blank page in her typewriter could be merciless in its taunting, carrying on like some opaque mirror demanding that rather than looking passively at her reflection, she would have to create it, with unsparing honesty and full detail. In the face of so burdensome a prospect it was easy to look away from the typewriter and find any number of small tasks begging to be taken care of. This afternoon, for instance, the falling sun cast its light across the flowerbeds framing the thin strip of land passing for the cottage's backyard. Flowers tipped in the breeze, bending to catch the light just right, so that Jane couldn't look at them without being overcome by the urge to pick them. *Yes, Jane. Pick me. And me. Yes, Jane, imagine all of us mingling together in a vase. Beautiful, yes? You can put the vase on your desk, right in front of the typewriter. For inspiration, right? Can't do your best work without inspiration, can you? Come on, Jane, you can take a few more minutes. There's more to writing than just camping out behind the typewriter all day. You need a break. You've earned it, Jane.*

She got up from her chair and grabbed a pair of trimming shears from the ledge in front of the kitchen window. Down the steps she bounded, glad to have liberated herself from the patio, even if it was only for a few minutes. She carefully eyed the flower beds, trying to recall which blooms had come up that day and which had already been around long enough to have drawn sufficient nourishment to withstand the trauma of being cut for the vase. She clipped mostly tulips, red and orange petals like flames in the sunlight. On the way back to the patio, she smelled the flowers and smiled. Jack was still in bed, staring out at her. She waved the flowers slightly. He smiled stiffly back at her, then turned his gaze down at the newspaper in his lap. As she went inside and filled a vase to put the flowers in, she recalled her accident with the breakfast tray that morning and chuckled lightly to herself. She'd planned it all, having overloaded the tray with careful consideration and practiced several different ways of walking before deciding that the balancing act with her nose against the orange juice was the most apt to provide them both with some much-needed comic relief. The past week had been extremely trying, for her as well as him. Starting work on her book was challenge enough. Having to contend with Jack's mercurial moods had required even more concentration. How many times had she worked out on the patio with her attention divided, pecking slowly at the typewriter as she kept her ears tuned to the opened window behind her, hoping to judge from Jack's sighs and the way he shifted in bed whether he might want or need her presence? She was glad to give what she could of herself, even grateful for the forced breaks from her work required by the need to prepare meals, clean the cottage, and run errands. In many ways things were proceeding much as she had expected. Her biggest concern had been the lack of spontaneity, the absence of frivolity that had marked their earlier week together. Of course the circumstances had changed, but it seemed that now Jack was trying too hard to be the good patient, the valiant soul in the face of adversity, while she was guilty of her own charade, of being some modern-day Florence Nightingale, stoic and compassionate to the point of absurdity. The "accident" had been a step in the right direction, a breaking-through of their diligent façades. Now she just had to see to it that they kept it up. Today, a good laugh, tomorrow . . .?

Back out on the patio, she set the cut tulips next to her typewriter and resumed her battle with the blank page. She had gotten to a chapter about her failed marriage, the bitter years with Andrew that had led to her drinking problem, that had ended with her decision to divorce him only a few days before he was murdered by J. T. Aames, an old high school flame with deadly designs upon her. This was to be the heart of her book, of course, the reason the public would rush to buy it. How could she come across some fresh perspective on those painful events that would give them a ring of honesty without sounding as if she were milking her hardships for all the pathos it was worth? That seemed such an easy way out, to paint herself as a poor victim of foul circumstance, a helpless innocent brutalized by the men in her life. She knew there was far more to it than that. She had had a hand in her undoing, and somehow she had to own up to it while keeping things in balance. No easy task.

Several times she tried to commit her thoughts to paper, but the words came out awkward, clumsy. None of them rang true. She fussed with the flower arrangement, cleaned the typewriter keys, tried propping objects of different heights under her feet to reduce back fatigue. When it became clear that she was spending more time on her distractions than her work, she abandoned the typewriter altogether and busied herself with neatening the stack of pages she had already written. She decided to read what she'd done so far in hopes of both polishing her prose and building momentum. But she only succeeded in escalating her sense of growing despair. How could she have written this, this sophomoric, amateurish babble? How bland, how pretentious, masquerading trite clichés in gaudy adjectives and adverbs. How had she managed to fool one of the country's leading editors into believing she actually knew how to write? Bad. It was all bad, terribly bad. And to think she had been so impressed with this same shallow effort only days before, bragging to Jack that she was going to go ahead and mail out the book, chapter by chapter, written off the top of her head with unmistakable brilliance.

Jane had to fight an urge to crumple her work, to take it to the edge of the property and give it a heave into the breeze, watch the pages flutter into Lake Superior, bound for decomposition, a most deserving fate. Instead, she slipped the pages into a file folder and carefully put it inside the desk beneath her typewriter. Perhaps tomorrow it would read better. Perhaps tomorrow she would be in a better mood, would be more inspired. For now, well, the sun was going down. It was time to make dinner. Beef stew, made from scratch. They would have steaming bowls and sit before the fireplace. Maybe tonight they would talk, the way they had talked before.

The kitchen was fragrant with the aroma of beef stock and vegetables simmering in a large pot. Jane raised the lid and stabbed at a floating chunk of potato. It was still a little too hard. The broth was excellent, however. Rich, thick, and brown. And the loaf of bread in the oven was rising nicely. She'd closed off the kitchen from the rest of the cabin and had even draped towels along the crack beneath the door in hopes of keeping the smells from reaching Jack's room. As far as he knew, tonight's menu was oatmeal and Campbell's soup for the second night in a row. She couldn't wait to see the look on his face when she brought out his favorite dish, his favorite bread. And Dr. Glover had said Jack could drink a little wine. A fine chardonnay was chilling in the refrigerator. For herself, Jane had sparkling cider on hand.

She left through the back door and circled around the cottage, trimming a few more flowers to make an arrangement for the coffee table in the living room. They'd eat there tonight, in front of the fire. As she stacked wood and kindling in the hearth, she sniffed the air, glad that she couldn't smell the stew. So far so good. Her mood was brightening by the moment. To hell with the book for now. There were things more important.

She freshened up in the bathroom, brushed her hair so that it filled out, the way she knew Jack liked it. Fidgeted with the buttons of her blouse, found herself blushing in the mirror with embarrassment. *Here I am, carrying on like a teen-ager on her first date.*

Jack was still busy with the newspaper when she came in and sat beside him on the bed. He set the paper aside and they kissed, a haphazard peck that she stretched into a longer embrace, giving him a chance to smell her perfume. When their lips parted and she opened her eyes, she could see the preoccupied cast to his gaze. She was hurt, but caught herself, didn't let it show. Instead, she ran her fingers through his hair.

"Getting hungry?" she asked.

He nodded, still with the faraway eyes.

"Jack, what is it? Something we can talk about?"

Jack looked at her. "When I first got out of surgery, Dr. Glover said there was a chance they could go back in after that bullet lodged against my spine. All I had to do was regain my strength."

"It's more complicated than that, Jack. You know it."

Jane dropped her hand from his hair, put it in his lap. "I talked to him about it, too. There's risks, big risks. And no guarantees you'd come out of it better off than you are."

Jack clasped Jane's hand tightly, looked her in the eyes with a purposeful gaze. "I want that operation," he said.

Twenty-one

Even though it was the state capital, Bismarck was a small town, and, as in most small towns, it was difficult to get through the day without somebody else knowing your business. Hal Dewez and Jake Morrison had quickly learned that they needed more than the pretense of their dairy farm to cover for the various activities that took place on their property. Flaunting bogus military credentials, they had set up the training ground in the back woods as part of a periodic survivalist training program they would provide for anyone within a hundred-mile radius who could pass a physical, pay a tidy fee, and sign a waiver releasing Dewez and Morrison from any responsibility for what might happen to "students" while they subjected themselves to torturous regimens modeled after exercises engaged in by the Navy SEALS, Delta Force, and other paramilitary organizations. The old lodge served as headquarters for the survival programs, but the men had also gone so far as to set up a small shop in downtown Bismarck that specialized in the wares most often sought out by doom-conscious souls ranging from devout Mormons to right-wing religious zealots and closet Nazis masquerading behind haughty monikers. Christened Darwin's Den in tribute to the man who first made "survival of the fittest" a household phrase, Morrison and Dewez's supply shop took up the middle space in a cramped mini-mall built on the site of a former service station. Flanked on one side by a take-out Chinese restaurant and on the other by a trinket-and-antique shop, the Den was a decidedly low-profile enterprise, advertised by only the smallest of storefront signs and relying primarily on word of mouth for business. Operating both the store and the survivalist outings gave the men a bona fide cover for their more clandestine operations and also provided them with a visible means of support, allowing them to keep at a minimum any loose talk around town about their spending habits or the nature of the merchandise that tended to pass through their hands.

Morrison was at the shop the day after the incident in Oregon. As agreed upon, Dewez hadn't tried to make radio contact with the ranch for fear of being overheard, but the plan had been for him to place a call at four-hour intervals to a pay phone located down the block from Darwin's Den. The night Dewez and the Syrians had departed for Oregon, however, a drunkard had taken it upon himself to practice an inebriated approximation of Kung Fu on the phone when it had failed to refund his money after he'd misdialed a number. With the phone out of service, Morrison was dependent upon the media for information on the heist, and he took partial consolation in the fact that apparently no one had been apprehended in connection with the incident. He'd checked with the ranch periodically to see if Dewez might have called in with a coded message, but there was no news. For all Morrison knew, their Huey might have crashed into the Rockies, killing all aboard and unleashing nerve gas upon an unsuspecting population of mountain goats and cougars.

He was alone in the store with Brady, one of the ranch hands. They were unloading a shipment of dried foods, stacking them on shelves next to the bottled water and across from the bookracks containing tomes that dealt with such survivalist concerns as purification of chlorinated pool water, stockpiling of nonperishable foodstuffs in an erosion-proof environment, and ways to kill a man with your bare hands or other normally nonlethal objects.

"Should have that phone fixed by sundown," Brady said as he stacked bags of freeze-dried apricots on a shelf. "Any luck and we can catch Dewez next time he calls."

"Provided he *does* call," Morrison muttered. When the door opened and a beer-bellied man walked in looking for a month's supply of instant potato flakes, Morrison let Brady handle the sale so he could go to the back office and take care of some other business. The office was a cramped space made even smaller by loose clutter. Morrison put a call through to the ranch. Still no word from Dewez. He was about to place a long-distance call to an answering service in Washington when the rear door to the office swung open. Dewez strolled in, his mouth a grinning sickle of yellow teeth.

"Hey, Jake!" As Morrison hung up the phone, Dewez told him, "I checked out the phone on the way here. No fucking wonder I couldn't reach you guys."

"Never mind that," Morrison said, rising from his desk to shake Dewez's hand. "It's good to see you. We were concerned —"

"Yeah, well, I would have called the ranch, but I had my hands filled getting those camel jockeys out of my hair and tying up loose ends. Sorry."

"I take it everything worked out."

Dewez nodded, taking an envelope from his pocket. It was similar in size to the envelope Argvai had given

Morrison upon the Syrian's arrival at the dairy ranch.
It was also similarly filled with large denominations of
American currency. "Three canisters down, three to go,"
he said. "I've got 'em out in my car, tucked away like
babies. Hoummari decided if she's gonna adopt any of
'em?"

"She's still talking with her people," Morrison said.
"It'll be a few days before we know."

"Well, if she doesn't want it, somebody else will, right?"
Morrison nodded. "True."

Dewez noted Morrison's downbeat mood for the first
time. "Hey, what's the problem? Things are shaping up
nicely. We made ourselves a quick kill here and our hands
are still clean as far as anyone knows. That's what it's
all about, eh?"

"Something's come up," Morrison replied.

"Oh, yeah?"

"I had a call from Winslow today. Somehow the FBI
caught wind of the Syrians' Chicago connections." Morrison looked at Dewez. "They still plan on moving the
gas out of there, don't they?"

Dewez's smile faded. "Yeah, that's the plan, all right.
Shit! How much do they know?"

"Winslow wasn't sure," Morrison said. "Washington's
clammed up and the guy he was tapping for info just
flew to Chicago to check things out."

"That's fucked." Dewez hit the wall with his fist and
swore some more, then tapped out a cigarette. "Hell, I
thought those friggin' Syrians were out of the picture."

"Far from it."

"Ain't that the truth." Dewez blew smoke. "We have
to do something."

Morrison nodded. "I think you should give Arlo Kendall a call, see if he can help out."

"Jesus!" Dewez moaned. "Not Arlo."

"He's our best bet," Morrison insisted. "We need to find out if we've been linked with the Syrians. Kendall knows Chicago better than anyone else we have ties to."

Dewez grimaced as he took a long draw on his cigarette, spilling ash to the floor. "Shit! Not fucking Arlo ..."

Twenty-two

Jane was trying to be supportive, but Jack could see the fear behind her taut smile, the slight trembling in her hands as she stroked his forearm.

"I'm strong, Jane," he tried to assure her. "Trust me."

Jane's eyes were damp. "I want to," she whispered. "I don't like worrying. It's just that ... Jack, you never had a chance to see yourself those first few days in the hospital. You were so frail. I swear, it broke my heart to look at you. I know it's partly just selfishness on my part, but I don't want to see you like that again. It was too frightening."

She was still stitting at the edge of the bed. Jack drew her into his arms and leaned back. Her head on his chest, they both stared out the window at the sunset. He ran his fingers through her hair, kissed the loose strands. "I want to watch that sun go down from the docks someday."

"I could wheel you down there."

"That's not what I mean. I want to walk down there, sit on planks, stick my feet in the water and feel it. You know what I mean?" He laughed lightly. "I'm talking Otis Redding here."

"Jack . . ."

"I'm serious. I want to be able to pick you up and throw you in the water, then go swimming after you. It'd get dark and we'd have to hurry inside, start up a big fire in the living room. Make love in front of the flames like we did in Chicago . . ."

The tears were flowing freely. They both wept, turned to face each other and kiss, holding each other close. Jack left unsaid his other, equally firm desire — that he could be well enough to rejoin Seamus and the others out there trying to track down the men responsible for his condition and the other acts of terror they'd sprung on the world with a brash, insidious defiance. As he lay silently with Jane, letting the room go dark with the coming twilight, he couldn't help wondering about a spate of unanswered questions concerning the terrorists. The assassination attempt and the raid on the nerve gas shipment in Oregon had both been full-scale military assaults, so unlike any other related incidents he could think of. Assassinations in America had traditionally been the acts of lone individuals or the smallest of groups, and most documented acts of domestic terrorism involved time bombs or other similarly passive acts where the perpetrators removed themselves from the scene of violence as much as possible. The guerrilla nature of what had been happening of late had all the markings of Third World subversives or Middle East terrorist squads. Was there an actual foreign involvement, or was some fringe group inside the States merely using international events as inspiration? And, too, there was the disturbing likelihood that those forces behind the attacks had contacts within both the U.S. government and its intelligence community.

"Penny for your thoughts, Jack."

They'd been lying there for some time, their tears already dry. Jack's arm had fallen asleep where Jane was leaning on it.

"A penny? Is that all you think they're worth?" Jack teased, avoiding an answer. As Jane shifted her position and sat up, Jack sniffed the air. "Hey, what's that smell?"

"Oh, shit!" Jane bounded to her feet and rushed for the door. "I can't believe I forgot about it!"

"Forgot about what?"

Both the stew and bread were slightly burned, but they were still a welcome surprise. They ate out in the living room, Jack in his wheelchair, facing Jane and the fire. He could feel the wine halfway through his first glass and he let go of his worries about the world outside their cabin. Jane related her frustrations with work on the memoirs, and Jack took advantage of the opportunity to provide support. He heard her out, listening intently to her reminiscences of life in Los Angeles in the years before she moved to Washington. Just talking gave Jane some new insights and perspectives and her mood brightened as the night wore on. The had ice cream smothered in chocolate syrup for dessert and dozed off holding hands before the fire. It was close to midnight when Jack awoke, feeling a dull headache. Jane was curled up in a chair beside him, snoring lightly. He quietly wheeled himself away from her, going to a hall closet, where there were two sleeping bags on one of the lower shelves. It took some doing, but he managed to pull the bags out and unroll them on the carpet in front of the fireplace. There was still a glow in the embers and he wheeled close enough to stir up a flame, letting it catch a handful of kindling and spread to the small branches he carefully tossed onto the grating.

"Jack?"

He turned, saw Jane stirring in her chair, yawning as she rubbed the sleep in her eyes.

"Want to help me put a few logs on?"

"But it's late, Jack. What's with the sleeping bags?"

Jack grinned. "I thought we'd camp out for a change."

"What?"

"You heard me. C'mon, give me a hand."

The whole time they'd been at the cottage, Jack and Jane had spent their nights separately, he in his customized bed, she on a cot in the room next door. It had been an unspoken arrangement, unquestioned until tonight.

"Are you sure?" Jane asked as she got up from her chair.

"Positive," Jack told her. "I want to be with you when I wake up in the morning. Any objections?"

"No," Jane whispered, kneeling next to Jack and embracing him. "None at all . . ."

Twenty-three

Tony Bex finished his cigarette near a two-story-high Picasso sculpture of a baboon head that filled most of the courtyard between two of the countless skyscrapers passing for trees in Chicago's asphalt jungle. The brightly colored sculpture reminded him of a criminology instructor from his early days with the Bureau. He'd covered a lot of ground since then, tackled as many varied assignments as any other agent he knew. This one was shaping up to be the biggest of them all. *Crack this one and I can retire on top*, he thought. Grab some kudos, tell anecdotes at a banquet tribute, then move to California and get a cush job as creative consultant for some movie outfit in Hollywood. It was amazing how much money they'd pay just to have someone around to give their shit a whiff of authenticity. He'd buy a nice car and line himself up with a steady diet of starlets who couldn't get enough of a lawman who talked dirty and bought them pretty things.

Rush hour was ending and the city streets began to swell with colliding shadows as the sun dipped below the skyline. Bex flicked his cigarette at the baboon and fell in with the flow of pedestrians heading toward the nearest intersection. He stayed behind when the crosslight changed, keeping his eyes on a news kiosk halfway down the block. Among the half dozen people skimming through papers and magazines was a short man with a skimpy goatee, wearing a military jumpsuit two sizes too big for him, splotched with paint. A riding cap was cocked to one side of his head, and his eyes were hidden behind tinted granny glasses as he nosed through a smut magazine. He glanced up, saw that Bex was watching him, and slipped a scrap of paper into the magazine before setting it back on the rack. The kiosk was next to a bus stop, and the small man clambered aboard an eastbound bus as Bex strode to the kiosk and bought the magazine. He didn't open it up until he was inside a cab he'd flagged down at the curb.

The note told him:

Fifth and Summit. Old stockyard gate.

Bex repeated the directions to the cabbie and sat back, fingering the lapels of his overcoat, glad to feel the inconspicuous button transmitter relaying his position to a back-up team of agents waiting in an unmarked sedan parked around the corner. There was a second, larger transmitter taped to his chest and attached to a microphone that would hopefully pass along his conversation with the little man in the jumpsuit. Bex had a bad feeling about him, but when the person he'd planned to meet about the Syrian connection had skipped their rendezvous and apparently left the city in a big hurry, the Bureau feared they'd come up with a dead end, only to receive an anonymous call offering information on the missing contact and further insight into Middle Eastern involvement in the failed hit on Houril. This informant had resisted offers to meet in a public place, preferring to call as many of the shots as he could. Bex had no idea if the man with the goatee was, in fact, the new contact or merely a go-between, just as he was in the dark as to whether the meeting would take place at the stockyard gate. Picasso's baboon and the news kiosk were only two of nearly a dozen landmarks Bex had been forced to seek out over the past two hours, each time receiving a fresh clue as to where he should go next. The little man had been on hand at half the spots, but Bex had also encountered a rail-thin woman, an acne-ravaged young man in a motorcycle jacket, and a lumbering hulk who could have made a good bookend with Refrigerator Perry. Maybe this new mystery contact was just trying to impress Bex and the FBI with the manpower at his disposal. More likely he was trying to shake off anybody tailing Bex. Then again, Bex bleakly theorized, this could be nothing more than an elaborate hoax, some prize jerk's way of getting his rocks off. Bex would find out soon enough, because he decided during the cab ride to Fifth and Summit that he was through playing hide-and-seek. He was going to stay put at the old gate until the person he wanted to meet came to him.

"Fuck this shit!" as he put it.

It was dark by the time he got out of the cab and started across a grassy field surrounding the old stockyard gate. It was built along the lines of the Arc de Triomphe in Paris, though much smaller in size and significance, commemorating, after all, the arrival of doomed cattle destined for the meat departments of America's supermarkets. Not surprisingly, there were no wreaths laid at the base of the arch, no tourists crowding before it and saying *cheeseburger* for the camera. The park seemed deserted and stank, not of bovine slaughter, but of wino piss and cheap port.

Bex checked his watch in the spotlight shining up at the arch. He was a few minutes early still. Leaning against the brickwork, he rolled a quick cigarette, pinched it between his fingers before poking it in his mouth.

"Need a light?" the little man with the goatee said as he stepped out of the shadows, holding a Bic out before him, flame reflecting off his tinted lenses.

Bex lit up on his own, stepped away from the arch. Cool, not about to let the man know he was fed up with the runaround. Not yet, at least. He blew smoke in the little man's face, told him, "I thought they gave away free razors with those lighters."

The little man put away his lighter, stroked the stubble on his chin with a grin. "I don't shave when I'm on vacation."

"I was hoping you were here on business," Bex said. "How about we get down to it? I take it you're in charge on your end."

"Correcto, Mr. B."

"You have me at a disadvantage," Bex said. "I don't know *your* name."

"How about that?"

Bex pitched his cigarette into the shadows. "Okay. I came into town to see a guy named Omar about Syrians running around in our backyard. I go to meet him and he doesn't show. Instead, I get a bouquet of flowers with a card that sends me on a wild-goose chase. I'm supposed to find out what happened to Omar and what's going on with these Syrians, but instead I get blisters on my feet and shell out enough cab fare to buy my own fucking taxi. For what? How's that saying go? 'Are we having fun yet?'"

The little man laughed. "Yeah, I had a blast. But, sure,

you wanna get serious, fine." He put his hand out. "One of those notes mentioned a finder's fee. We saw you go to the bank, so I assume you have it on you."

"Not so fast," Bex told the man. "You talk first. Then I pay."

The little man sighed. The shadows let loose another man, the Goliath Bex had run into earlier at the stop before Picasso's sculpture. The big man was also fast on his feet. Bex wound up with his arms pinned behind his back before he could get to his gun. The little man took Bex's weapon and pressed it against the agent's neck as he searched him.

"Wrong answer, Mr. B."

Although this was the quieter end of town, there were still plenty of night sounds. Traffic a few blocks over, a few cooing pigeons up in the arch. Off in the distance one particular sound grew increasingly louder. Bex saw a helicopter finally clear the rooftops of a warehouse across the street and flutter toward the grass clearing. He stayed as calm as he could when the little man ripped his shirt open at the chest, revealing the larger transmitter.

"Got a heart problem, Mr. B?" The little man ripped loose the transmitter wiring. "Naw, I don't think this is a pacemaker after all."

"What's with the chopper?" Bex asked as the helicopter set down in front of the gateway and kept its rotors turning. It was a small Bell, one man at the controls.

"You're bitching so much about cab fare, we figured the next ride should be on us."

Bex's captor had a skull as thick as he was big, and a butt from his forehead was enough to knock the agent out.

"Hold it right there!" came a shout from the far end of the clearing. "FBI!"

Three other agents were running toward the gateway, waving handguns in front of them. As the big man dragged

Bex to the chopper, his smaller partner leveled Bex's gun and fired at the approaching lawmen. One of them crumpled to the grass while the other two fanned out, taking refuge behind trash cans. Once Bex had been stuffed inside the copter, the big man hauled out an Uzi and pinned down the surviving agents with steady fire while the little man scrambled aboard. He took a bullet in the arm as he got into the chopper and closed the door behind him. The aircraft lifted off and banked away from the two agents on the ground, who ran in pursuit, firing a few more wasted shots before giving up and heading back to see if they could help the third man before he bled to death.

Twenty-four

Jane sat alongside Jack's bed in the pre-op wing of Marquette City Hospital. The nurses had been able to tap into a vein in his arm for the intravenous drip, freeing his hands so he could play cards with Jane as he awaited his turn for surgery. They mostly went through the motions of playing, not keeping score, in no apparent hurry. It gave them something to do, something to focus on besides Jack's pending return to the operating table. He'd called to request the surgery the morning after their fireside dinner, and although Dr. Glover had voiced the same concerns as Jane, he hadn't been able to change Jack's mind, and he ultimately put the agent on schedule for the following afternoon. Jack and Jane had spent yesterday together, driving down the coast to Pictured Rocks National Lakeshore, yet another of the Upper Peninsula's many natural wonders. It had been a warm, clear day and they'd spent most of it quietly watching the scenery, each of them lost in their own thoughts. Because Jack was under doctor's orders to fast completely after ten o'clock that evening, they indulged in the most lavish lunch and dinner they could find within his dietary restrictions, and it was while they ate that they shared their thoughts, their hopes for the future. Their conversations were invariably optimistic and they talked as if his full recovery was almost a foregone conclusion. But beneath this façade of mutual hope, neither of them was able to clear their minds of certain dark realities. Dr. Glover had put it to them plainly and succinctly. As with any surgical procedure requiring a general anesthesia, death was always a possibility, however remote. And there was also another disturbing possibility — that the surgery would do nothing to reverse the paralysis of his lower limbs, or, worse yet, that tampering with the bullet lodged in his spine might lead to further nerve damage. It was not inconceivable, Glover had gravely maintained, that Demarrest would emerge from surgery a quadriplegic.

Now, as Jane dealt out another hand, she and Jack continued to battle back against a sense of dread and foreboding. They shared small talk, teased each other as they played, but during the lapses between the distractions their concern rose to the surface. They would look to each other, feeling a sharp tug of emotion, realizing there was that distant chance that these were the last few moments they might ever share.

The plastic curtain blocking their view of the rest of the room was pulled open by an orderly and nurse. The nurse was the same woman who had been washing Jack's back the first time Jane had come to see him at the hospital. She commented on how much better he looked now, then told Jane she would have to leave while Jack received a preliminary injection prior to going under anesthesia. Jane slipped the cards in her pocket and stood up, leaning over Jack.

"I'll be fine," he assured her, clutching her hand.

Jane smiled but her eyes were filled with worry, shimmering with the verge of tears. "I love you, Jack," she whispered, kissing his lips. "I'm behind you, no matter what."

"I know."

Jane blew him a second kiss and started out, turning her gaze from the sight of the nurse readying a syringe. She felt light-headed and took a deep breath on her way to the rest room across the way. Inside she leaned over the sink and splashed her face with cold water. She glanced at her reflection in the mirror and was startled by the terror in her eyes.

She'd brought her manuscript with her, and as she took a seat in the waiting room, she fingered absently at the pages, trying to focus her concentration on the words. With some difficulty, she was finally able to read. To her amazement, her prose didn't seem quite as appalling as it had the other night. She wondered if she were just being less critical now. After all, with one's lover about to have his life put on the line, all other matters tended to lose some of the would-be importance they might otherwise lay claim to. There was a clock on the wall and her gaze strayed up to it, recalling Jack's surgery schedule and imagining where he was at any given moment.

There was a family seated across the room, a mother and father keeping an eye on the young boy playing on the floor between them. They whispered to one another periodically, and, as it did for Jane, the clock held a special significance for them, demanding far more of their attention than the television in the corner with its sound turned down.

Jane had been there an hour when a surgeon, still wearing the outfit he had worn in the operating room, walked in. He offered Jane a soft smile, then sought out the family. Jane could make out only a few random words, but from the reaction of the parents she could tell that the news was good. The mother was weeping, smiling at the same time, hugging her boy. Her husband looked stunned, pleasantly so. The doctor gave them a last few words of encouragement, then turned to leave the room.

"Are you here for Jack Demarrest?"

"Yes." Jane's voice cracked as she spoke.

"They just took him in," the doctor said. "He's in good hands."

The doctor left and Jane stared at the floor, trying to calm the rapid increase in her pulse. She wasn't religious by nature, hadn't been so for more than half her life, but she found herself twisting the doctor's words in her mind.

"Jack," she murmured.

He's in God's hands ...

Twenty-five

Seamus McTeague was on a Chicago-bound plane within an hour after hearing of Tony Bex's abduction. He arrived at O'Hare shortly after midnight, already exhausted from the double shifts he'd been working on almost on a daily basis since a link had been established between the events in Michigan and Oregon. When he called the FBI's regional office in Chicago and was told there were no new developments since he'd spoken to agent Dan Carlisle, McTeague decided to wait until morning before plugging himself into this latest wrinkle in the convoluted quagmire of domestic terrorism. He took a cab to Palmer House and checked in for the night, leaving instructions for a wake-up call at nine the following morning. When the call came, he found himself sprawled across his bed, fully dressed, having collapsed from fatigue moments after taking his shoes off. The sleep had done him good. He ordered up breakfast and sent his suit out to be pressed while he ate, showered, and skimmed the morning papers. To his relief, he found no mention of Bex's abduction on the front page. Newsworthy as the story might have been, both the *Tribune* and *Sun-Times* had relegated it to small print in the back sections after receiving word from the President's task force not to play into the hands of news-hungry fanatics who might take a cue from the media saturation recent terrorist activities had received.

It was shortly after ten thirty when McTeague reported to the local FBI headquarters and was ushered into the office of Dan Carlisle. Carlisle was young for a man of his seniority, with small but intense eyes and large ears. A lot of his colleagues called him Batman, but never to his face. He greeted McTeague with a solemn expression that did not alter in the slightest during the entire course of their meeting. Once they had dispensed with greetings, Carlisle waved McTeague into an armchair and settled himself into a padded rocker behind his meticulously neat desk. There was a manila file on the blotter and he opened it, revealing the initial reports on Bex's kidnapping.

"They whisked him away in a Bell chopper," Carlisle said, flipping through pages. "No identifying marks, of course. Probably a few thousand like it in the area, so we aren't getting our hopes up on that front, although there are men out working on it."

"What size?" McTeague wanted to know.

"Four-seater," Carlisle told him. "Definitely not the same one used in Oregon."

"Christ! What do they have, their own air force?"

Carlisle leaned back in his chair, squeezing one of his pendulous earlobes in an obviously idiosyncratic gesture. "I could give you figures about missing military supplies that would make you want to crawl into the nearest bomb shelter and never come out. Choppers, Jeeps, jet components ... we have records of tanks mysteriously vanishing from supply depots."

"Meaning what?"

"Meaning if this band of cutthroats is as well connected

as we think they might be, they might not only have their own air force but a whole mini-armed forces."

"And they go around raising hell right under our noses," McTeague said, frustration in his voice. "Making us look like a pack of goddamned Keystone Kops.

"Well, losing our heads won't help matters, will it?" Carlisle quit fiddling with his ear and went back to the file, pulling out a scrap of newspaper. "Here's the best thing we have in the way of a lead."

McTeague took the paper from Carlisle and looked it over. It was from yesterday's morning edition, part of the metro section, filled with horoscopes, weather charts, shipping schedules, and obituaries. Carlisle told McTeague it had been found during a search around the base of the old stockyard gate.

"Nothing's marked," McTeague said after checking both sides of the paper.

"No, but it strikes us that the most valuable information is the shipping schedule at Navy Pier. We're putting most of our money on that."

McTeague gave the paper back to Carlisle. He didn't care much for the other man's dispassionate demeanor but kept his feelings to himself, almost mimicking Carlisle. "If it was a straight kidnapping, we would have heard something by now," he surmised. "Some kind of ransom note."

"Nothing."

"What about the person he was supposed to meet? Omar?"

"Omar's still missing, too." Carlisle pulled a black-and-white mug shot from the file. "This is who Bex ended up meeting. Name's Arlo Kendall. Nickel-dime thug, but he knows the streets around here. We used him as an informer a few years back on a weapons-smuggling case. It didn't work out."

"How so?"

"We were after big fish and all he turned us on to were minnows," Carlisle said. "I think he was just playing along while he sniffed us out, got some ideas on how to keep his nose clean in the future. So far it's worked."

In the photo, Kendall was without his goatee and glasses, staring out at the world with a smart-ass leer, like he knew something important and wasn't about to let on what it was. "Does he have any inside connections?" McTeague asked.

Carlisle shook his head. "We haven't worked with him in years, so I can't say for sure. I was his contact back then." As an afterthought, he added, "And I'm clean."

McTeague slumped back in his chair, adding up the new bits of the puzzle. He didn't like the shape it was taking. "If any of that loose gas gets put on an outbound freighter, there's no telling where it will end up."

Carlisle said, "We're just going to have to make sure it doesn't come to that . . ."

Twenty-six

Tony Bex awoke slowly, dazed, temples throbbing. Cold cement pressed against his face, his hands. He opened one eye, then the other, seeing only dark gloom. *Where am I? Why can't I see?* Questions ran frantically through the fog inside his skull, making his head ache when they collided. His whole body was sore. It hurt to move. He remained still, fighting the disorientation. When his eyes became attuned to the darkness, he made out a door across from him, shut tight. He turned his head slightly, realizing he was lying face down on a floor. The room was small, empty. *Where am I?* he wondered again. He backtracked in his mind. Chicago. A baboon. Little beatnik and his big stooge. The helicopter. He was still figuring it all out when a light flashed on over his head. He sat up, traced the glow to a bulb in the ceiling, recessed behind a mesh screen, throwing checkered shadows across the floor. His hand went to his chin. A day-old beard. *Where am I?*

"Did you sleep well, Mr. Bex?"

There was a small speaker next to the light, also built into the ceiling and covered with protective mesh. The voice was pleasant but unfamiliar. A man.

"Where am I?" His tongue was dry, thick, slurring his speech.

"I think it would be best if we asked the questions, Mr. Bex."

Bex closed his eyes, fought off his pains. He rose to his feet, legs feeling like lead. He eyed a mirror built into the wall across from him. He looked into it, ignoring his reflection, addressing people he couldn't see.

"Who are you?"

Jake Morrison and Koura Hoummari were on the other side of the two-way mirror, watching the prisoner. This room was larger than Bex's, carpeted and paneled. They sat in swivel chairs, side by side. Morrison was closest to a control box mounted on the wall next to the mirror, equipped with a bank of toggle switches, a condenser microphone, and small speakers the size of half dollars. He had to push a button next to the microphone to speak to Bex, who was now standing before the mirror, pounding it weakly with his fist.

"Save your strength, Mr. Bex."

Bex stepped back from the mirror, rubbed the back of his head as he looked up at the ceiling again. This time he talked to the light. "What do you want from me?"

"I think you know, Mr. Bex."

"I know who the fuck I am, all right? Lay off the 'Mr. Bex' shit."

"If that's what you want, fine. Cooperation is what this is all about."

"Oh yeah?" Bex spat on the floor. "Shit! I thought I was goin' on a game show. What's behind door number one over here?"

"We have all the time in the world," Morrison told

Bex. "Play games if you like, but sooner or later you'll have to do things our way."

Bex stood in the middle of the room, arms crossed and silent. A minute passed. Two. Then he calmly walked back to the mirror and spat on the glass.

Hoummari instinctively recoiled in her seat. "Insolent bastard!"

"What's this? A lady, too?" Bex taunted. "You guys got a strange idea of a hot date, don't you?"

"I think you could use a lesson in manners, Mr. Bex," Morrison intoned as he leaned toward the control box and flipped one of the switches.

Inside Bex's cell, an intense, ear-piercing siren blared down at Bex from the ceiling. Morrison flipped another switch so that he and Hoummari couldn't hear the shrill sound or Bex's pained howls as he covered his ears and staggered across the room, eyes closed so that he banged into the unyielding door.

"Stop it, you fuckers! Fuckers!!!"

Half mad from the torturous noise, Bex charged the wall separating him from Morrison and Hoummari. He leaped up, scuffing his stocking feet against the equally reinforced glass of the mirror. He landed hard on the concrete and groaned, writhed in agony, hands still clamped to the sides of his head.

As abruptly as it had begun, the siren stopped. An after-ring echoed in Bex's ears even after he uncovered them. He sat up slowly, blinking away tears of pain. Another sudden blast of the siren brought forth a scream and Bex fell down again, curling himself in a fetal position. The noise stopped much sooner this time, and in the ensuing silence Bex remained contorted, grimacing, waiting for the next jolt.

"I won't have to do it again if you cooperate, Mr. Bex," Morrison told him. "I can be reasonable."

Bex warily unwound himself, rose to one knee. "You

have someone on the inside," he said, eyes back on the mirror. "They know as much as I do."

"If that were true you wouldn't be here, would you? Come on, Mr. Bex. Don't be a fool. Talk to us."

Bex stood up, looked in the mirror. A doomed man stared back at him.

Twenty-seven

Hal Dewez and Arlo Kendall drank beer on the front porch of the hunting lodge, staring at the Bell chopper parked in the clearing beneath camouflage netting.

"Decent of you guys to take that off my hands," Kendall said between swigs. "I sure as hell wasn't going to fly back with it."

"Extra bird can always come in handy," Dewez muttered. He finished his beer and crushed the can against his knee, then pitched it across the grass, missing a trash can by several feet. "By the way, Arlo, what happened to that Omar fellow?"

"Ask me no questions and I'll tell you no lies." Kendall belched and reached to his side, pulling another two cans of beer from a Styrofoam ice chest. He gave one to Dewez and started in on the other, snickering, "Let's just say he went on a deep-sea cruise."

"You run into the Syrians?"

Kendall shook his head. "I figure the less I know the better, right?"

"Yeah, right."

They drank silently, watching squirrels play tag in the nearby trees. Kendall finished his beer, picked up the ice chest, and poured some of the cube-chilled water over his sweating forehead, gasping at the sensation. "Ahhhhh! Damn! That feels good!" As he wiped his face on his shirt sleeve he looked over at Dewez. "C'mon, man, quit leavin' me in fucking suspense, would ya? I know you guys are behind all this shit that's been hitting the fan. What's the lowdown?"

"Don't know what you're talking about, Arlo," Dewez responded coolly, still working slowly on his beer.

"Hal, buddy — This is Arlo . . ."

"Forget it."

"The way I figure, there's always room for a good man, right?" Kendall's voice bubbled with enthusiasm. "I just proved to you that I can deliver, not that you didn't already know I was reliable. Look, you cut me in on the action and I can make it worthwhile. Guns, explosives . . . you name it, I can get my hands on it for you."

"We already have a supplier, Arlo," Dewez told him.

"So I gathered." Kendall was petulant, feeling his beer. "Seems to me I shoulda had the inside track on that, huh?"

"Arlo, you did what we asked and you got paid a god-damned pretty penny for it, okay?" Dewez was fed up with the smaller man's obstinacy. "Why don't you quit while you're ahead?"

Kendall sighed, stood up, and walked out onto the grass. He'd spilled water on his glasses and he took them off, wiped them clean with a loose flap of his jumpsuit. "You know, Hal, the reason I didn't bother tracking down the towelheads was because Omar and I had a nice chat before he went to feed the fish."

"You're lying."

Kendall smiled, put his glasses back on. "Yeah, you're right. Of course, Hal, whatever you say."

Dewez had had enough. He grabbed his gun, fired a bullet into the grass between Kendall's legs. Kendall froze, looked at the scarred ground, heard Dewez's cold voice riding the wake of gunfire. "You've wore out your welcome, Arlo."

"You can't hurt me," Kendall told Dewez. "My people are expecting me back tomorrow. I don't show up and they start making some anonymous phone calls."

"Spare me the threats, Arlo." Dewez waved his gun to one side, pointing out a rental car parked alongside the lodge. "Just get the hell out of here."

The men faced off a few seconds. Then Kendall turned, walked to the car. As he was getting in he glanced back at Dewez. "Hey, man, thanks for the brews."

"Any time, Arlo." Dewez stood up, took a few steps closer so Kendall could hear him as he started his engine. "You don't know how big we are these days," he warned the driver. "You want to find out, though, just threaten us again sometime, okay?"

Kendall said nothing. He put the sedan in reverse, backed out onto the dirt road leading through the woods. Dewez watched until the dust clouds settled, then circled around to the side of the lodge. There was a recessed lean-to attached to the main building with wide wooden doors like the entrance to a storm shelter. Dewez sprang the combination lock and let himself down a flight of steps leading to the farthest-reaching of the many cement-lined tunnels running beneath the sprawl of the dairy ranch. The passageway was ten feet wide and nearly as high, dimly lit by well-spaced low-voltage bulbs. Just inside the entranceway were two old, paint-flecked golf carts hitched up to battery rechargers. Dewez unplugged one of the carts and rode it down the long tunnel until he reached the main underground chamber beneath the old barn. Trent and Brady were near the big doors, working on the engine of a customized Jeep.

"Morrison get anything out of the G-man yet?" Dewez asked.

"Beats me." Trent shrugged.

Brady said, "They're still grilling him. I heard Hoummari saying something about wanting to see how the gas worked."

Dewez plugged the cart into another recharger and strode down one of the other tunnels, passing the bunker where he'd first reported news about the botched assassination attempt in Michigan. Around the corner he saw another of the ranch hands standing in front of a steel door, face pressed against a peephole.

"What the fuck are you doing?" Dewez demanded.

The hireling spun away from the door, too flustered to talk. He eyed Dewez like a schoolboy caught peering into the girls' bathroom.

"Get lost."

When the younger man had left, Dewez went to the door and checked through the peephole. Inside the small cell where he'd been held for questioning, Tony Bex was twitching grotesquely on the floor, clearly having no control over the spasms. The agent's eyes were half open, but there was no life in them. He continued to jerk about for several more seconds. Then he lay still on the concrete, face turned upward at an unnatural angle, limbs contorted.

"Jesus!" Dewez muttered, moving away from the peephole. He went to the door a few yards farther down the corridor and pulled it open. He couldn't believe what he was seeing. Morrison was standing up, back against the two-way mirror, his pants to the floor as he held on to Koura Hoummari, who had her skirt hiked up to her thighs as she straddled the man's loins, panting and grinding herself against him as she looked over Morrison's shoulder and through the two-way mirror at the prostrate body of Tony Bex. Caught up in the throes of her ecstasy, she ignored Dewez and continued to groan. Morrison glanced at Dewez, his face expressionless. Dewez took a step back and closed the door.

Twenty-eight

There was a phone in the waiting room and it rang seven times before Jane was jarred from her thoughts enough to realize she was the only one around. The phone rang again before she got to it.

"Hello?" Her voice was dull, hoarse.

"Yes. Is there a Jane Britland in the waiting room there, please?"

"Dad?"

"Jane, is that you?"

"Yes, yes." She cleared her mind of what she'd been thinking about. "How on earth did you know to reach me here?"

"Jack talked to Seamus the other day and mentioned something about another operation. When I couldn't reach you at the cottage, I tried the hospital."

"Is there anything wrong, Dad?"

"Well, we're in the thick of a crisis that dwarfs anything I went through as President, but that's not what I called for. How's Jack? Have you heard yet?"

"No, I haven't." She glanced at the wall clock. "He went into surgery two hours ago. I've been going crazy waiting for word. They said it was probably only a half-hour operation. Dad, I'm scared."

"Try not to be, honey. Maybe there were some complications, but you have to hope for the best."

"I've been telling myself that for the past hour."

"Well, keep it up. Talk to me about something else. The book. How's it coming?"

"Terrible. I've done about thirty pages and it's all a big mess. I try to keep it simple and it ends up full of all kinds of wretched clichés, so I start changing things around and pretty soon it's gotten so pretentious I can barely stand to read it. I'm thinking of giving the advance back and just giving it up."

"You don't mean that, Jane."

"I know." Jane sighed, leaning back against the wall, just realizing how stiff her spine was from all the time she'd spent in one chair without changing positions. "It's just very discouraging, and of course I'm always thinking about Jack, too, so I don't have much in the way of concentration."

"Can I ask you something?"

"Of course you can, Dad."

"Who are you writing this book for?"

"What do you mean?"

"I mean, if you're writing it for someone besides yourself, that might be the problem."

"Dad, I don't think they want four hundred pages of 'Dear Diary.'"

"Probably not, but I know Frank Tennleton, and if there's one thing he always looks for in a biography, it's honesty. You have to tell it like it is, Jane, to borrow one of those wretched clichés."

"You're starting to sound like my old analyst, Dad."

"Sorry."

"Don't be. You're probably right. You always were, after all."

George Britland laughed in his daughter's ear. "I never thought I'd live to hear those words from you, my dear. I'd better hang up before you take them back, hmm?"

"Thanks for calling, Dad. I love you."

"And I love you. Your mother sends her best, too. We're at home for the next two hours or so. Why don't you call us collect once you hear word on Jack?"

"Okay, I will."

"Good. Hang in there, honey."

"Thanks again, Dad. 'Bye."

She hung up the receiver and sighed. Next to the pay phone was an in-house line, above which was a posted note giving a number people could call for information regarding patients. She picked the other phone up and started to dial the number, then stopped and set down the receiver. Her hand was trembling. She was afraid to ask how Jack was. It was a superstitious reaction, an irrational fear that her calls would somehow magically flow through the phone wires and seep into the operating room, killing Jack where he lay. She found herself laughing out loud, a ragged, frightening laugh like that of a cackling witch. *God, what's happening to me?* She sat back down, closed her eyes, drawing in deep breaths. *Yes, in slowly, out slowly. Think peaceful thoughts.* She'd learned relaxation techniques at the rehab center and she put them to use, fighting off the hysteria. When a semblance of calm came over her, she opened her eyes and saw Dr. Glover standing before her, blood on his gown.

Jack's favorite recurring sensation in his dreams was that of being weightless, able to move about in great, graceful leaps without concern for gravity, like a dolphin in water. Here he was loose in the woods, toying with armed soldiers who plodded slowly in their pursuit of him, moving as if they were wading through chest-high water instead of airy ferns. He would let them get close to him, maybe even take aim with their incredibily bulky rifles. Then he would twitch slightly and be off skimming above the foliage, caroming noiselessly off the sides of trees like a swimmer kicking off the edge of a pool. He would avoid one soldier, veer, and deftly kick the rifle from the hands of another. When he tired of this game, he merely set his sights on the blue sky visible above the treeline, and with fluid strokes of his arms he would surge upward, a man in flight, racing birds to the clouds . . .

As the anesthesia began to wear off, the clouds thickened, blotting out the dream. The real world crept in with its hospital sounds and antiseptic brightness. He opened his eyes.

"Hello, Jack."

Jane was far away, near the end of the bed, drifting in and out of focus. Smiling but also crying. His legs were uncovered and her hands were on his feet, massaging his toes.

"How does that feel?" she asked.

"It feels," he told her. "It feels . . ."

Twenty-nine

Navy Pier jutted out into Lake Michigan, where long gray freighters plied the choppy waters. The sky was leaden, bleak with dark clouds that whipped wind through Chicago's Loop. Activity along the docks was frenetic, noisy, from the squeal of the winch and rumble of forklifts to the profanity of longshoremen tending to the unrelenting flow of cargo, some of it coming ashore, the rest to be loaded aboard the big ships for the meandering journey through the Great Lakes and St. Lawrence Seaway to the Atlantic Ocean and points beyond. It was concern over the myriad export possibilities that had brought about increased security precautions on the Pier. In addition to the usual measures, an extra security force roamed the area, waving sensors like magic wands over all crates and boxes slated for transfer to cargo holds. Trained German shepherds were led about by leash, lending their olfactory prowess to the proceedings. Should any of the probing turn up the deadly substance authorities were looking for, several small white trucks were parked at equidistant points along the Pier, outfitted with gas masks, radiation suits, and other appropriate equipment that might prove essential in the handling of volatile nerve gas.

McTeague and Dan Carlisle were on hand near the entrance to the Pier, where Coast Guard officers manned a checkpoint and inspected all incoming vehicles. Off to one side, two Chicago policemen were in the process of arresting a crew-topped young man dressed in leather from head to toe. While one of the officers directed the suspect to lean spread-eagle against a patrol car, the other carefully dropped a small glass vial and two half straws into a clear plastic bag.

"Another cokehead," Carlisle groused, annoyance finally breaking through his emotionless façade. He stopped tugging his earlobe and crossed his arms. "That makes three drug busts and one guy we've nabbed for smuggling bogus Levi's. America can sleep easier tonight."

"Maybe we're too visible," McTeague suggested, puffing at his long-stemmed pipe until a small cloud rose from the glowing bowl.

"It's not so easy to be discreet and still get the job done with this sort of layout."

A foghorn blared out in the bay. McTeague turned up the collar of his trenchcoat, trying to keep wind from slipping down his neck and adding to his discomfort. He wasn't sure if it was the ominous weather, his incompatibility with Carlisle, or just the cumulative tension of the past few days, but ever since coming to the Pier two hours ago he'd felt a vague dread gnawing at his nerves, not unlike the caffeine jitters that used to plague him before he cut back on his coffee intake. He tried to force the sensation from his mind and keep his attention on the bustling around him, looking for that one subtle clue betraying someone with a grim, ulterior motive. His vigilance bore fruit several minutes later, as he saw a red

Ford van pull out of the line of vehicles waiting to pass through the security checkpoint at Navy Pier's entrance. He caught a glimpse of the driver and pulled his pipe from his mouth, quickly tapping the loose ash out onto the concrete as he strode to a two-door sedan parked a few yards away.

"What's up?" Carlisle asked, instinctively following McTeague's lead and joining him in the car.

"Put a call out on that van," McTeague said, gesturing at the Ford while he started up the engine. "It's our baby."

"You're sure?"

"Just call it in!" McTeague jerked at the steering wheel and drove around a skid stacked high with stereo crates. Although the sedan was unmarked, the Coast Guard authorities were familiar with it, and a gateway barrier was hastily pulled aside so McTeague could leave the Pier and join traffic along Lake Shore Drive.

"What makes you so sure about this?" Carlisle asked after he'd placed a call over the car's dispatch radio.

"Driver had a headband," McTeague said, scanning the busy thoroughfare.

"Can't get much more criminal than that," Carlisle drawled sarcastically.

"You want to be a comedian, rent a hall," McTeague retorted. "The guy could have been Syrian and it looked like the same kind of headband we saw up in Michigan. Damn it! My gut says this is it."

"I hope to hell you're right."

Arlo Kendall had lied to Hal Dewez about a number of things, including his supposed lack of involvement with the Syrians who had participated in the raid on the nerve gas shipment. Before he'd slain Omar, the would-be government informant, Kendall had pumped the man for all he knew about the Syrian connection. Omar had told him that Argvai and one other of his comrades were coming to Chicago to arrange for the safe passage of their deadly contraband to the Middle East. Their middleman was supposed to have been a Persian rug dealer working out of an exclusive downtown gallery, but after dropping Omar into the Des Plaines River with an old Frigidaire chained to his neck, Kendall had met with Argvai and cut his own deal, agreeing to grease the appropriate skids at Navy Pier for a fee equal to what he was eventually paid for abducting Tony Bex and delivering him to the dairy farm in North Dakota.

Now, as he guided the Ford van through traffic, Argvai cursed himself for having ignored his reservations about Kendall. He'd been betrayed, he was sure of it. The American had taken their money, given them this barely running vehicle and a clipboard filled with forged documents, then had called the authorities so they could set their trap at the Pier. It had almost worked, too, Argvai mused sullenly, turning off Lake Shore Drive at the last possible moment and peering into his rearview mirror to see if anyone had yet picked up his trail. His partner had pulled out an automatic pistol from under his seat and set it on his lap, finger close to the trigger as he checked the side mirror, equally paranoid. They both wore the rigged headbands, this time of their own volition. It was, of course, their highest hope that they would succeed in bringing the nerve gas back to their homeland for use against their enemies, but in the event circumstances prevented the success of that mission, they were determined not to have acted completely in vain. Rather than peacefully surrender and turn over the gas, they were prepared to blow themselves up, killing as many American pigs as they could. With any stroke of fortune, such an act would also destroy the canisters they were carrying, setting loose a death cloud that would make them heroes in the eyes of their people.

Argvai noticed McTeague's sedan gaining on him at

the same time he was slowing down at an intersection where the light had changed. Down the cross street, a police car suddenly swung into view, lights flashing, sirens screaming as it lurched against the flow of traffic in the next lane. Before the squad car could reach the intersection, Argvai pressed his foot to the accelerator and leaned hard on the steering wheel. The van rear-ended a Porsche, shoving it into the intersection, then sideswiped a pickup truck as it shot through a narrow gap between cars, leaving a snarled multivehicle pileup between it and its pursuers. The man riding with Argvai rolled down his window and leaned out, firing a burst from his gun back at the congestion.

McTeague braked just in time to avoid being sideswiped by a station wagon that was, in turn, trying to swerve clear of the pileup, which by now reached all the way into the intersection, preventing the police car from getting through.

"Hold on," McTeague told Carlisle as he cut sharply to his right, bouncing the car onto the sidewalk and scattering pedestrians as he circumvented the mass wreckage. He guided the sedan back onto the cross street just in time to see the red van turn the next corner.

Horns blared as the van hurtled the wrong way down a one-way street, clipping one car and nearly colliding head on with another. When McTeague followed in pursuit moments later, several angry motorists hurled objects at the car; a coffee cup shattered against Carlisle's side of the front windshield, leaving a web of cracks in the glass. Off on the sidewalk, a pedestrian lay sprawled on her back, a bullet in her chest and her groceries spilling from a shopping bag next to her.

"Jackals are taking potshots!" Carlisle shouted as he grabbed the microphone and called in with an update on the van's position. "Don't lose them!"

"I don't aim to," McTeague asserted, leaning to one side so he could see past the blighted part of the windshield.

Two blocks away, a pair of squad cars screeched to a halt in the middle of the intersection, lined up one next to the other to form a makeshift barricade. Officers piled out, using their opened doors for shields as they waited for the van headed their way. One of them shouted to civilians on the street and sidewalk, telling them to duck for cover.

Outdistancing McTeague by more than a hundred yards, the van barreled down the street, its sides battered from glancing blows to other vehicles. Up ahead was the roadblock. Argvai could see at least two riot guns aimed at his vehicle. Rather than slow down, he once more floored the accelerator and took aim at the two-foot gap between the patrol cars. The other Syrian ducked to one side as a shotgun blast took out his side window and the upper part of his bucket seat. A second later, the van pounded its way between the two police cars, spinning them apart with the force of impact and crushing three of the officers in their way.

McTeague aimed his sedan down a narrow section of street to the right of the wrecked cruisers. He was able to squeeze past, but as he began to pick up speed in hopes of gaining ground on the van, which had slowed down due to front-end damage received in the collision, a teen-aged boy on a skateboard suddenly appeared from around the corner of a bank building, heading directly into McTeague's path. To avoid the boy, McTeague hit the brakes and turned sharply to one side, skidding up onto the curb and shearing a hydrant before coming to a stop amid the sidewalk display in front of a florist's shop.

"Are you all right?" he asked Carlisle. The agent was

leaning against the door, bleeding from a gash across his forehead and holding his right shoulder.

"I'll live," Carlisle conceded, swinging his door open. "Let's go."

Leaving their disabled vehicle, the two men continued their pursuit on foot, waving badges along with their guns to keep pedestrians from getting in their way. The air was alive with sirens now as ambulances, paramedic vans, and fire trucks began to converge upon the area along with all available units of Chicago's finest.

Grant Park was a stretch of well-kept greenery between Navy Pier and Soldier Field. Despite the gloomy weather, the park was busy. Separate softball games were taking place at opposite ends of the grounds, and in between there were isolated pockets of activity — couples tossing Frisbees, young children trying to loft kites into the cloud-choked skies, men and women out walking their dogs. There were picnics under the taller trees, people reading near the spouting waters of Buckingham Fountain. It was a Norman Rockwell atmosphere, Americans at their leisure on a quiet, lazy day.

Then came the sirens. First one, then another, finally a frantic chorus. In the midst of it all, the sound of squealing brakes, the shattering of glass, the slamming of vehicles into one another. Those in the park were at first unperturbed by the noise. Chicago was a bustling town, after all, seething with life and the cacophony that came with it. There was always someone dying, someone being born, ambulances racing back and forth to tend to those leaving or entering the world. But as the distraction grew louder, nearer, it was impossible to ignore. People throughout the park looked up, saw a battered red van burst forth from the side streets, hell-bent for the green expanse. There were screams as the Ford jumped the curb and plowed through a cluster of pedestrians. The Syrian riding in the front seat was bleeding, one arm out the window, shooting blindly until his gun was empty.

Police cars raced into view from other directions, heading more cautiously through the park. One officer with a riot gun rolled out of his cruiser, seeing the van on its way across the grounds, breaking up one of the softball games. He raced toward the van, trying to head it off. When he was close enough to get off a shot, he dropped to one knee, took aim, and fired at the driver. The shotgun shook in his powerful arms as it sent its volley of lead at the van.

Argvai shouted in pain as the windshield exploded and he felt a series of hot, jabbing pains in his shoulder. Blood was seeping through his shirt, down his face. He lost control of the van and was clawing at his seat belt when the Ford careened wildly to one side, splintering a picnic table before tottering onto its side atop the steps that led to Buckingham Fountain.

McTeague and Carlisle were crossing the park on foot when they saw the van brought down like some wild beast in a game preserve. They slowed down, catching their breath, figuring the chase was at long last over.

They were wrong.

Argvai and his comrade crawled out of the crippled vehicle, dropped to the grass. Neither man looked well enough to get far, and the cop with the riot gun drew aim on the Syrian closest to him, begged him not to surrender so that the shotgun would have to stop him once and for all. Argvai was on the other side of the van, hidden from the view of the police. He rose to his feet, straggled away from the fountain, favoring one leg injured in the final crash. That part of the park had already been abandoned by fleeing citizens, thwarting his search for a hostage.

"Freeze!" McTeague shouted, pulling his service

revolver from a shoulder holster. Argvai was less than fifty yards away. Carlisle had the Syrian covered with his gun as well.

Argvai stopped, stared at the agents, blood still flowing from his wounds. He put one hand in the air, tried to indicate that he couldn't raise the other one because he'd been shot in the shoulder. That arm he cocked in front of him at an unnatural angle so that it looked useless. He slowly dropped to his knees, eyes still on McTeague and Carlisle, waiting until they came out of their firing stances and started toward him. Then, in a blur of motion fed by fanatical passion, he pulled the remote transmitter from his belt and stabbed his finger at the switches.

"Get down!" McTeague shouted, lurching to one side, shoving Carlisle to the ground. There was an explosion off near the van. Without looking, McTeague knew that the other Syrian's headband had gone off. Argvai was still in one piece, though, much as he continued to flail at the transmitter. McTeague and Carlisle got back on their feet and rushed over to apprehend the terrorist. McTeague took away the transmitter and pointed at Argvai's bleeding scalp and the intact headband.

"Must have fouled up the detonator when you hit your head," he told the Syrian. "Looks like you aren't going to be able to take the easy way out after all..."

Moments after the explosion, a sparrow landed on the grass between the headless Syrian and the ravaged van. It took two frisky hops and was starting to peck at a shred of the terrorist's brain when it was suddenly seized by convulsions, flapping its wings in place for a frenzied second, then lying still. The policeman with the riot gun started toward the van, eyes on the man who'd lost his head before he'd had a chance to be shot. Out of the corner of his eye he saw a slight twitching of the sparrow's wings. As he turned for a closer look, the cop dropped his gun and began to shake uncontrollably. Losing his balance, he pitched forward into the grass, wracked by more spasms.

"Jesus Christ!" Carlisle shouted as he slapped handcuffs on Argvai. His eyes were on the area around the fountain. "What the fuck's going on?"

McTeague also glanced across the park, seeing three more people being felled as if pounded by an unseen surf. There was something unreal about the sight, a nightmarish quality that held the agent mesmerized for several seconds before he broke off the trance and sprang into motion. Telling Carlisle to keep an eye on the prisoner, he rushed off on foot, running at an angle away from the offshore breeze, toward a throng of curiosity-seekers creeping its way toward the fountain.

"Clear the park!" he shouted. "There's been a gas leak! Clear the park!"

Once the people were aware of the reason for the strange activity near the fountain, they gave in to mass hysteria. Police on the scene did their best to make the evacuation as orderly as possible, but as more men and women were pulled down by the drifting invisible cloud, the pandemonium only heightened. There were casualties among several handicapped students on a field trip who were abandoned by their escorts and then knocked to the ground when they were unable to clear themselves from the path of the fleeing mob. Wails of anguish and fear vied with the sirens. When men in full-body emergency suits poured out of trucks and made their way to the van, they had to wade through the fierce human flow.

McTeague helped lead the masses from the park, down a cross street to a parking structure several blocks away. By the time he'd reached the top level less than ten minutes later, the park had been fully evacuated save for the victims and emergency personnel. He could see them from where he was, standing out starkly in their bulky white outfits, some sealing off the van and transferring nerve gas canisters into other leakproof containers, others gathering bodies together at an abandoned picnic site where smoke still rose from a barbecue roasting pieces of chicken to a black crisp.

Thirty

Jack sat at the edge of his hospital bed while Dr. Glover tested his reflexes with a triangular rubber mallet. A tap to the knee and Jack's right foot shot outward.

"Good," Glover pronounced, shifting the mallet to Jack's other knee, repeating the test with similar results. "Good."

Jack winked at Jane across the room. She was back after a fitful night at the cottage. Her excitement had kept her up until past three in the morning, optimism and joy wrestling with a die-hard residual of disbelief at Jack's recovery. Now that she saw him, legs and feet responding to the peck of rubber, smiled back at Jack, exultant despite her fatigue.

"That's some pack of angels you've got watching over you, Jack," Glover said as he set aside the mallet and moved his chair away from the bed. "This kind of progress rates right up there with miracles."

"You can't keep a good man down," Jane said.

"Well, I don't know about the good part," Jack scoffed, dropping his hospital gown back over his knees.

"Do you feel strong enough to stand?"

Jack braced his hands against the bed and pushed himself to his feet. "Doc, I'm ready to do jumping jacks."

"I don't think so, Jack." Dr. Glover crossed the room and picked up an aluminum-frame walker leaning against the wall. "Let's just take it one step at a time, okay?" He unfolded the walker and placed it in front of Jack.

"C'mon, Doc, I don't need that."

Glover smiled sourly. "You keep calling me 'Doc,' so I assume you know what I'm here for, right?"

"Yeah," Jack said, gripping the walker's handles. "Sorry."

"Apology accepted. Now, start out nice and easy."

Jack raised the walker forward a few inches, then set it down and leaned on it for supoort as he took his first step. His forearms trembled under his weight. He took a second step and stopped, chest heaving as he gasped for breath. He looked at Jane, then Glover. "I don't get it," he wheezed.

"On the contrary, I think you *do* get it, finally." Dr. Glover helped Jack back to bed and took away the walker as Demarrest eased back onto the mattress, exhausted. "Don't get discouraged, though. Like I've been trying to tell you, this is to be expected. You have to give yourself time."

"How long?"

"We'll draw up a rehabilitation regimen for you," Glover told him calmly. "Some physical therapy, exercise, a few supplements to your diet —"

"How long?" Jack demanded.

The surgeon sighed. "A month at the absolute minimum. Two or three, more likely."

This wasn't news that Jack wanted to hear. Unlike Jane, he'd been riding on a crest of certainty since awakening from his operation. He had visions of being back on his feet, back on the job in a matter of days — a week, tops — with just a few scars and minor pains to show for his brush with death. The thought of a prolonged rehabilitation frustrated — depressed — him. Jane came over to the bed, pulling a chair behind her. She sat next to Jack, taking his hand.

"Come on, Jack," she said, trying to inject cheer into her voice. "This is wonderful! Don't you realize that? You're going to get better."

"Yeah," he drawled blandly. "But why so long?"

Dr. Glover grabbed his ever-present clipboard and scrawled a few quick notes, then eyed Jack, charm and patience gone from his gaze. "Okay, let me give it to you without the sugar coating. Even if you go through rehabilitation on schedule and come out with flying colors, your spine's going to be vulnerable for a long, long time. You pull any macho routine and try coming back too fast, you're asking for trouble, and I don't have to tell you what kind. Try to remember that."

After Glover left the room, Jane took a towel and dabbed at the sweat on Jack's brow. "We'll get through this," she assured him. "You've already cleared the biggest hurdle."

"Yeah, yeah, yeah," Jack muttered, staring at the wall.

"I don't believe you!" Jane said. "Why are you acting like this? You'd think the operation was a failure the way you're taking it."

There was a reason for Jack's anxiety that he hadn't mentioned and he leaned away from Jane a moment, retrieving a copy of the morning paper from his nightstand. "Here!" he said, thrusting the headlines before Jane's eyes. "Damn it! They're still out there!"

This was the first Jane had seen or heard of the incident at Grant Park. The death toll had reached almost two hundred before the nerve gas had dissipated in the Lake

Michigan breeze. The men in the photograph looked like they were in spacesuits on another planet, cleaning up after an intergallactic war. "My God!" she whispered, skimming the headlines and first lines of the several articles on the tragedy.

"And while they're out there, I'm stuck out here in the middle of nowhere trying to learn how to walk again!"

Jane set the paper aside and looked at Jack, not sure what she could say to calm him. For several minutes they were both silent. Jack's breathing gradually slowed and his pulse dropped to its normal rate. He finally cupped his hands around Jane's forearm and gave her a gentle squeeze. "I don't mean to take it out on you."

"I understand," she said. "You know, Jack, you might not have to be stuck up here all that long. If Dr. Glover approves it, we could leave, go back to Washington. I'm sure he can transfer your records and put you in touch with a good clinic."

Jack looked at Jane. "You wouldn't mind?"

Jane smiled. "How could we ever top that last night we had at the cottage, hmm? I say we go."

Jack smiled back, spirits rising. "Your place or mine?" he asked.

Thirty-one

The news from Chicago didn't sit well with Hal Dewez.
Minding the survivalist store along with Brady, he'd spent
most of the morning in the back office, twiddling knobs
on the television and radio in a constant search for the
latest update. With Argvai in custody, head still on his
shoulders, America was pointing its collective finger at
the Middle East. Congressmen were rattling sabers in both
the Senate and House, calling for the direst of sanctions
against Syria and its allies. Some were going a step further,
demanding a declaration of war, despite Houril's impas-
sioned plea that reason rule the day until the facts could
be sorted out and the blame laid where it belonged. After
all, the Syrian government denied any involvement in the
outbreak of terrorism on American soil and further
claimed no knowledge of the lone prisoner linked to the
incidents. Several countries of the Persian Gulf were similarly vociferous in their cries of innocence, although scattered splinter groups in those same nations and others
throughout the globe continued to boast that it was their

efforts that were giving U.S. citizens a taste of the terror and bloodshed that were part and parcel of life in most other parts of the world.

Cal Winslow had yet to contact the ranch with the inside track on what headway the intelligence community was making in its investigations, and until such time when he heard that there was no reason for concern, Dewez felt chained to a beast-sized paranoia, wary that at any moment, in some small room like the cell where Tony Bex had been killed for keeping his silence, the Syrian Argvai would be talking his fool head off, intimating the full details of his involvement with a certain pair of former CIA agents now free-lancing for the highest bidder from their scenic lair in rural North Dakota. In such a frame of mind, Dewez's roaming of the media airwaves had an air of desperation about it. The last thing he wanted to have to contend with was the buzz of the office intercom and the matter-of-fact announcement Brady rendered from his post at the front counter.

"There's a sheriff here to see you, boss."

Dewez snapped off both the radio and television, stared at the intercom. No, he was just hearing things. He stayed put, calculating the time it would take him to grab his gun from the top drawer of the desk and slip out the back door.

"Boss? You there?"

Dewez pressed the intercom button, leaned close to the built-in microphone. "Tell him I'll be just a minute. I'm on the phone, long distance."

"Will do."

Dewez checked the back alley. It was deserted. He walked quickly around the building and checked the sheriff's car in the front parking lot. No one there. No backup, no reinforcements. He breathed a little easier, backtracked to the office, left the gun behind as he joined Brady on the main floor. The sheriff introduced himself, name of Moore, medium height, in his late forties but in good shape, tanned muscle against the light brown of his uniform, high cheekbones and a pointed jaw, face like an African tribal mask. He stood with a confident nonchalance, a man used to being in charge of situations. Dewez mirrored the cop's cool, offered a smile and handshake when he introduced himself, asked, "What can I do you for, Sheriff?"

Moore talked while his eyes roamed the store, taking inventory. "You folks run some kinda hard-ass training camp outside of town, right?"

"We call them survival outings, actually," Dewez corrected, poker-faced, ready to play out the conversation. "Yeah, we put 'em on every few months."

Brady circled around the counter and busied himself with some shelf work, putting himself behind Moore, ready to take the sheriff out if it seemed necessary.

"I got a nephew went through the one you had last spring," the officer told Dewez. "Passed with flying colors and now he thinks he's the toughest piece of shit around. Joe Moore. He ring a bell?"

Dewez calmed himself within, relaxed slightly at the counter. "Yeah," he said. "Big jock out of Aberdeen."

"Big jock's right, with a mouth to match." Moore stuck his thumbs behind his gun belt, shifted his weight. "He's been givin' me grief about going soft on the job. Askin' to be brought down a few notches, if you catch my drift."

"Not exactly."

Moore picked up a shovel that could double as a pick. It was heavy but he held it in one hand, choking up on the handle, like a horse trader testing the merchandise. "You got another outing comin' up soon?"

Dewez checked a wall calendar next to the register. "Four weeks from tomorrow."

"That'll be perfect." Moore put the shovel back and leaned on the counter. "Sign us up, would ya? Me and Joe."

Under the counter Dewez tracked down a clipboard and file box, stalling for time. No fucking way did he want a lawman on the ranch. *Think fast, Hal, buddy.* He shuffled through papers, pretending to know what he was looking for. "Might be a problem, Sheriff."

"Yeah? Why's that?"

Dewez found a sheet with names on it. "Ah, I was afraid of that. Sorry, but we've already filled that class up."

"Gee, that's too bad." Moore clucked his tongue, taking it too well as far as Dewez was concerned. "You're sure you can't make room?"

"Program's set up for a certain number of people," Dewez explained. "We go over that and things start going wrong. What I could do is put you down on an alternate list, in case somebody has to cancel at the last minute."

"That's not good enough." Moore put one hand on the counter, drummed it with his fingers. "I tell ya, from what Joe tells me, you do some shit at that camp you're really supposed to have permits for. Be a damned shame if I had to come out there as a cop instead of a customer, don't you think?"

Dewez didn't answer right away. His eyes were on the front entrance, where a bell over the door had just rung, announcing the arrival of still more bad news. Koura Hoummari strode in, dark eyes ablaze. She checked her anger at the sight of the sheriff and drifted over to a bookrack.

"I gotta paint you a picture, friend?" Moore asked.

"No, no," Dewez replied, turning back to the sheriff. "Sorry. Yeah, we can make room for you."

"I thought so."

While Dewez pried free a few blank forms from the clipboard, Hoummari moved away from the bookrack and got his attention long enough to gesture that she wanted to meet him in the back room. As she walked past Brady, Dewez handed the forms to Moore and told him, "Just fill these out, okay?"

Moore pulled a pen from his pocket. "I don't recall Joey sayin' how much this shindig costs."

"No charge for lawmen," Dewez said.

"That's what I like to hear."

"I have to see to another client, Sheriff," Dewez said as he waved Brady over, "but I'll have my assistant answer any more questions you might have."

"Good enough," Moore said. He looked up from the forms, eyeing Dewez. "One more thing, though."

"Name it."

"I don't want no special treatment when we're out on the course. Joey's gonna get his butt shown up fair and square."

Dewez nodded. "You got it."

Hoummari was looking out the back window when Dewez joined her in the office. He closed the door behind him and glared at her. "You trying to blow our fucking cover?" he demanded. "What's the problem?"

Hoummari turned around to face Dewez, pointing a small handgun at his midsection. The fire was back in her eyes. "Who else were you supplying with nerve gas?"

"Put that popgun away," Dewez said. "Jesus! I got enough problems."

"Answer me!"

"What makes you think we were giving gas to anyone else?"

"I read the papers, you idiot!" Hoummari took a step closer, gave Dewez a better view of her handgun. A cheap .22, he figured. *Just my luck to die from a fucking cap pistol.*

"So you read the papers," he said. "What's the connection?"

"That gas in Chicago was the same kind you sold us,"

Hoummari claimed. "Morrison said he was selling us *all* of it."

"He must have meant all we had left," Dewez guessed. "Come on, Koura. You're in America, land of free enterprise. Don't get so bent outta shape about this, okay?"

Hoummari raised her gun, pointing it at Dewez's face instead of his chest. "That prisoner they took. They think he's Syrian. Syria is our enemy."

"They're guessing. He won't talk," Dewez insisted. "And he's not a fucking Syrian, for crying out loud. You think we'd deal with —"

"Liar!"

Brady swung the door open and stuck his head in. "He's gone . . ."

Hoummari's attention was diverted momentarily, giving Dewez enough time to torque his body and lash out with a well-placed karate kick. Hoummari let out a cry as the gun flew from her hand. Dewez lunged at her and fought his way past her flailing arms, grabbing her by the waist, flipping her across his outstretched leg onto the desk and pinning her there while Brady tracked down the loose gun.

"Give me that," Dewez said, taking the gun as he let go of Hoummari. She stood up, eyeing him hatefully as he took his own gun from the desk and let her compare the two barrels.

"Pig!"

"Oink, oink," Dewez drawled. He waved Brady out of the room and let his gaze linger on Hoummari's body. "You fuck Morrison and then you come at me with a gun," he told her, faintly amused. "Hardly seems fair."

"Go ahead, shoot me," she taunted. "My men will track you down."

"Gee, I haven't been threatened like that in, oh, say, twenty-four hours." Dewez emptied Hoummari's gun and slid it across the table to her. "You cut a business deal with us and we held up our end. No need to come by here trying to jerk us off, okay?"

Hoummari slipped the gun in her purse. "After Chicago, security everywhere will be stronger," she complained. "We won't be able to get our gas out of the country now."

Dewez opened the door to the back alley. "Sorry, Koura, but we don't deliver. That's your problem, not ours. Maybe you should get to work on it, hmm?"

Hoummari started for the door, paused in front of Dewez. "You may think it's not your problem, but you're wrong."

"I'm trembling."

Hoummari slapped his face. "Fuck you!"

"I'd like that," Dewez told her. "I've got a few kinky habits, too. It'd be fun."

Hoummari left the office and started down the alley, not looking back.

Thirty-two

While working at the *Sentinel*, Jane had rented out part of a town house within walking distance of work. It was an old brownstone, thick with ivy on the south face, its garden in full bloom and partially shaded by a pair of elegant cherry trees showing off their pink blossoms. The late-day sun looked as if it were doing a balancing act atop the distant point of the Washington Monument and huge clumps of dark cumulus clouds huddled in various groups, conspiring to merge and fulfill promises of evening showers. An ancient Checker cab rolled down the street and stopped in front of the town house. Jane got out first, followed by the cabbie, a gangling Jamaican with dreadlocks weaving out in all directions beneath his cap like vipers entranced by his humming of selections from the Bob Marley songbook. As the cabbie unlocked his trunk and removed luggage and a wheelchair, Jane opened the door for Jack and helped him to his feet. As Dr. Glover had predicted, the plane trip had proved a physically draining experience, and Jack's euphoria at being back in Washington wasn't enough to shake off the effects of jet lag and the natural fatigue one might expect only a week after surgery as complicated as what he'd gone through.

"You are going straight to bed, Jack Demarrest," Jane ordered as the cabbie rolled the wheelchair over.

"Yes, boss," Jack mumbled through his grin, easing himself into the chair.

"You want I should help take de bags in, miss?" the driver inquired, his Caribbean accent as thick as the smell of incense clinging to his clothes.

"That's all right, I'll handle it," Seamus McTeague called out, already halfway across the street from where he'd just parked his car. He beamed at Jack and Jane. "Hi, guys. Thought it might be nice to have a welcome wagon." He pulled out a quart of double-chocolate ice cream from a shopping bag.

"How nice." Jane kissed McTeague lightly. The two agents traded high fives.

"You look a little green around the gills, Jack," McTeague said.

"Nothing an overdose of ice cream wouldn't cure," Jack replied. He gave Jane a slight nudge. "Going to let me stay up past my bedtime, Nurse Ratched?"

"As if I had a choice."

Jane paid off the cabby, took the ice cream in one hand and her overnight bag in the other, while McTeague put a suitcase on Jack's lap and wheeled him up the walk. The town house was a duplex, with Jane renting out the ground floor. There were five rooms besides the kitchen, and she needed them all, having accumulated a trove of belongings during her married years in a huge Colonial-style home in the suburbs just outside Washington. She was in the process of changing her tastes, and the apartment's decor reflected as much. Pseudo-Colonial antiques clashed with her newer Art Deco furnishings, and some pieces belonging to neither period were mixed in haphazardly like unwelcome guests told not to make themselves too comfortable. Although Jack had been here several times before, he found himself more keenly aware of the details this time. He planned to be living here for a while, after all, and when he brought some things over from his apartment across town, the decorative anarchy would be further incited.

"It's stuffy in here," Jane said, starting to open windows. "Could you give me a hand, Seamus?"

"Sure."

"I can help, too, you know," Jack said, getting out of the wheelchair. His voice was testy, but after taking a few steps he realized how tired he was, and after shifting a house plant from one side of the coffee table to the other, he sat down on the sofa, offering an embarrassed grin. "There," he muttered sheepishly. "I helped."

None of them had had supper, so they took a quick poll and decided to order take-out pizza from a nearby establishment best known for a seven-topping, deep-dish creation called the Filibuster. Jane called in the order, then excused herself to go upstairs and get her mail from the duplex's other tenant. Left alone in the living room, Jack and Seamus batted small talk back and forth for a few minutes. Jack salvaged enough strength to walk to the kitchen for a couple of beers.

"What's with this guy they caught in Chicago?" he asked McTeague, handing him a bottle.

"Hasn't said a word," Seamus told him. "They're watching him around the clock, figuring if he doesn't try to kill himself again somebody else might try to help do it for him."

"Any clues from the van?"

"Nothing yet, but the lab boys are still working on it."

"How much gas got loose to kill that many people?"

McTeague shook his head. "There were three canisters in the van. One of them was jarred loose when it crashed. We could barely find the leak in the seam, and they say what got loose was just the tip of the iceberg as far as what's still out there unaccounted for. Serious shit. You should have seen what it looked like in that park." McTeague shuddered. "I keep ending up there in my dreams, and it's not by choice, believe me."

Jack leaned forward on the sofa, glancing over his shoulder and then pushing the wheelchair away, banishing it as if to keep it from influencing what he was about to say.

"Seamus," he told his friend, "I want to get back into it."

McTeague bought time looking for a coaster to set his beer on. "It's a little soon still, isn't it?" he finally said.

"It can't be soon enough as far as I'm concerned," Jack countered. "Damn it, I'm going crazy with this convalescence crap."

"It's not crap, Jack," McTeague told him. "Look at yourself, would you? You look like death warmed over and you know it. Going to the fridge for a couple beers is enough to wipe you out, for Christ's sake! I'm not trying to be cruel, but face facts. Besides, you're still classified disabled with the Service. It's going to take more than snapping your fingers to change that."

"Fuck the red tape!" Jack snapped. "Look what's going on out there! We need all the help we can get."

"That's true, but —"

"No buts. I want in, Seamus."

McTeague sighed. "I'll see what I can do," he conceded. "No promises, though."

"I'll take what I can get," Jack insisted.

Jane walked in while Jack was talking. "What's that?"

Jack thought fast, lied. "We were talking about pizza. I was saying at this point I want all the solid food I can eat . . ."

Thirty-three

Morrison and Dewez had bought the dairy farm jointly after a six-month search for a base of operations. Hal Dewez had grown up on a cattle ranch and was familiar enough with the life-style to oversee successfully the running of the dairy business. Even with his attention divided by the other covert activities he was involved in, he'd been able to turn a modest profit each year, and there were times, when he'd get particularly fed up with the mercenary trade, that he found himself yearning for a simpler life, a return to his roots, if not his hometown. He fancied himself well suited to the life of a cattle baron in the Sun Belt somewhere, lording over a vast spread and reaping enough of a profit to allow himself a life of leisure. After what he'd been through with Arlo Kendall and Koura Hoummari the past couple of days, the longing was stronger than ever. To hell with having to deal with scum and degenerates, he mused, entering the walk-in cooler and inspecting the sides of beef hanging from meat hooks. He ought to kiss all this behind, take his cut and head south, buy a spread in Texas and find himself a hot-blooded little college coed to marry and knock up every other year until he had a house full of noisy, snot-nosed kids who would call him Daddy and beg him to come out and play with them in the backyard. Damned straight, that's what life was supposed to be about. *Who needs all this fucking gloom-and-doom shit all the time?*

He found a good slab of meat and hauled it over to the butcher's saw in the corner, carving up enough portions for a decent barbecue. When he was finished he loaded the meat on a platter and dropped his bloodied apron in a hamper just outside the cooler. A pair of maids was already cluttering the kitchen with fixings for supper. Vegetables on the chopping block, bread in the oven, ears of corn wrapped in foil and stacked like ingots on a serving plate. He spoke to them in Spanish, asking one of them to take the corn out to the patio and the other to track down Brady and have him call the airport to find out what the fuck was keeping Morrison. He was supposed to have been back from Washington five hours ago.

Rowdy was out on the back patio, a used-brick layout the size of a tennis court, running out from the main house and built around a massive sycamore that rustled its leaves in a faint afternoon breeze. He stirred the coals in a huge brick barbecue taking up one whole corner of the patio. When Dewez and the maid came over and set down the meat and corn, Rowdy used tongs to transfer the food to the grill, which gave off a sharp sizzle and fragrant wisps of smoke.

"Good-lookin' cow," Rowdy said as he sprinkled seasoning over the cuts of meat.

"Yeah, well, make sure mine's done rare enough to moo," Dewez said on his way to an outdoor bar, also framed with brick and a tiled counter. He was fixing himself a drink when he saw Morrison heading up the driveway in the ranch Jeep. Morrison pulled up to the patio and got out.

"About fucking time," Dewez complained.

"What are you so upset about?" Morrison joined Dewez at the bar after greeting Rowdy with a slight nod.

"You got a week, maybe I can tell you." Dewez drained half his drink and refilled it before heading over to a picnic table under the shade of the sycamore. Morrison followed moments later and sat across from him. Dewez told him about his encounter with Hoummari the day before. Morrison smirked at Dewez's wisecrack about Hoummari's sexual appetite but didn't seem worried by the threat she'd made.

"She won't give us any problems, Hal. She knows we just have to leak a little info ourselves and she'll be shut down permanently within twenty-four hours."

"Speaking of leaks, what's the word from Washington? Argvai started singing yet?"

Morrison shook his head. "Not that Winslow knows of."

"Meaning what?"

"Meaning that security's tight," Morrison said. "This special task force is keeping to itself, and the best Winslow can come up with is second-, third-hand rumors. He's hoping things will change when they bring Argvai to Washington."

"How so?"

"He's wrangled his way onto security detail." Morrison paused to sip his drink. "He should be able to take care of our Syrian friend."

Dewez finished his drink, waiting for the alcohol to bathe his nerves. It wouldn't be soon enough. "How'll he pull that off? Jesus! It ain't like he's gonna be able to play Jack Ruby. They'll have Argvai's ass covered six ways from Wednesday and you know it."

"It'll work out, Hal," Morrison said, eyes on the barbecue, where Rowdy was flipping steaks and shifting the wrapped ears of corn. "Let's not worry, okay? I see we've got a nice feast lined up. How about we enjoy it, eh?"

"Don't think I wouldn't like to," Dewez grumbled. "It's just that there's been too goddamned many screw-ups lately. Jesus! We just try to make a few lousy bucks and it's lookin' like World War Three. We're damned lucky our butts haven't been nailed five times over by now."

"I have to agree with you there." One of the maids came out with a pitcher filled with iced tea. Morrison emptied his drink and held the glass out so she could fill it. Dewez left the table long enough to get his refill from the bar. When he came back, Morrison suggested, "Look, we've got a bit of a nest egg and the dairy's bringing in some spare change. It might be a good idea for us to lay low for a while. What do you say?"

"I say that's fucking music to my ears."

"Good, good. Let's toast to it, then."

The men chinked their glasses and drank slowly. Dewez stared out at the rolling hills, the distant woods. "Oh, shit!" he suddenly blurted out, remembering Sheriff Moore's visit to the survivalist store and his enrollment in the upcoming training session at the lodge. He filled Morrison in on the details and was surprised at his partner's reaction. Instead of frowning at the news, Morrison seemed upbeat, almost pleased.

"I've heard a few things about this Sheriff Moore," Morrison explained. "Seems he's had a few run-ins with a mutual acquaintance. You know the Skowron brothers? They got us ammo those couple months when Jensen was in prison." Dewez nodded. Morrison continued: "Moore's on the take with them and a few other people, too."

"Interesting."

"Very," Morrison replied. "I think we could use somebody like him ..."

Thirty-four

"I want a cigarette."

Thus ended Argvai's silence.

He was in an interrogation room, seated at a table across from Dan Carlisle and Seamus McTeague. Dressed in prison grays, he looked less like a firebrand revolutionary, more like a foreign exchange student dragged before the dean for academic and extracurricular transgressions. He'd hardly slept since his apprehension in Chicago, and the flight to Washington had only compounded his fatigue and subsequent irritability. Carlisle, who'd spent most of the past few days trying to crack the Syrian's cool exterior, was no model of patience himself.

"We want information," he told the prisoner. "You help us, we help you. It's very simple."

"I want a cigarette," Argvai repeated sullenly, clasping his hands on the table.

"You speak English. That's a good start." Carlisle took a pack of Old Golds from his coat pocket and pried a cigarette out, rolling it across the table to Argvai. The

Syrian placed it between his lips, waited expectantly for a light. Carlisle flicked the lid off a sterling-silver lighter and coaxed a flame, letting the Syrian see it before he closed the lid and grinned.

"You want a light? Earn it."

"I know your American laws," Argvai retorted. He looked away from Carlisle, trying his luck on McTeague. "I don't have to talk. Where is my lawyer?"

McTeague motioned for Carlisle to give Argvai a light. The FBI agent complied, an embittered expression on his face. He and McTeague had already agreed upon their strategy for dealing with the prisoner. Carlisle would play tough, leaving McTeague to counter with the soft touch, the attempt at camaraderie. It was an old ploy, still widely used because of its effectiveness.

"You realize the people you work for don't care what happens to you," McTeague told Argvai. "Why are you so hell-bent on protecting them?"

"You are not a friend, so don't pretend to be." Argvai leaned back in his chair, pursed his lips to blow smoke rings in the air.

"It's not too late to save your neck, you know," McTeague reminded the prisoner. "You want to live or you would have forced me to shoot you in Chicago, right?"

"I tried to blow myself up," Argvai said. "If it would have worked, you might have died, too. You owe me a favor, American. Bring me my lawyer."

"You're not an American citizen, shitface!" Carlisle shouted, slamming a fist against the table and startling both McTeague and the prisoner. "What makes you think you get a lawyer?"

Argvai shrugged and calmly blew smoke in Carlisle's face. "Who says I am not an American?"

"Just a lucky guess," Carlisle deadpanned.

McTeague stood up, started pacing the room as he

skimmed through the contents of a file folder. "I have to tell you, it was a mistake to have had your fingerprints surgically removed. You see, there's different techniques for doing that, and by figuring out the technique we can usually come up with a good guess as to where the work was done."

"So?" Argvai said.

"So, we figure you're either Syrian or Palestinian. Once we've circulated your picture to our sources over there, we'll know who you are and what group you belong to."

Argvai shook his head, dropped the cigarette on the floor without bothering to crush it out. "You are bluffing."

The door to the interrogation room opened and in walked Cal Winslow. He saw the stray cigarette and stepped on it as he looked at fellow FBI man Carlisle. "They're ready to meet down the hall."

McTeague closed the file, kept it in his hands, and looked at Argvai on his way out. "Think about what I told you."

Carlisle told Winslow, "Keep an eye on him."

"Will do," Winslow said, holding the door open for Carlisle and McTeague. Once they left, he closed the door, leaving him alone with Argvai. He smiled at the prisoner.

In a conference room down the hall, the steering committee for the special task force sat around a table, waiting on Carlisle and McTeague. Kopp, Daniels, Britland, and White: between the four of them they might have had a total of eight hours' sleep the past night. To a man they looked haggard, grim, stymied by the lack of progress in dealing with this, conceivably the most serious threat to the United States government since the Cuban missile crisis several decades before. When McTeague and Carlisle joined the group, their dour faces did little to raise hopes within the small chamber.

"He's still not talking, I presume," the Secretary of State said.

"He's talking, but just enough to be a nuisance," McTeague said as he took a seat. Carlisle plopped into a chair next to him.

"Where does that leave us?" former President Britland asked, directing the question at Carlisle.

Carlisle took the file from McTeague and pulled out a map of the United States. He held it up for the others to see and explained, "The van was stolen in Billings, Montana, the night after the ambush in Oregon. We found a pack of matches on the dead man from a truck stop in Fargo, North Dakota. Both towns are located off Interstate 94, which also runs through Chicago." He traced the route with his finger.

"And we already figure they fled in a chopper after the gas heist," White put in. "Must have used it to clear the Rockies."

Carlisle nodded, kept his finger on the map. "I think our best bet's to focus on this strip of Interstate. That's still five states, but it's a damned sight better than fifty."

"Of course," CIA chief Daniels said, "there's still a chance we can get this guy to talk. I say we give him some sodium pentothal and a few other 'incentives.'"

"I'm all for putting the bastard on the rack if that's what it takes," Kopp said. "But if the way he's been acting up to now is any indication, my guess is he's been trained to counter anything we can throw at him."

"Well, we have to do something!" Britland sat forward in his chair. "There's still three canisters of gas out there, and what happened in Chicago's going to seem like a trifle if the rest of that stuff gets used to its full potential."

Britland's words cast a brief pall over the group. McTeague broke the silence several moments later, keeping his promise to Jack Demarrest. "We're going to have to bring in more people to cover all this," he began. "I know somebody we can all trust, and —"

There was a knock on the door and a federal marshal let himself in without waiting to be formally admitted. He eyed the group somberly. "Trouble with the prisoner," he announced.

McTeague was the first man to his feet. "What kind of trouble?" he asked on his way to the door.

Argvai's trouble was that he was dead.

A paramedic was hunched over the inert body lying on the floor near where Argvai had been sitting. Cal Winslow stood off to one side, looking flustered. As McTeague and Carlisle rushed into the interrogation room, he told them, "I can't figure it out. He was just picking his ear. Then he put a finger in his mouth and keeled over before I could get to him."

"He's gone," the paramedic confirmed, rising to his feet. "Cyanide, from the smell of it."

"Cyanide!" Carlisle exclaimed. "Christ! We searched him head to toe back in Chicago and the minute we got him here!"

"It doesn't take much," the paramedic replied. "You must have missed it."

A second attendant entered the room with a gurney and body bag. Carlisle kicked the table in frustration. McTeague watched the paramedics slip Argvai into the body bag and hoist him onto the gurney with quiet efficiency. Then he let his gaze drift upward, taking in Cal Winslow. The agent was lighting a cigarette, doing his best to look miserable.

One Month Later

Thirty-five

Her father's advice had proven the key.

When Jane went back to work on her memoirs the third day after her return to Washington, she'd discarded the pages she'd written in Marquette and had begun anew. This time she sat down at the typewriter the way a devout and penitent Catholic might enter the confessional, with no thought on her mind but to bare her soul and speak truths, whatever the consequences. She was determined to write honestly, pulling no punches, sparing no details in the name of timidity or discretion. Perhaps once she'd finished the first draft she would allow herself to go back over the manuscript with an editorial eye and concern herself with cosmetic touches. Perhaps. But she vowed not to concern herself with revisions until she'd put it all down once, beginning to end.

It wasn't easy. The first pages came slowly, agonizingly slowly. Hours spent on troublesome paragraphs, trying to find the right array of words to convey the more difficult times in her life, striking a balanced tone between dispassionate recitation of facts and passages wrought with a flurry of emotion. But she stuck to a firm regimen of two-hour shifts each morning, afternoon, and night. After the first week the discipline came more easily, as did her narrative voice. Instead of dreading her turns behind the typewriter, she began to look forward to them. Two-hour shifts stretched into three, then four, and finally she reached a point where she would write for hours on end, locked into a state of near entrancement, as if she were a mere bystander, a conduit through which the tumult of her thoughts raced down to her fingers, filling page after typed page as the day raced by.

Jack's presence in the apartment did little to deter her literary output. If anything, he was yet another source of inspiration. Having taken over the all-purpose room and filled it with equipment shipped down from Marquette and brought over from his apartment, he had his own schedule, supervised periodically by a visiting physical therapist. His progress had been initially slow, but once he'd shaken off his dependence on the walker and had bolstered his diet with supplements, he, too, had begun to exceed expectations in terms of his activity. From the walker he advanced to a stationary bicycle and walks through the neighborhood, doing the latter when Jane was ready for a break and they wanted to spend time together, sharing their thoughts and cheering each other on. Eventually, Jack was cleared to run on a treadmill, logging mileage on a pedometer. By the end of three weeks he was running three miles in place, ready to test himself on an outdoor surface. Seamus McTeague joined him for morning jogs, at the same time filling him in on details with the task force's ongoing investigation into the terrorist incidents, which had abruptly stopped after the death of the prisoner apprehended during the debacle in Chicago. Jack had been cleared to join the task force in a limited capacity. When he wasn't working out or resting from the exertion, he was usually on the phone, talking to field agents in the five target states where they hoped eventually to make a breakthrough in their search for the string-pullers behind the earlier episodes. The progress of that investigation, however, did not mirror the success of Jack and Jane's personal endeavors. With the exception of scattered bits of circumstantial evidence, nothing had turned up to shed any new light on the situation. A theory emerged that the man who had died of cyanide poisoning shortly after his transfer to Washington was the true mastermind behind what had happened, and that with his death his followers had disbanded, leaving little trace behind.

Four weeks after she had resumed work on her memoirs, Jane had placed a call to Frank Tennleton in New York, telling him she had seven hundred twenty-eight pages of rough draft. On his vow that he would refrain from divulging any unprintable material he might come across while reading the manuscript, Jane entrusted him with full editorial control over the pages, having decided that she was far too subjective to go back over what she'd written and start making changes. Tennleton had flown to Washington the following day and stopped by the town house to pick up the manuscript on the way to his hotel suite. He forewarned Jane that it would probably take him three or four days to carefully read the manuscript and jot down some preliminary comments. A day later, she and Jack had come home from a walk around the block to find a completely neutral message on her answering machine, Frank Tennleton requesting that she come by the hotel as soon as possible. Frantic with expectation, Jane had rushed out the door and flagged down a cab, leaving Jack behind in her determination that, good news or bad, she wanted to face Tennleton alone.

Jack was hungry and busied himself for the next half hour making a supper of ham and home-fried potatoes. He took a call from Dan Carlisle, who had spent most of the past month roaming Montana, both Dakotas, Minnesota, and Illinois, supervising his small army of investigators who were still looking for their first solid clue. Carlisle was coming back to Washington over the weekend for a strategy meeting scheduled on Monday.

After he ate, Jack cleaned the kitchen and slept for an hour. When he woke up, Jane still hadn't returned. He was sore from the day's workouts, but it was a welcome soreness, that of muscles tightening into shape. His only real source of true pain was some of the scars, and even they were healing well, thanks to regular applications of aloe vera lotion and liquid dosages of vitamin E. It was dark out now, with a breeze coming through the windows, taking an edge off the day's heat.

Slipping into a pair of gym shorts, Jack went to his workout room and slipped on a cassette. He stretched to slower music, then started in on the weights to rock and roll, working up a quick sweat. He'd started growing a beard a couple of weeks before and already had a chin full of hair for the first time since his college days. He wasn't sure how long he'd keep it, but for the time being he liked the change. Finished with the weights, Jack was doing pushups when he heard the front door open. He stood up, grabbed a towel to wipe his face. Jane strode across the living room, stood in the doorway, a blank expression on her face.

"Well . . .?" Jack asked.

A smile split Jane's face. "He loved it!" she screamed, taking two long steps into Jack's embrace. "He absolutely, no two ways around it, loved it!"

"You sound surprised," Jack said calmly. "I mean, was there any doubt?"

Jane laughed, pummeled his chest with her fists. He

wrapped his arms tightly around her, kissed her, raised her off her feet. She stopped laughing, concern flooding her eyes as she looked down at Jack's legs.

"Jack," she said worriedly, "what are you doing?"

"What does it look like I'm doing?" He shifted her in his arms, honeymoon-style, and carried her to the bedroom. He set her down slowly, then leaned over. Their lips met again, long and passionately. His fingers reached for the buttons of her blouse, began to undress her. She whispered his name, drew him close to her.

He licked her ear, stroked her bared breast, whispered back at her, "What's a good book without an exciting climax . . ."

Thirty-six

While they kept a low profile in terms of involvement in endeavors requiring the sort of media-grabbing violence that had predominated their recent agenda, Dewez and Morrison didn't pull themselves entirely out of circulation. A few days after their barbecue at the ranch, the men were approached by one of their military contacts, a supply officer at a navy weapons depot in Arizona. The officer had been a primary source of weapons for Dewez and Morrison for the past two years, and now he'd graduated into heavier arms, managing to steal almost two million dollars' worth of F-14 navy jet parts. For a twenty percent commission, Morrison agreed to fly to Washington, South Africa, and Tripoli to act as middleman in setting up a smuggling operation that would eventually place the jet parts in Libyan hands. While Morrison was in Washington, he'd managed a brief, surreptitious meeting with Cal Winslow, who had been forced to curtail his spying efforts on behalf of Morrison and Dewez for fear that he was under considerable surveillance and suspicion as a result of his having been alone with the Syrian prisoner Argvai before his mysterious cyanide poisoning. Although the official explanation had been that the man had committed suicide, Winslow suspected that that position had been announced more as a ploy meant to bait him into becoming overconfident and making another false move. In his meeting with Morrison, it was agreed that Winslow would refrain from further work on behalf on his secret benefactors, although he would begin the search for a possible replacement and report back to North Dakota if and when he'd tracked down someone who could provide an insider's view of the government investigation into domestic terrorist activities.

Back in North Dakota, Dewez contented himself largely with the running of the ranch and making the necessary preparations for the upcoming survivalist outing at the lodge and training camp. During the weeks before the outing, there was only one alarming disruption to the ranch routine. With the government offering a reward of one hundred thousand dollars for information leading to the arrest and conviction of anyone connected with the attempted assassination of President Houril or the gas heist in Oregon, two employees at the dairy farm had made a pact to go to the authorities when they made their next trip into nearby Bismarck. Rowdy Trent happened to overhear their plans, however, and the two men were summarily executed and cast into the same vats of quicklime behind the barn where Tony Bex's earthly remains had been tossed. News of the executions spread quickly enough throughout the compound to serve as an incentive for others to resist any attacks of conscience the offer of reward money might lead to.

The survivalist outing took place the following week. Joe and Sheriff Moore were two of twelve recruits who had signed up for the five-day course on what Dewez so modestly referred to as "a few self-help tips." On the same course where Syrian guerrillas had trained in preparation for their raid on the nerve gas shipment, Dewez and Trent led the recruits through prolonged periods of torturous calisthenics, taught courses on topics ranging from gun cleaning and blindfolded assembly of seven different types of firearms to ways of sanitizing water in the wilderness and to what parts of which insects one should avoid eating when forced to forage for one's supper. Each day there was a war game in the woods, each game played with a variation in the rules, played at a different time of day, so that the recruits might learn to accommodate themselves under the most divergent of circumstances. No live ammunition was used in the actual games, but bruises from club wounds and cuts from hurled sticks or stones were not uncommon injuries incurred during these exercises, when sheer competitiveness fueled by strained tempers and bursts of adrenaline escalated the means of warfare beyond the use of handguns that fired pellets filled with red paint.

Although Joe Moore had been through the program before, the presence of his uncle unnerved him periodically, much to the sheriff's delight. By arrangement with Dewez, the two relatives took separate sides during each of the war games, with the elder Moore invariably singling out his nephew for one-on-one confrontations, which the sheriff just as invariably won. Flustered and dispirited, Joe Moore was the first recruit prepared to leave when the outing ended. Fresh from his first shower in five days, Joe's face was bandaged where it wasn't black-and-blue, and he limped on one leg as he carried his tote bag from the lodge and started for his Olds Cutlass in the dirt parking lot. His face was downcast.

"Hey, don't take it so rough, Joey," Sheriff Moore called out, taking long strides to catch up to his nephew. Now that he had humbled the youth, Moore felt he could afford to play the Dutch uncle. "Look, I was doin' this shit in the marines back when you were in diapers. Stands to reason I'd have a few more tricks up my sleeve, right?"

"Yeah," Joe Moore mumbled. "Maybe so."

Sheriff Moore gave his nephew a good-natured slap on the back. "Don't worry, I ain't gonna rub it in your nose any more than you force me to. Now go on home, get yourself a cold six-pack, and fill up on some of your ma's cooking."

"You aren't comin' with me?"

"I got a little business to attend to with these gentlemen here." The sheriff gestured back at the lodge, where Hal Dewez stood on the porch with Jake Morrison, who'd just returned from his globe-trotting mission the day before. Moore told his nephew, "I'll see ya at your folks' Sunday, hear?"

Joe Moore nodded, then dragged himself into his Cutlass, leading the procession of recruits leaving the ranch grounds. Sheriff Moore lingered behind and made his way back to the porch.

"What sort of little business did you have in mind, Sheriff?" Morrison asked.

Moore looked out at the rugged, tree-choked surroundings. "You guys put on a decent training, I gotta admit."

"Thanks, but that doesn't answer my question."

Moore paused to light a cigarette. Dewez did the same. Moore blew his smoke slowly, lazily. "Between this here 'school' you run and all the shit you peddle back at your store, you could be a big help to some friends of mine."

Morrison smiled blandly. "Those friends wouldn't happen to be the Armageddon Brotherhood, would they?"

Moore's cigarette dipped precariously, almost fell from his mouth. The existence of the Brotherhood was supposed to be a highly guarded secret, not to mention his involvement with the sect. He pretended ignorance, without much luck or conviction. "Who?" he murmured.

"Little band of right-wingers holed up north of here

a ways. Planning some kind of bomb-proof country club they can all run to when the big one hits."

There was a railing that ran the length of the porch and Moore leaned against it. The bravado he'd rubbed his nephew's face in the past week was gone, replaced by a defensive trepidation. He looked hard at Morrison and Dewez. "How do you know about this?" he wanted to know.

"That's not important, Sheriff," Morrison told him.

"Like hell."

"The point is, I think we can help each other," Morrison confided. "That's what you wanted to talk to us about, after all, wasn't it?"

None of the men spoke for a few minutes. Dewez waved to the last couple of recruits driving away from the lodge, then told Moore, "How about if you tell us what you need, and we'll see if we can come up with some kind of deal?"

Moore relaxed a little, drew some pleasure out of his cigarette. The guarded edge left his voice when he spoke. "We're tryin' to keep down our overhead and stock up on supplies at the same time."

"Not an easy thing to do," Morrison commented.

"Not unless you know the right way to go about it. Problem is, most of my people get a little pantywaisted when it comes to things like that." Moore stubbed out his cigarette and grinned at Dewez. "When my nephew told me about this place, I figured you might be just what we were lookin' for. After goin' through this meat grinder course of yours, I'm convinced. You guys got some balls."

"Yeah," Dewez replied, returning Moore's grin with one of his own. "Yours..."

Thirty-seven

"These shots are from our Middle East office," Interpol agent Benson White told his fellow members of the special task force. He was holding enlarged black-and-white photographs as he spoke, pointing out details as needed. Some were crowd shots; other showed small groups huddled in conversation. There was one picture of a man walking down a busy Damascus street. There could be no mistaking him.

"Most of these are from a rally in Damascus last winter," White said as he started passing around the photos, keeping the shot of the lone walker, holding it out for all to see. "You'll see him in all the shots. His name was Argvai Kalim. Syrian nationalist, by all reports. They paint him to be their version of James Bond, but I can think of some less flattering comparisons."

"That's him, all right," President Houril said, picking the Syrian out in one of the crowd shots. They were in the White House Cabinet Room, and from his seat Houril could see the Rose Garden, red blossoms bobbing in the wind, a tranquil counterpoint to the armed soldier pacing vigilantly alongside the trimmed hedge. He sighed, remembering the few weeks early in his term when he and Cecile had walked through the garden, then blooming with hyacinth, tulips, and columbine, and mused about how a few minutes spent amid the flowers every day would be a sure tonic, the way he'd managed to get through one, possibly two terms without looking as if he had indeed borne the weight of the world on his shoulders. How naïve he'd been. Ever since returning from the nightmare in Michigan, he hadn't set foot in the garden once, and these few distracted seconds were the most he'd allotted himself even to enjoy the view. When Secretary of State Kopp passed him another of the photographs, Houril snapped out of his reverie. "I'm glad we know who he was," he told the others, "but I'd feel better if we knew who was working with him here in the States."

CIA chief Daniels glanced at Seamus McTeague and the newest member of the task force, Jack Demarrest. Wanting to leave the option open for undercover work, Jack had convinced the others to let him keep his beard. A turtleneck still hid the scars around his neck. Daniels asked him, "You've had this Winslow fellow under the microscope for a month. He hasn't stepped out of line yet?"

"We had to back off a few weeks ago because it looked like he was on to us," Jack said, "but just the past week it looks like he's up to something again. We aren't sure what it is, but we're on the verge of cracking his routine for making and placing calls."

"Well, that's good news, provided it's not a false lead," George Britland said. "I was beginning to think it was a mistake to have left him off the hook."

McTeague insisted, "Any luck and we can pin his contact within a week. I'm almost sure of it."

"Presuming there *is* a contact," Kopp said. "Like George was getting at, aside from our suspicions and a little flimsy evidence, we really don't have any proof Winslow's tied into any of this."

Dan Carlisle scoffed, stabbing at one of the photos. "Hooey! This guy was thoroughly searched — twice, in fact — before he was left alone in that room with Winslow. There's only one way cyanide could have come into the picture."

Before the issue could be dragged out into a debate, Houril intervened, suggesting they move on to the other, even more pending, problem. All month Carlisle had been pressing for a more coordinated, better-staffed effort to look for clues in the states between Oregon and Michigan that were linked by Interstates 90 and 94. After considerable discussion, it was decided that instead of having Carlisle act as supervisor of the entire area in question, there should be one person placed in charge of investigation efforts in each state and that the overall manpower devoted to the effort should be doubled, using carefully screened personnel from all law enforcement agencies cooperating with the task force.

Jack Demarrest lobbied hard for an assignment and was given the reins to North Dakota.

When the meeting was over, George Britland took Jack aside and guided him out to the Jacqueline Kennedy Garden, away from the others.

"Does my heart good to see you up and about, Jack," the former President said, hands clasped behind his back as he walked, nodding a greeting to the soldier stationed nearby.

"Thank you, sir."

"Don't bother calling me 'sir,' Jack. These days we're equals, at least as far as this task force is concerned."

Jack grinned. "Sorry. Just force of habit, I guess."

"Yes, I suppose so." Britland stopped walking, waited for Jack to do the same. "And I also owe you a debt of gratitude for the influence you've had on my daughter. I haven't seen Jane this contented in years."

"I can't take all the credit for that," Jack said. "She wrote that book on her own."

"So she did." Britland was beating around the bush, and they both knew it. He finally dropped his pretense and said straightforwardly. "What kind of plans do the two of you have?"

Jack stared at Britland, disbelieving. "Plans?"

"For the future, Jack. Do you two know where you stand with each other?"

"We haven't made any binding commitments, if that's what you mean," Jack said. "I wouldn't be surprised if we did eventually, but for now we're just trying to take it a day at a time." Jack could see the concern still welling in Britland's eyes and he assured the older man, "You know that I care about her. She's someone special to me."

"How special?"

"What?"

"I know I'm being a bit of a nag here, Jack, but bear with me, please." Britland put a hand briefly on Jack's shoulder, then pulled it away. "It's just that after all these great strides my daughter's taken the past few months, I'd hate to see anything happen that might jeopardize that."

"Such as...?" Jack had to check his voice, hold back a trace of impatience and indignation.

"I don't want her hurt, that's all," Britland told him.

Jack laughed awkwardly. "Well, join the club, sir. And you really shouldn't concern yourself. Things have been working out well with Jane and me. I don't see that changing."

Britland exhaled nervously and gestured at Seamus

McTeague, who was crossing the garden toward them. "I swear, I had this same conversation with Seamus while you were in the hospital. How much convincing is it going to take for me to butt out once and for all?"

"I don't think either of us wants you to do that," Jack said. "If you could just trust our judgment..."

It was Britland's turn to laugh, with equal uneasiness. "All I can say to that, Jack, is that you've never had children of your own."

McTeague reached them, wasted little time on formalities. "We just got word from Chicago," he announced. "They've arrested Arlo Kendall."

"Kendall," Britland repeated the name, trying to place it.

"He was the one behind the kidnapping of Tony Bex," McTeague explained. "He's being flown down here. Wants to cut a deal with us to save his ass."

Jack and the former President let their earlier discussion fall to the wayside. As all three men headed from the garden toward the White House, Britland said, "I just hope we get to him before someone else does again."

"We've got orders that he have at least three men watching him at all times," McTeague countered.

Jack had a sudden thought. "This might be the breakthrough we've been looking for on all fronts. If Winslow finds out we have Kendall, it might force him to make a move."

"Bingo!" McTeague said on his way up the steps. "We're already setting him up..."

Thirty-eight

Jane's small manual typewriter hadn't been intended for the workload she subjected it to during the weeks she had hammered out her memoirs. Twice she had taken it into a repair shop for minor adjustments, and a third mechanical breakdown had required more complicated repairs, making it necessary for her to rent a backup machine. She'd chosen a sturdy office electric and had been amazed at the increased efficiency the bigger, more advanced typewriter had provided her. Now, having finished the incredibly few revisions Frank Tennleton had prescribed for her manuscript, she had just splurged on a new home computer, complete with letter-quality printer and a state-of-the-art word-processing program. In the few hours that she had been tinkering with the computer, calling upon user knowledge picked up during her stint at the *Sentinel*, she could already see the potential for greater speed in her performance. Tennleton had complimented her extensively on her ability to turn out pages, suggesting that between her discipline and typing prowess she'd developed a natural knack for writing that was often never achieved by slower, more deliberate authors he'd dealt with who were constantly plagued by the inability to get their thoughts down on paper anywhere near fast enough to maintain a fluid, coherent narrative style. The editor had gone so far as to say that the nature of Jane's particular talent was such that she could expect her work to get better in proportion to her ability to keep improving her means of output. If ever there was a writer destined to use a computer, he'd said, it was Jane Britland.

And so she sat before the glowing screen, fingers flying across the computer keyboard, writing a preface to her upcoming memoirs. Mozart on the turntable, a view of the setting sun outside her apartment window those few times she took her eyes off her work, the aroma of baked chicken wafting from the oven. She had a glass of sparkling cider on the table beside her, and she was pausing to sip from it, admiring the bands of color streaking across the horizon, when the front doorbell rang.

She wasn't expecting company, and Jack was supposed to be dining out with Seamus. Getting up from her table, Jane went and opened the door, stunned at the sight of the man standing out on her front porch.

"Mr. Pierce?"

The bespectacled editor of the Washington *Sentinel* had what he hoped would pass for a humble smile. "Hello, Jane."

"What are you doing here?" There was more bewilderment than anger in her voice.

"I owe you an apology and thought I'd deliver it in person," he told her. "May I come in? Or is it a bad time?"

"No, no." Jane took a step back, opened the door wider. "Please, do."

Pierce strode past her into the living room, smiling wider at the sight of the computer. "Ah, got yourself an electronic monster. I could have given you a deal on one of ours, you know."

"It didn't occur to me to ask," Jane admitted, still trying to gather her wits and figure out the reason for the man's visit. "I'm a little confused here, Mr. Pierce. I didn't think I left the paper under the most amicable of circumstances, particularly as far as you were concerned."

"And the mistake was mine," Pierce confessed, doing a commendable job of maintaining this new role of benevolent well-wisher. Jane found it hard to believe this man was the same chauvinist taskmaster who'd browbeaten her constantly during the months she worked for him. "Please accept my apology."

"On one condition," she told him. "Why the change of heart?" In the next breath she pulled wine from the refrigerator and looked inquiringly at Pierce.

"A small glass would be fine, thanks." Pierce waited until he had the wine in hand before telling Jane, "I had a change of heart because I had a chance to see what kind of work you're capable of."

"Come again?"

"I read your memoirs," he said. "Stayed up until dawn finishing them, too, I'll have you know. Splendid stuff. Absolutely wonderful, Jane."

Jane refilled her glass of club soda and sat down across from Pierce on the sofa. "I still don't understand. How? I didn't even know the galleys had been typeset."

Pierce sipped his wine, found it to his liking. He smiled less bashfully at Jane. "You forget the *Sentinel* and Collins Press are owned by the same conglomerate. Word travels fast, especially between a pair of old farts like me and Frank Tennleton."

Jane was dumbfounded. "Frank sent you the manuscript?"

Pierce nodded. "We bought first serial rights. For a tidy sum, too, I'll have you know."

"I don't believe this."

"It certainly is a small world, isn't it?" Pierce took a long sip of the wine, complimented Jane on it, then went on. "At any rate, the irony of this whole thing is that you'll be getting that front-page by-line you wanted, and you don't even work for me anymore. How's that for a perverted bit of poetic justice?"

"I'm stunned."

Pierce finished his wine and stood up. He wasn't about to leave, however. He began pacing the room, looking at the posters on the walls, the house plants, the opened doorway leading to Jack's exercise room. "An apology isn't all I had in mind in coming here," he told her, pausing near the home computer and resting his hand on the monitor. "I'd like a chance to make things up to you."

"How's that?"

"When we last talked, you said you had a special perspective on that assassination attempt in Michigan." Pierce went back to his pacing, found his way to Jack's doorway. Subtle. "I understand you still have that special perspective, and I thought you might be interested in following through on it, writing about what's happened since then."

Jane turned on the sofa to keep up with Pierce's meanderings. "I'm not much on reading between lines, Mr. Pierce. What are you getting at?"

His tour of the living room complete, Pierce returned to the chair, sat down with an air of finality. "I'd like to hire you back at triple your former salary."

Jane laughed, almost spilled her drink. "You're joking, right?"

Pierce shook his head. "We want an investigative piece on this whole domestic terrorism thing, from a fresh angle. Front page, staff backing, expense account. Name your terms; you're the one to do it."

The flattery had done its job, and it took Jane a few moments to sort through what Pierce was offering and see the small print, the unmentioned bottom line. Her face hardened; her voice took on a harsh tone. "I'm the one to do it because the man I'm living with is involved in a top-secret capacity," she surmised. "That's it, right? I'm supposed to spy on him, try to sneak some juicy tidbits past the press blackout."

Pierce wasn't put off by her anger. He'd been playing hardball since before she was born. "Let's not forget that *you* were the one who first pointed out your special qualifications."

"I think this discussion has gone far enough." Jane got up from the sofa and went to the front door, opening it for Pierce. "Good day, Mr. Pierce."

Pierce sighed, shook his head, a new kind of grin on his face. "I think you're being a little too self-righteous here, Jane," he told her on the way outside. "At least think about what I said."

"I already did," she replied curtly. "Longer than I should have. The answer's no."

"If you should your mind, you know where to reach me."

"Don't hold your breath."

Once Pierce was on his way down the steps, Jane closed the door. She took the glasses into the kitchen and rinsed them out, set them on the drainboard, becoming angry at her inability to shake Pierce's buzz words from her mind. They floated about inside her head like pretty butterflies. Triple salary. Front-page by-line.

Name your terms . . .

Thirty-nine

It felt good to be back in action, Hal Dewez thought. There was just something about having one's life on the line that couldn't be duplicated by simulated war games or any of the other intrigues he'd been involved in since the assault on the gas shipment in Oregon. There was no replacement for that jackhammer pulse of anticipation, the full heightening of the senses, that feeling that one's every action was of absolute importance. No, he wasn't here for the money, which was negligible compared to what he could pull in through other ventures, and there were other ways that Moore could have been brought into the fold without offering to run errands for his friends in the Armageddon Brotherhood. Dewez was here because he wanted to be.

Minot was a small city a hundred miles north of Bismarck, an hour's drive away from the cattle ranch. It had recently celebrated its centennial anniversary, and there were still a number of sun-bleached banners dangling from light posts lining streets in the heart of town. Meat packing was one of the main industries, along with the production of farm machinery and building supplies. Dewez had been here often on business, either to bring cattle in for slaughter or to purchase the countless tons of cement and other materials that had gone into the creation of the ranch's underground network of tunnels, bunkers, and storage areas. Accordingly, it had been easy enough for him to case out the industrial park where he and Rowdy Trent now waited for the arrival of a certain eighteen-wheel semi. It was almost two in the morning, and they were crouched behind a shaggy clump of bushes flanking the main road accessing Minot's warehouse row. They wore ski masks and were dressed in black.

Two minutes later the truck rumbled into view, gears rattling as it approached the entrance to a fenced-off sprawl of buildings located beneath a glowing neon sign touting EDIBLE NEST EGG, INC. The truck bore the company logo on its side.

A security guard manned the main gate, and as the truck approached, the guard stepped out of a small wood-and-glass booth to unlock the gate and wave the truck through. He was a man in his late fifties, twenty pounds heavier than he'd been upon his retirement from the Minot police department two years ago. For him, this was a low-key job that supplemented his pension and gave him a little extra money to spend on three grandchildren.

As the truck rolled past him, he turned to head back into his booth, where a late-night movie flashed across the black-and-white screen of a portable television. There was an unfamiliar sound coming from the back of the truck, and as the guard glanced over his shoulder to investigate, he saw Hal Dewez jump down from the truck's rear bumper and aim a gun at him. Rowdy Trent was still clinging to the backside of the truck like an armed shadow.

"Keep your mouth shut and say your prayers," Dewez advised the guard, "and you just might see the sun rise."

After he'd backed up to the warehouse loading dock, the driver left his truck idling and climbed down from his cab. He was a thick, burly man with long curls of unwashed hair sprouting out from beneath a baseball cap. On his way up the steps to the loading dock he spat out the last splinter of a toothpick he'd been chewing on since Fargo. His mind was on the long shift ahead of him and he didn't bother glancing off to his right, where Rowdy Trent had taken refuge behind an overfilled trash dumpster.

Up on the dock, a short full-blooded Cheyenne in dungarees and a flannel shirt was driving a forklift filled with bound crates of Edible Nest Egg survival foods. During the next eight minutes, he managed to transfer another dozen similar loads from the warehouse stockroom to the idling truck. The driver helped guide the goods into place and counted off the stock as they went, checking numbers against a bill of lading on his clipboard.

"Eight fifty-nine, eight hundred sixty cases," he mumbled as the last load was eased down off the forklift. "Lotta chow."

"No shit," the Cheyenne said, backing the lift out of the truck and parking it. "Feed a small army for a year on that, long as you don't mind powered eggs and peanut butter every night."

"We won't mind it a bit," Rowdy Trent proclaimed as he scrambled up the steps and joined the men on the dock. They saw his mask and his gun, not necessarily in that order, and instinctively put their hands in the air. Dewez followed Trent and peered into the truck's hold, grinning at the full load.

"My, my," he snickered. "Looks like Christmas comes early this year."

"Don't shoot!" the driver pleaded. For a big man he had a very small voice. "I got a family."

"Good for you," Dewez told him. "Play it smart and they'll go on having a daddy."

"I'll do whatever you say," the driver promised. He looked like he meant it. The Cheyenne kept silent and glared at the gunmen, pissed.

"Put 'em in back," Dewez ordered Trent.

Rowdy translated the command with his gun, waving it at the other two men until they took a few tentative steps toward the truck.

The Indian finally spoke. "Where are you taking us?"

"Company picnic," Dewez told him.

Rowdy shoved the men inside the truck and Dewez helped him close the doors. They rushed up to the cab and clambered aboard. Dewez had never driven anything that ran on more than four wheels, so Rowdy took the driver's seat and geared the engine out of idle.

Skull throbbing, the security guard slowly sat up, feeling the egg-sized knot behind his left ear. His vision was blurred, filled with constellations, and he felt like his lunch was going to come up any second. He'd also struck his hip against something when he'd fallen and it was hard for him to get up. He grabbed the booth doorway for support. The portable television was still on, telling him the best place in town to get a deal on a used car. Once he was on his feet, his stomach felt even more queasy and he doubled over as he reached for the phone. Before he could dial, he heard the piston growl of a semi and turned toward the warehouse. The stars in his eyes were blinded by the twin suns of the truck's headlights. He dropped the phone and tried to rush out the doorway. He never made it. The semi clipped the side of the booth, wrenching it off its shallow foundation. Crushed by the rupturing enclosure and the rolling front end of the truck, the security guard fell in a mangled heap amid the rubble left behind as Rowdy Trent drove off into the night.

Avoiding Highway 83, Dewez and Trent took country back roads south toward the ranch. They hadn't spoken since leaving the warehouse. Dewez sat enveloped in a cloud of cigarette smoke while Rowdy hunched over the steering wheel, jaw clenched, gaze bouncing from mirror to mirror, on the lookout for the law.

"He was going for the phone, I'm telling you!" he finally shouted. "You saw it, right? I had to cream him."

Dewez crushed his cigarette out in an ashtray already half filled with twisted butts. "You creamed him all right."

"What do we do with those guys in back?" Trent wondered. "We can't let 'em go now ..."

"That's right," Dewez told him calmly. "We can't."

Five minutes later the truck pulled off onto the shoulder. They were still off in the country, nothing but dark hills and empty road around them. Dewez stayed inside as Rowdy hopped down from the cab and circled around back. The hostages were bartering for mercy even before the doors were opened. Trent fired two shots and dragged the bodies from the truck. There was a culvert running alongside the road, overgrown with weeds and mesquite. Trent shoved the bodies down the slope and closed the truck doors before getting back behind the wheel. He and Dewez had nothing to say to each other the rest of the way back to the ranch.

Forty

Unlike his Syrian predecessor, Arlo Kendall had a lawyer at his side well before he so much as stepped into the Washington interrogation room where Argvai Kalim had met his untimely demise. His attorney was Ike Iovine, a fair-haired, ruddy-faced veteran with almost twenty years of experience dealing with legal squabbles on and around Capitol Hill. Kendall was no stranger to plea bargaining, either, and he sat calmly before his inquisitors with an aura of bemused detachment. Across the table from Kendall and Iovine, Seamus McTeague, Jack Demarrest, and Dan Carlisle sat with the determination of avenging archangels, waiting for the attorney to finish perusing a three-page document that had been drawn up in advance of the meeting. Off near the door two armed guards posed like statues. Another two were posted in the corridor outside.

"This all seems in order," Iovine finally said, passing the document to Kendall along with a ball-point pen. The small man, who had shaved and had his hair neatly trimmed since his apprehension, scribbled his signature, then leaned back in his chair, clasping his hands behind his head.

"Okay, boys," he drawled lazily, "fire away."

McTeague started the interrogation, asking a few background questions that had more to do with technical formalities than making any headway concerning the matter at hand. Once the ritual had been perfunctorily dealt with, the Secret Service agent got down to specifics.

"What happened to Tony Bex after he was abducted in Chicago?"

"Who's Tony Bex?"

"He was an FBI agent who had flown to Chicago specifically to make contact with a Syrian named Omar Mentou regarding the alleged involvement of his countrymen in the assault on a delivery train transporting a shipment of nerve gas from Oregon to a port on the California coast," McTeague explained slowly, enunciating his words for the benefit of a tape recorder monitoring the conversation. "Instead of Mentou, he encountered you at an old stockyard gate just outside of Chicago. He was kidnapped and flown off in a helicopter following a skirmish during which two backup FBI agents were shot, one fatally. Does that refresh your memory?"

Kendall chuckled. "Hey, that was pretty good. You get tired of this line of work, you could always cut it as a newscaster, you know?"

McTeague looked at Iovine. "Could you kindly instruct your client to answer our questions directly and dispense with the levity?"

Iovine nodded at Kendall, who turned his smile into a sneer and lowered his arms to the table as he sat up.

"What happened to Tony Bex after he was abducted in Chicago?" McTeague repeated.

"I don't know," Kendall said. "I was just playing matchmaker."

"Then who did you set him up for?" Carlisle demanded.

From his preliminary conversations with Iovine, Kendall had already figured out what scoops of truth he would give to the feds along with those well-crafted untruths meant to protect his bargaining position. He was prepared to go halfway when it came to the men who'd paid him to get Bex into their clutches. "Couple ex-CIA guys," he divulged with practiced reluctance.

"Names?"

Kendall hesitated again. "Jake Morrison and Hal Dewez," he said finally. "They got the boot a few years back and decided to go into business for themselves."

"Doing what?" Jack wanted to know.

"Little this, little that. You know, entrepreneur-type work."

"Like terrorism and espionage," McTeague said.

Kendall's smile came back. "Yeah, maybe some of that, too."

Carlisle scribbled a few quick notes and rose from the table. "I'm going to check this with Daniels at CIA," he told the others on his way out the door.

Jack took over the questioning. "Where do they base their operations?"

Kendall shrugged. This was where he drew the line. "I never asked," he lied. "If they invite me to their Christmas party this year, maybe —"

"I'll warn you one more time," McTeague interjected. "Keep rubbing your immunity in our faces and we'll see to it that you —"

"Objection," Iovone cut in. "My client's cooperating as agreed upon."

"Bullshit!" McTeague retorted. "You tell him that he might walk out of here, but we can't guarantee he won't end up back behind bars for other offences we might happen to 'stumble upon.'"

Iovine turned to Kendall again but the prisoner waved him off. "Okay, okay. Look," he told McTeague and Demarrest, "we always met on neutral turf or else I dealt with go-betweens. That's the way they wanted it and it was fine with me."

"Was one of those go-betweens named Cal Winslow? FBI?"

"Outside of Morrison and Dewez, I don't know names," Kendall said. "I meet a guy he's gonna be callin' himself Red Dog One or Poontang Pappy, right? Cloak-and-dagger, just like the movies. Winslow doesn't ring a bell, but that doesn't mean anything."

McTeague glanced over notes he'd prepared. "How were Morrison and Dewez connected with the hit on the President and the raid in Oregon?"

"I wasn't in on those. God's truth," Kendall said.

"But they were. How?"

"They might have been suppliers," Kendall speculated. "Consultants, something like that."

"Consultants for who?" Jack asked.

"Like I said, I don't know names."

"What about faces?"

"What do you mean?"

"We have a who's-who book of terrorists, here and abroad," McTeague explained. "Maybe you can check the mug shots, get some people Morrison and Dewez do business with."

Kendall made a referee's signal. "Time out." He pushed his chair away from the table and motioned for Iovine to join him in a huddle. As they traded whispers, across the table Jack and McTeague looked at each other.

"Think he's on the level?" Jack asked softly.

"When he wants to be," McTeague replied. "I'd feel better if we could have gotten him to agree to a polygraph."

"Fucking legal system," Jack muttered bitterly. "You'd

think Monty Hall was on the Supreme Court the way things are run around here."

"Okay, boys," Kendall announced, breaking his huddle with Iovine. "Bring on the dirty pictures . . ."

Forty-one

"Another double for you, sweetie?"

Sheriff Moore glanced up at the waitress, a buxom woman in her late forties with a beehive hairdo and low-cut blouse that made her breasts look like twin Kilroys about to peek above the fabric line. Moore nodded and handed her his salt-rimmed glass. "Please, Marge."

"I thought that first one would have put you in better spirits," Marge said. "What's the problem?"

"Just a long day, that's all, Marge," Moore groaned, shoveling a nacho into a shallow bowl of salsa.

"Don't worry, you'll snap out of it," she told him. "You always do. Say, what's the name of that guy you're waiting for?"

"I'm sure he'll be able to find me," Moore answered evasively before slipping the chip into his mouth.

Marge winked at him. "I read you, sweetie, loud and clear. I minds my own business, right?"

The waitress wandered over to the next table, leaving Moore to his misery. He was out on the terrace of the

El Coyote Cantina, his favorite drinking hole and dining place. A combination of wide-limbed elms and tall shrubs blocked the terrace off from Main Street, although he could still hear five o'clock traffic rushing by. He took out his restlessness on the nachos, finishing the platter and signaling to a busboy for more. He got the chips and his second margarita at the same time. Jake Morrison showed up and took the seat across from him a minute later, apologizing for being late. Marge came by to take his drink order, then sashayed off. The men got down to business.

"Your people didn't have a problem with the shipment, did they?" Morrison inquired.

"Feeding dead men to the coyotes wasn't part of the bargain," Moore said.

"It couldn't be helped."

"Maybe not. Point is, I gotta cover your asses now on top of everything else. I don't like it." Moore chomped down hard on a nacho for emphasis.

"You'll be compensated," Morrison replied, unperturbed by Moore's foul mood.

"How?" Moore shoved away the chips and started on a cigarette. Morrison calmly stirred his bourbon after Marge had set it down before him, giving him a none too subtle once-over before moving out of earshot.

"Your Brotherhood's going to need a security force of some sort, correct?" Morrison asked the sheriff.

"Yeah. What about it?"

"Perhaps they'll need training."

Moore was finally beginning to feel his first drink, and a healthy draw on the second helped his disposition further. He relaxed in his chair, stopped burning up the cigarette like a fuse. He smoked slowly, let clouds tumble out between his nicotine-stained teeth.

"Matter of fact," he said, "that's one of the other things I wanted to talk to you about. We got five, six eager beavers we can get to do just about anything as long as they get to wear a uniform. Problem is they're on the young side. Greener than month-old oranges."

Morrison reached for his menu as he told Moore, "We could take care of that for you."

Moore nodded, licked a little salt off the rim of his glass. "I believe you could at that."

"I'll have Dewez set up a time when you can bring them in."

"The sooner the better," Moore said. "Lot of the brothers don't think you can put doomsday on hold."

"I'm sure we can accommodate your schedule." Morrison took a moment to skim the menu. Then he folded it, set it aside. "Now that we have that matter settled, how are you coming along with your end of the bargain?"

"Slow but sure," Moore said. "I'm just sniffing around so far, showing my face and trying to be helpful. I don't want to come on too strong or they might start raisin' eyebrows."

"Of course."

"You have to realize, too, that most feds are too goddamned highfalutin to give a country dick the time of day, much less any priority info." Moore smiled across the room at Marge, who had glanced at their table while waiting for drinks at the bar. He told Morrison, "I'm warmin' up to a skirt that's close to the inside track, though. Just a matter of time before I prime her like a country pump."

"Fine," Morrison said. "But remember, we're a little concerned about the time element, too."

Moore nodded, finished his second drink. He was feeling up, brimming with confidence. "Just out of curiosity, Jake, what happened to the truck?"

"Truck?"

"Yeah, the fucking semi you hauled all that shit away in."

Morrison smiled. "Our commission," he said.

"Fair enough," Moore told him. "Just do me a favor and keep the fucking thing off the road until things blow over. You got me on your side, but I can't be responsible if any of my men catch you guys breakin' laws and decide to do their duty."

"You don't throw them on our scent and there won't be any problems on that front."

"That's good. Real good," Moore said, dive-bombing his cigarette into an ashtray. "So's the enchiladas they make here..."

Forty-two

Jane was out when Jack returned to the apartment with Seamus McTeague and CIA officer Quinton Daniels. They'd brought along take-out burgers and fries as well as Daniels's information on former CIA operatives Jake Morrison and Hal Dewez. He briefed the two Secret Service men while they ate, cluttering the living room coffee table with fast-food wrappers.

"Back in '74, Schlesinger was running our outfit," Daniels explained, wiping stray ketchup off his ever-disheveled suit. "Morrison and Dewez were two of about two thousand people he let go that year."

"Two thousand?" McTeague said. "I remember it being quite a purge, but not that big."

"Well, it was definitely a major turnover," the older man went on. "Some of it had to do with Watergate fallout, but mostly it was routine housecleaning. Making way for new blood."

"These people that got canned," Jack said, "were they incompetent or what?"

Daniels shook his head. "By and large, they were at their peak. Longtime veterans who knew the ropes. You'll find a lot of them still working for the private sector. Corporate security, things like that."

"Or sponsoring terrorism," Jack put in, crumpling a wrapper in anger. "What do you have on Morrison and Dewez after they split the Agency?"

The CIA man glanced over his notes, though he already had memorized the information. It gave him time to finish his fish fillet sandwich. He wiped his lips with a napkin and proceeded. "For a couple years they were partners with four other ex-company men, trying to get a self-run intelligence network off the ground. I guess they figured they could go on milking their old contacts and hire themselves out without having to answer to the government. A real mercenary-type operation."

"Sounds like our boys," Jack said. "Didn't it work out?"

"In theory, it might have sounded good, but it didn't pan out in practice," Daniels said. "Naturally, we weren't about to put up with some kind of renegade outfit wandering around our turf — who knows? — maybe working against us. All we had to do was plant some bogus information and throw a few other monkey wrenches into their operations. They had a streak of big-money deals that blew up in their faces and had to close shop. It wasn't a pretty breakup either. One of the guys, Howie Lands, murdered a partner and got life. Another got himself killed working as a hack man for some private eye in Los Angeles."

"And Morrison and Dewez?" McTeague prompted. "Where are they now?"

Daniels's craggy face wrinkled even more when he frowned. "That's, as they say, the $64,000 question.

"We kept tabs on them a few years after their partnership folded, but they kept clean. When we ran into budget cuts last administration, things like surveillance on ex-personnel had to be curtailed, even dropped. The most recent info we have on Morrison and Dewez is from four years ago. They were running an import business out of New Jersey."

"Something tells me we aren't going to find them there," McTeague speculated.

"I already ran a check through phone books there," Daniels said. "Last time they were listed was three years back."

"Figures." The front doorbell rang. Jack got up from his chair. "I'll get it."

It was Carlisle.

"Kendall went through the whole rogue's gallery," he told the others as he strode into the living room with a large envelope tucked under his arm. "Picked out two ringers. One was Winslow."

"I knew it!" McTeague exclaimed between bites of his burger.

"Who else?" Daniels asked.

Carlisle pulled a photo from the envelope and passed it to the CIA agent, telling him, "Kendall figured her for Morrison's mistress."

One look at the eight-by-ten blowup and Daniels smirked maliciously. "Mistress, my ass," he muttered, passing the photo to McTeague.

"She looks vaguely familiar, but I can't quite place her," the Secret Service agent said.

"Her name's Koura Hoummari," Daniels said. "Born in Lebanon, schooled in the States. New York, if I remember correctly. She heads up a splinter group of Middle East misfits from half a dozen countries."

"I know her now," McTeague said. "She's some kind of militant feminist, right?"

Daniels nodded. "She doesn't like the way they treat

women over there, so she shifts allegiances depending on who's most likely to free the sisters once the shit stops hitting the fan, if you'll pardon my French."

"Is she the one who called Houril a marked man for pushing aid to the Saudis?" Jack asked.

"Right again."

"You know what this all means, of course," Carlisle said, not bothering to sit down with the other men. "If Hoummari's the one that sent that hit squad after Houril in Michigan, she's going to have a chance to kill two birds with one stone this weekend when the Saudis come visiting."

"Jesus! What a mess!" Daniels swore. "I guess our next step is to check around and see if we can't track down this nice little lady."

McTeague glanced at his watch and quickly rose from the sofa. "You can get started on that if you want, but Winslow's our bird in the hand, and if we've done our homework right, he's going to be making a move in less than an hour. Cross our fingers and maybe he'll link us up with Hoummari and we'll nail both of them . . ."

Jane was heading up the walk when the door to her apartment swung open and the four men headed out, determination in their strides.

"Jack!" she called out as he approached her. "I didn't expect you back so soon!"

"Things are starting to break," he told her, giving her a quick kiss. The other men continued past him.

"You won't believe the job offer I got a couple of hours ago," Jane started to tell him.

"Tell me when I get back, okay? I gotta run." Jack gave her a pat and hurried down the walk to catch up with McTeague. Jane frowned, followed him with her gaze.

"Wait a second! Can't you at least tell me what's the big hurry? Where are you going?"

But Jack was already inside Carlisle's sedan, closing the door behind him. Jane watched from the walk as the vehicle lurched away from the curb. When its taillights disappeared around the next corner, Jane stopped looking and went inside. The men had left their mess behind in their rush, and she grumbled to herself as she started gathering together the sea of wrappers and empty cups. Then she slowly sat down, finding something besides the remnants of a fast-food extravaganza. Jack's notes on the commode, an envelope filled with photographs. Her first instinct was to leave the material alone, or at least put it in Jack's room. But she also had a second, persuasive instinct, known in journalistic circles as a nose for news. She sat there with her conscience, trying to decide between the two.

Forty-three

Moonlight shone over Washington. With most of the major tourist haunts closed for the night, traffic thinned, the sidewalks became less crowded, fewer people walked the streets depending on maps for directions. One by one, vending vans that had spent the day parked along strategic curbs rolled away, bound for their nightly quarters, their silvery exteriors gleaming under streetlights. Tomorrow they would be back, restocked with food and drink for the masses, offering a quick meal on the run for sightseeing out-of-towners and time-pressed locals alike.

Koura Hoummari was behind the wheel of one such van, driving northwest on Pennsylvania Avenue after leaving her day-long job peddling Chinese food in front of the NASA museum. Elsewhere in the vehicle were two young men from Lebanon, in town with student visas, working part-time out of the vending van between classes at nearby Georgetown University. At school the two men were vehemently apolitical, cultivating an image among their colleagues as typically money-hungry law students willing to struggle the long years required to establish lucrative careers as attorneys. Theirs was an effective façade, allowing them to maintain a low profile, free to involve themselves in certain extracurricular activities. One of those activities was providing lodging for Koura Hoummari and assisting her in what was shaping up to be the latest of her desperate ploys on behalf of her self-envisioned revolution.

She'd come to Washington after her confrontation with Hal Dewez, three canisters of nerve gas secreted in the trunk of her rental Impala. Moving into the house shared by the two men and three female students, also hailing from the Middle East, Hoummari spent the next two weeks haunting the area around Capitol Hill. Oversized tinted glasses and a variety of large hats helped disguise her adequately as she played the part of tourist, snapping off roll after roll of film, always using a wide-angle lens so that her shots could take in security arrangements throughout the city without drawing attention to herself. Through intermediaries, she kept in contact with certain foreign embassies, monitoring the necessary connections to secure financing and forged documents in a successful effort to establish her present identity as owner and chief operator of the food-vending van she was now driving across Rock Creek on her way to Georgetown. She'd found that with the van she could secure close access to the areas she wanted to be near when it came time to put her master plan into operation. The vehicle also provided a large enough enclosure in which to make the necessary preparations without falling under the eye of security personnel.

On the way to her safehouse, Hoummari detoured to the outskirts of Georgetown and pulled into a service station attended by a gum-smacking man wearing headphones bringing him play-by-play reports of an early season contest between the Baltimore Orioles and Detroit

Tigers. The man had swarthy skin, dark eyes. Hoummari rolled down her window, told the man she was having problems with a slow leak in one of her back tires. The attendant motioned her to back into the service garage. She did so, easing into the cramped space while the two men inside the van slipped back toward the rear doors. While the attendant whistled his way from tire to tire, checking pressure and pretending to plug a nail hole, the other two men slipped out of the van. Along the back wall of the service bay, hidden from view of the street by the parked van, was a stack of boxes boasting the brand names of various long-life batteries. The men quickly shifted the stacks and transferred two of the boxes into the van, then climbed inside and closed the doors behind them. Moments later, the attendant finished his chore, winked as he told Hoummari she owed him five bucks for fixing the leak. She gave him an envelope filled with fifteen thousand dollars and drove off.

Twenty minutes later the van was parked at the food service lot and the two boxes were transferred to the back of Hoummari's Impala. She and the two men drove to the safehouse and took the boxes inside. The house was in a respectable part of town, modestly furnished. The three female students were already there. One of them, a tall, lean woman with close-cropped hair, used a box cutter to slice through the cardboard of both containers, opening them and taking out the contents. Instead of containing batteries, the boxes held a miscellany of tubes, control boxes, and other disassembled parts. She quickly inspected the separate pieces and confirmed to Hoummari that everything was there.

Hoummari smiled tightly. As the short-haired woman began assembling the parts at one end of the dining room table, Hoummari sat at the other, unfolding a large map of Washington, D.C. The two men moved off near the windows, making sure the shades were drawn all the way.

The other two women took a Frisbee and left the house, turning on a front porch light so they could see while they played catch and kept an eye on the neighborhood.

With swift efficiency, the short-haired woman fit the various pieces together, turning them into an Israeli-made Kylar-27B rocket launcher, easily one of the most accurate and powerful of such weapons in existence. It had a firing range of more than a mile, although its accuracy was best assured at half that distance. When she'd finished the transformation, she showed the launcher to Hoummari, who asked a few questions and handed a drafting compass to her. The short-haired woman calibrated the compass and gave it back to Hoummari. Hoummari placed the metallic tip of the compass against the outline of the White House on her map, then slowly drew a circle around the presidential residence, establishing the radius within which the rocket launcher would have the greatest likelihood of striking its intended target. Hoummari then drew a second circle, the center of which was the nation's Capitol Building. With great pleasure, Hoummari noted that there was an area where the two circles overlapped.

Forty-four

Cal Winslow leaned against a cherry tree, protecting himself against bugs with smoke from his cigarette. His eyes were on a pay phone twenty feet away, where an obese woman in a flower-print dress was in the midst of a conversation requiring her to nod her head constantly and reply in a steady chorus of affirmatives to the party on the other line. Winslow was amazed; the woman had tied up the phone for the better part of five minutes without ever speaking a sentence of more than three words. He checked his watch, imagined Morrison's temper flaring half a continent away as he tried without success to get through. Another minute, Winslow finally decided, and he was going to have to intervene, have the woman end her call. There was no way he wanted to miss connecting up with Morrison and have to wait another day to pass along the news about Arlo Kendall. Winslow wanted to blow the whistle, tell Morrison he'd have a new contact lined up by the end of the week, then start making preparations for the vacation time he'd just put in for with the Bureau. He was going to fly to the Bahamas, rig a fake death, and take on a new identity, courtesy of tricks he'd learned through a friend working with the government's witness relocation program. It would cost him a bundle, but it'd be worth every penny. For him, the past four weeks had been an orgy of paranoia, living on an ugly edge that robbed him of sleep and spawned an ulcer that even now was flaring up on him like a pair of hands wringing his intestines.

Forty seconds had passed when the fat woman finally hung up and started away from the phone. It rang before she'd taken ten steps and she began backtracking to answer it. Winslow beat her to it, breaking from the cherry trees and taking long strides to the phone, assuring the woman the call was for him.

" 'Lo," he muttered into the receiver, watching the woman head off for her car, one of several parked along the curb flanking this side of the tidal basin. "Yeah, it's me," he told Morrison, cupping his free hand over his other ear and turning away from the traffic, giving himself a view past the phone stand and through the cherry blossoms. Out on the still waters of the basin he could see a reflection of the moon and the Jefferson Memorial.

Winslow hadn't been the only one seeking refuge in the cherry trees surrounding the tidal basin. McTeague and Jack Demarrest were crouched behind trash cans less than twenty yards away on either side of Winslow. Both men had walkie-talkies. McTeague, as agreed upon before the men had staked out their positions twenty minutes ago, made the call to their backup, whispering as low as he could, "Okay, roll 'em."

Dan Carlisle knelt inside a van parked across the street from the phone booth. The van's exterior was painted with wild colours in designs borrowed from the Peter

Max school of sixties psychedelics. Carlisle used binoculars to peer through a slit in the black velvet curtains. He, too, had a walkie-talkie to his ear, and on McTeague's cue, he signaled a technician beside him to start up the recording equipment and begin a trace on the call. A small speaker relayed Winslow's conversation with Morrison.

"All I know for sure is that they've brought him here for questioning and he wants to cut a deal," Winslow was telling Morrison as he fumbled with his pack of cigarettes. "I can't find out more without putting my own neck in a noose."

"When will Eckland be ready to take over for you?" Morrison was calling long distance from a pay phone down the street from the survivalist store in Bismarck, but his voice was clear on the line. Calm, reassuring.

"Next week, I'm hoping." Winslow lit a fresh smoke, shifted the phone to his other ear. "He's got a few loose ends to take care of before they clear his transfer."

Out of the corner of his eye, Winslow saw the fat woman trying to wriggle her Cadillac out of her parking space. Even before the faint collision, he could see that she was going to back into the rainbow-colored van behind her. The van jostled sharply from the Cadillac's impact. Simultaneously, Winslow heard an abrupt crackling sound over the phone.

"Shit!" he cursed into the receiver. He asked Morrison, "Did you just hear something on the line?"

"Yes. Probably —"

The phone went dead as Winslow hung up. He stole a quick glance back at the van, then headed the other way, into the cherry trees. He took a few slow, casual steps, but when he heard the van doors opening he broke into a run, heading for the shoreline of the tidal basin. Jack Demarrest stepped clear of a trash can, blocking his way.

"It's over," Jack told the man. "Hands up."

Winslow hesitated, started to raise his arms, then suddenly bolted to one side, ducking behind a tree. He jerked out his own gun and fired wildly at Jack before dashing off.

"Stop!" Jack shouted at the man, following in pursuit. When Winslow reached the water's edge he stopped, swung around to confront Jack. Before he could get off another shot, Jack's gun fired and Winslow staggered backward into the water, dropping his gun, clutching at his chest. By the time McTeague had run to his friend's side, Jack was watching Winslow's body float facedown, giving off ripples that seemed to slice the moon's reflection.

"You okay?"

"Yeah," Jack said, putting his gun away. Dan Carlisle joined them, saw the body.

"Can't say the same for him." Carlisle and McTeague braced themselves, holding on to Jack's hand as he leaned out far enough to reach Winslow and drag the body ashore.

"He mentioned somebody named Eckland as his replacement," Carlisle told the other two men.

"Name doesn't ring a bell here," McTeague said. "My guess is it's code."

Stepping away from the body, Jack looked down at his victim, angry at himself. "I sure as hell didn't want to kill him. Hell, all this time trying to set him up and it's wasted."

"Not entirely," Carlisle told Jack. "We managed to get a partial trace before he hung up. Somewhere in the middle of North Dakota."

Jack smiled for the first time in hours. "Well, well," he said, "that's my territory . . ."

Forty-five

The freshly repainted semi, now bearing the logo of a fictitious wholesale supply company, rolled into Bismarck as bells in the town churches chimed two times in the darkness. The truck's front end had been repaired, showing no signs of damage from its collision with the guard booth in Minot on the night its ownership had changed hands. Like then, Rowdy Trent was behind the wheel, and, also like then, he was armed and ready for gunplay if the need arose. He guided the huge truck down the deserted streets of Bismarck, past the principal milk buyer's office, a two-story white brick building atop which stood a plastic cow the size of a one-car garage. A traffic light blinked red in one direction, yellow in the other. Rowdy turned the corner, slow and wide, giving himself room to maneuver into the narrow alley that ran behind Darwin's Den. Brady emerged from the back entrance of the supply store, helped Rowdy get as close to the building as possible.

Morrison was inside the store, wearing jeans and a flannel shirt rather than his customary suit. Sleeves rolled up, he was arranging stock into loads that could be most easily moved by handcart. With the truck ready for loading, he wheeled the first stack of crates out to the alley, trading quick greetings with Rowdy as he pulled the handcart out from under the goods. Two other ranch hands followed with a second load and helped both Trent and Brady muscle the merchandise up into the truck.

"That's it," Morrison told them. "Quick but quiet."

During the next hour, a quarter of the Den's stock had been transferred into the truck. Hal Dewez arrived, pulling his Jeep up next to the semi. He was still dressed up from a dinner date that had lasted until early morning, when the woman he was with had decided his sexual proclivities were a little too imaginative and degrading for her tastes. Liquor on his breath and the promise of a hangover blooming inside him, Dewez took in the activity behind the store with wary, bloodshot eyes. The message on his answering machine hadn't prepared him for this.

"What's going on, Jake?" he asked when Morrison emerged pushing another cartload of boxed potato flakes.

"They tapped Winslow when I called tonight," Morrison explained, taking a handkerchief from his back pocket to wipe sweat from his brow. "He hung up but they might have had enough time for a trace. No sense taking chances."

"Fuck!" Dewez muttered. He watched Rowdy hoist a box up to Brady, who was standing inside the truck's cargo bay. "Where's all this crap going?"

"To the ranch," Morrison said. "What we can't use we'll peddle to the Brotherhood.

"Thank God for the fucking Brotherhood." Dewez lit a cigarette and started rolling up his own sleeves. "Did Winslow call back?"

"Not yet."

Dewez kicked at the ground, scuffing his soles on

asphalt. "Damn it! I knew we should have cut him loose sooner!"

"No point dwelling on that now."

Forty minutes later the truck was almost half filled and they realized it wouldn't be possible to load all of the store's stock in one trip. With no guarantee that they'd be coming back, Morrison and Dewez began sorting through the merchandise, establishing priorities in terms of what could be most easily disposed of or put to use and what should be left behind. They were in the middle of this task when Rowdy leaned in the back doorway and called out to them, "We got company. Cops."

Morrison waved Rowdy inside, motioned for him and the other ranch hands to remain near the entrance while he and Dewez went out to deal with the police. Trent grabbed a shotgun from inside the back office while Brady unholstered his revolver and took up position on the other side of the doorway.

The patrol car was halfway down the block, heading slowly toward the semi. A searchlight streaked out from the vehicle, cutting through the darkness in sweeping arcs, half blinding Dewez and Morrison when it fell on them. The cruiser slowed to a stop and the driver's door opened.

"Trick-or-treat," Sheriff Moore said as he snapped off the searchlight and walked toward the other two men.

"That's really funny, Moore," Dewez told him. "Get your rocks off doing that, did you?"

"Lighten up," Moore told him, his eyes on the truck. He took a deep breath, grinned sourly. "Nice paint job, but I can smell it. You really think my boys would be fooled if they were here instead of me?"

"They aren't," Dewez retorted. "What the fuck are you doing around here, anyway?"

"It's my job, remember? I only moonlight as your errand boy."

"All right, there's no need getting on each other's

nerves," Morrison said. He paused long enough to signal to Brady and Trent that it was okay to resume loading, then turned back to the sheriff. "There's a chance we might have run into some trouble with our man in Washington." He went on to explain about the interrupted call to Winslow and the possibility that the call had been traced.

"You guys really know how to cheer a fella up," Moore drawled sarcastically. "I got half a mind to step aside and let 'em sniff you out."

"You got less than half a mind if you think you'd get away with it," Dewez warned him.

Moore was about to say something but thought better of it. He shook his head disgustedly and turned from the men, heading back toward his patrol car. Before getting in, he glanced over his shoulder, told them, "Oh, by the way, I finished lining up the boys we want you to run through your camp. I'll be dropping them off with you in a couple days. Any luck and I'll have some word about what the feds are up to as well . . ."

Forty-six

Jane loved going to movies. Sitting up close enough so that the screen would fill her vision, she could sit back and let another world wash over her. She took in all genres; only the worst of films would fail to hold her attention, lull her into a dreamlike state where her everyday concerns would be banished, however briefly. Then, upon leaving the theater, certain images, certain lines of dialogue, certain faces would linger in her mind, playing off the cerebral musings she'd put on hold. More often than not, there would be flashes of insight, new outlooks or understandings that helped her get a more rounded view of the life she was living. It wasn't at all uncommon for her to attend movies alone, because the whole process seemed even more intensified, less diluted by the stigma of shared experience.

Tonight she was on her own, walking home after taking in the latest Meryl Streep performance at a refurbished theater four blocks from her apartment. The strong-willed courage of the lead character was an inspiration to Jane, reminding her of some happier moments in her life, times when she'd faced difficult choices by trying to determine which course was most likely to challenge her, help her to grow. Those moments had been the pearls of her memoirs, the highlights that had made her recollection of more trying periods more tolerable. Now she felt on the verge of an important crossroad, weighing several options, none of which could be easily called more or less advisable than the others. She knew that she loved both Jack and her newly revitalized writing career, but she wondered to what extent she could commit herself fully to both. She cherished the past few weeks spent with Jack, but there was still part of her that clung to the miseries of her failed marriage. Once the uniqueness of their pairing faded, would she find herself succumbing to the same loss of self-identity she'd come to feel as Andrew's wife? It seemed unlikely. Jack and Andrew were so different, it was hardly fair to equate them. And yet, a relationship was a relationship, with inevitable clashings of wills and needs for compromise. Could she count on herself to be strong and hold an equal footing, or would the desire for ongoing harmony outweigh her insistence upon a life of her own, separate and independent from whatever part of herself she might choose to share?

She was still preoccupied with her inner debate when she returned to the apartment and found Jack sitting on the bed, inspecting his gun. He was dressed for travel, a packed suitcase lying on the sheets beside him. She stood in the doorway watching him, stunned, trying to chase her thoughts away. Jack seemed equally uneasy at the sight of her.

"What's this?" Jane finally managed to utter.

"We've had a major breakthrough," Jack told her, slipping the gun into his shoulder holster as he stood up.

There was still a stiffness to his movements, the slightest wincing of pain.

"You already told me that once tonight." The words leaped out instinctively, combative, filled with an anger Jane herself was startled by. Jack's defensiveness only served to bait her further. She found herself demanding, "Can't you be a little more specific?"

"We've pinpointed a search area in North Dakota," Jack told her. "I have to go."

"Have to?"

"Okay, I *want* to," Jack admitted. He took a step toward her. "Jane, you know how important this is to me." His voice was patient, but Jane knew him well enough to see the warning glint in his eyes. She was overreacting, taking cues from her daydreams instead of seeing the situation for what it was.

"Of course," Jane conceded, kissing Jack, embracing him long enough to rein in her emotions. Then she started for her closet, her voice taking on the tone of an accomplice. "But at least slow down enough for me to catch up with you, okay?"

Jack watched her pull out her overnight bag and start filling it with things from her dresser. "What are you doing?"

"I'm coming with you, of course."

"I don't think that's a good idea."

Jane glanced over at Jack, offered a smile. "Why not? You've already told me how short-staffed they are on this. I could be a big help. We could crack this thing together."

Jack shook his head, walked toward her. She closed her bag. He put his hand on hers, gently. "You'd stick out like a sore thumb, Jane," he told her. "You know that. They see the ex-President's daughter sniffing around and my cover'll be blown."

"Who says I have to go around saying who I am?" Jane countered. "You're using a cover. Why can't I?"

"Because Secret Service agents don't make the cover of *People* magazine and the front page of the tabloids four years running?"

However Jack might have intended the remark, it only served to incite Jane further. "And exactly what the hell's that supposed to mean?"

"You're taking this all wrong." Jack reached out, but she retreated from his embrace. He sighed. "Look, it just wouldn't work, okay?"

"You're talking about us?"

"Damn it, Jane! Would you knock off the martyr routine?" Jack shouted. "I'm talking about this assignment, for crying out loud! Look, you know damned well how much you've meant to me this past month, and I hope to hell you know I've cared about you for a lot longer than that. But this is my job, my first chance to prove myself since what happened in Michigan. I need to do that alone. You know, no crutches."

"Is that what you think I am?" Jane said. "Just a crutch?"

"No!" Jack looked up at the ceiling with a gesture of helplessness. "Jane, this is crazy!"

Jane had her overnight bag ready. She threw a few things into her suitcase and carried the luggage from the room, telling Jack, "Go ahead and suit yourself, Jack. Play hero and good luck."

"Jane —"

"I've got a career of my own to look after," she cried out over her shoulder as she opened the front door.

"What?" Jack cleared the bedroom, looked at Jane with continuing amazement. "What are you talking about?"

"You and your buddies left a few things behind with your burgers," she told him calmly. "I put them on the kitchen counter for you."

She slammed the door behind her and Jack could hear her heading down the walk. He went over to the counter and glanced over the notes and photographs. He cursed under his breath and bolted to the door, flinging it open, just in time to see Jane slip into the back seat of a taxi and head off into the night.

Forty-seven

Cal Winslow's Washington apartment had been searched on several occasions during the past weeks, each time without turning up any incriminating evidence linking him to known criminal elements or any other activity outside the law. This time would be different, however. The authorities no longer had to steal into the living quarters and take care to leave the place the way they'd found it, because Cal Winslow wasn't going to be coming home again. His cold body was halfway across town, lying on an even colder slab in the city morgue. The clothes he'd been wearing at the time of his death had been gone over, turning up nothing out of the ordinary, save for two full coin wrappers, one filled with quarters, the other with dimes. Although in certain circles these items might have passed as a poor man's brass knuckles, McTeague and Carlisle suspected Winslow carried the rolls as change for pay phones. He'd been observed making or taking calls away from his apartment all through the period he was under surveillance, and a computer checkout of his home phone bill hadn't turned up any calls to North Dakota or anywhere else outside the city limits. The extensive search of his apartment and car yielded nothing more substantial than a pocket-sized address book which, as both McTeague and Carlisle suspected, did not contain the name or number of anyone by the name of Eckland. The book was one of a handful of Winslow's belongings that were nonetheless put in plastic bags and tagged for later, more in-depth analysis in the hopes that they might reveal some faint clues as to the identity of the person Winslow had been supposedly grooming as his replacement.

"All this vacation shit on Bermuda was mailed to him just two days ago," McTeague mentioned, flipping through the travel brochures. He and Carlisle were back at the interim offices of the special task force, located in a wing of the U.S. Information Agency currently under construction. He and Carlisle sat on the same side of a table that filled almost half of the cramped room. A computer took up one corner and a pair of chest-high file cabinets another.

"Come from a travel agency?" Carlisle inquired. When McTeague nodded, he went on: "I'll get in touch with them come morning, see if Winslow mentioned when he was figuring to do his traveling. Stands to reason he wouldn't split until he was sure this Eckland character was in position. Hopefully we can come up with some date we can compare with our personnel records, figure out who was moving up the ranks around the same time."

There was a coffee urn at the end of the table and McTeague tilted it far enough to drain a last few drops into his coffee cup. It was only midnight but he was exhausted from cheating himself of sleep for so many days running. Thoughts of Bermuda and hammocks stretched taut between palm trees teased him as he rubbed at an ache in his lower back.

Benson White joined them several minutes later, bringing a tray filled with steaming cups of coffee along with him. He passed out Java with his latest update. "I've posted all our foreign bureaus, but nobody's seen hide nor hair of Hoummari for more than a month." He sat down across from his colleagues and savored the aroma wafting up from his cup. "I did overhear one rumor that says she was in cahoots with Libyans in the attack up in Michigan."

"Libyans, Lebanese . . . she gets around these days," Carlisle groaned. "She gets a few more people on her side and she's going to wind up twice as dangerous as she already is."

"Oh, wouldn't that be fun," McTeague deadpanned.

White let the wisecrack pass. He looked even more tired than the other men, even appeared to nod off for a quick second after he'd poured sugar into his coffee. He blinked several times and sighed with his lower lip jutting out so that he blew up into his face. "I just talked to Daniels," he said, shifting topics. "He's sending out word on Morrison and Dewez to every law enforcement agency in both Dakotas. With any luck, by the time Jack gets out there we'll have narrowed things down for him a little."

"Daniels is going with him, right?" McTeague asked.

White nodded. "We may as well put all our money on this one. If we don't nab those bastards quick, I got a feeling they're going to be long gone and we're going to be back at square one."

McTeague didn't even want to think in those terms. He excused himself and left the room, heading down the hall past two marines stationed there expressly to protect task force members. He told the soldiers he just needed a breath of fresh air. A short flight of steps led to a side door and McTeague opened it, stepping out into the cool, welcome breeze. This late it was relatively quiet.

He could hear a jet overhead and looked up, seeing its blinking lights through the limbs of a magnolia tree. A block away was Blair House, site of the bloodiest assassination attempt on a U.S. President prior to Houril's close call in Michigan. McTeague had studied that incident numerous times and he still marveled at how few precautions were made in terms of security back then, especially when compared to the exhaustive efforts now employed on behalf of the Chief of State.

McTeague's brooding was interrupted by the sound of footsteps behind him. He turned, saw Carlisle coming out to join him. He looked upset.

"I was just on the phone with Jack," the CIA agent told McTeauge. "We're going to have to send out word on Jane Britland, too."

"What do you mean?"

"Seems she's decided to play Woodward and Bernstein on us . . ."

Forty-eight

"I have to say, Jane, I didn't expect to be hearing from you quite so soon." Jess Pierce spoke through a diffident smile. "Naturally, I'm glad I did. This only reinforces my confidence in you."

"As long as we stick to my terms," Jane replied, "we'll all come out ahead."

They were in the back of Pierce's stretch limo, heading across the Potomac to the editor's estate in Alexandria, Virginia. She'd met up with him at the *Sentinel*, having taken the taxi there directly after leaving her apartment. She was familiar enough with Pierce's work schedule to know he'd be in that late. She agreed to take the assignment he'd proposed to her earlier, adding two conditions to the terms that had already been discussed. Foremost, she refused to use her personal relationships as a springboard to securing classified material for her story. Pierce had problems with this provision at first, feeling that without the benefit of her special "perspective" there was little to differentiate her from the hundreds of other reporters covering the same story. Jane countered that her name alone would provide a draw for readers and that she was already a step ahead of the pack in her knowledge that North Dakota was now the primary focus of the government's search for the key men involved in the plague of domestic terrorism. True, she was contradicting herself already in having learned the latter information through an oversight by Jack and the other members of the task force, but in her mind stumbling upon a lead was much different from deliberately setting out to exploit her associations with those same people.

The second provision was that, although she would use her own name in any by-lined story she might submit, for obvious reasons she wanted to travel to North Dakota under an assumed name and altered appearance. Pierce wholeheartedly supported Jane on this front, so much so that upon their arrival at his mansion, he'd turned her over to his wife, a former beautician who'd masterminded enough radical makeovers for Washington wives over the years to know exactly how Jane could go about altering her looks in a few simple steps.

As she entrusted herself to Felicia Pierce's care and half listened to the flamboyant woman's nonstop gossip about backstage drama on Capitol Hill, Jane's thoughts drifted back to her own bit of melodrama earlier that evening. She still couldn't believe the extent to which she had flown off the handle, but the more she thought about it, the more she was able to divine a certain method to her madness. Her outburst was, on the surface, both unreasonable and unwarranted, particularly from Jack's perspective, and she knew that an apology was in order. But looking back in terms of what she'd been thinking about after leaving the movie theater — about the need to make decisions in favor of the more challenging of two courses — she could see that in a way she might have subconsciously willed herself to make that more difficult and challenging decision, to turn the focus of her journalistic attentions away from herself and toward what was undeniably the hottest story going. How many of the great writers whom she most admired had paid their dues as war correspondents, throwing themselves into the fray and relying on their wits to get them through it all? Well, this was her war, and, like Jack, she wanted to go into it as independently as possible, to test herself without the buffer of someone to duck behind when the going got rough. Much as she loved Jack and hoped that her behavior wouldn't drive a permanent wedge between them, she now saw that, however unpleasant, a parting of sorts was inevitable — even necessary — for both of them. She was glad to be where she was now, being primed for the experience of her life, and she looked forward to some future time when she and Jack would be reunited, both stronger as individuals, both more ready to consider seriously the long-term commitments their relationship had been leading to.

Her hair trimmed, tinted, and restyled, Jane was already impressed with the first stage in her transformation. The following morning, after a fitful sleep and strange dreams that pitted her against Indians in combat fatigues in a North Dakota wilderness modeled more after old television Westerns than any real knowledge of the area, Jane sat again for Felicia, this time paying closer attention as the older woman showed her makeup techniques that would further enhance her disguise. By nine o'clock she had eaten and was riding with Jess Pierce to nearby Washington National Airport, wearing an informal outfit Felicia had given her as one final touch in her change of identity. She had trouble sitting still and her gaze invariably drifted to the rearview mirror. Was that really her?

"Relax," Pierce told her as they turned off the Jefferson Davis Highway and started toward the airport, visible a few hundred yards away.

"I hope you're right." Jane sighed, sitting back.

When they reached the terminal out of which Jane would be flying, Tracy Comstock, the *Sentinel*'s petite city editor, was waiting near the skycab booth. As a porter took Jane's luggage, Tracy handed Jane an envelope filled with press cards and other forged pieces of identification, a company charge card, airline tickets, and two thousand dollars in cash.

"Here you go, kiddo," Tracy said. "Gook luck."

"Thanks."

"Oh, I almost forgot. Jack Demarrest called the paper last night trying to track you down. He's worried sick about you."

"You didn't tell him that —"

"No, of course not." Tracy looked at her watch. "Look, you'd better get going or you'll miss your plane. Hang tough and I know you'll do fine."

Jane traded quick farewells with both Tracy and Pierce. Then the woman joined her boss in the limo and Jane followed the porter inside to a ticket counter.

"Can I help you?" a young woman in an airline uniform asked her, showing no signs of recognizing Jane.

"Yes," Jane told her. "I'm Holly Armstead. *Daily Sentinel.* I have a reservation on the morning flight to Bismarck . . ."

Forty-nine

It was lunchtime in Washington and business was heavy at Koura Hoummari's vending van. The egg rolls were going fast, and she'd already dished out the last burrito. Like most of the other vendors, she offered a variety of foods to cater to the multiethnicity of the tourist trade. She and her female cohorts wished customers a good day, keeping up the façade while they waited for word on the next step in their plan that could conceivably lead to the deaths of the same people who left the van chomping merrily on their fast food.

The van was parked on Constitution Avenue, near the National Art Gallery and the intersection of Pennsylvania Avenue, and 4th Street. Capitol Hill was less than half a mile away, the White House a little farther in the other direction. Hoummari's two male roommates were out playing tourist on nearby side streets, taking pictures of each other standing near predetermined buildings, hoping the resulting snapshots would help them to figure out the best place from which to use the rocket launcher.

The buildings' heights were naturally an important factor in determining trajectory, but other variables were being taken into account as well. Certain blocks were better bets in terms of security, and although Hoummari estimated it would take less than twenty seconds to get off a shot under ideal circumstances, with the increased presence of soldiers stationed throughout the capital, even that short time might not allow for success. She was also familiar enough with cities under siege to know that for every visible soldier there could be as many as three armed government agents either hiding in strategic lookout posts or roaming among the civilians in disguise.

When one of the soft-drink spigots poured out its last ration of cola and began hissing, Koura signaled to the woman operating the machine that she would change canisters. Behind the dispenser was a cluster of upright cylinders, some already hooked up, pumping carbonation and syrup to the spouts, others stacked and ready as refills. Hoummari wriggled aside the canisters for Mountain Dew and Cherry Coke to get at a replacement for the emptied container of cola syrup. She carefully avoided three canisters in the back of the cluster, anchored securely to the inner wall of the van. Although identical in appearance to the other containers, down to the brand-name labels and mounting nozzles, they held more than the promise of liquid refreshment. One of the canisters contained the disassembled rocket launcher. The other two housed modifed missiles packed with not only fragmentary explosives, but also doses of nerve agent.

It was nearly two o'clock when the two men returned to the van. Rather than joining their comrades, however, they got at the end of the line and waited for other customers to get their goodies before approaching the counter, shaded by a raised panel that served as a makeshift awning. The men ordered sauerkraut dogs and barbecued pork rinds, giving no indication that they knew Hoummari or the other two women inside the van. They paid for their orders and walked off, leaving behind a folded newspaper one of the men had set on the counter. Hoummari took the paper and left the counter area. Crouching in the back corner of the van, she unfolded the paper and took out three rolls of film and the map of Washington on which she had drawn circles the night before. Within the area where the two circles overlapped there was now a series of dots, each one corresponding to locations where photographs had been taken. Hoummari put the film and the map into her purse and told the other women she was taking a break. She left the van and walked three blocks to a camera supply store, where she had to wait in line to buy developing chemicals for the darkroom located back in the basement of the Georgetown safehouse. The store offered other equipment besides cameras, and as she stood in line, Hoummari's attention was drawn to a small television on a nearby counter. On the five-inch screen, President Houril was conducting a press conference with a swollen crowd of media representatives in the White House briefing room. Hoummari leaned closer to the set, turning up the volume.

"We haven't made a major breakthrough yet," Houril was explaining, "but obviously the matter's being given the highest priority."

"Could you be more specific?" a reporter from NBC asked, standing up amid his colleagues.

"I can't do that without compromising our efforts. You know that." Houril scanned the throng, where hands were waving in the air like stalks of corn in a summer breeze. He pointed to a woman in a red dress.

"With the Saudi delegation scheduled to arrive for meetings with you this weekend, are there any additional security measures being taken, particularly in light of rumors of Middle Eastern involvement in the recent terrorist incidents here in America?"

"Of course we're taking precautions," Houril responded crisply. "Again, I'm not about to go into detail."

Watching the press conference, Hoummari smiled to herself, sure that she could see a trace of fear behind the President's calm exterior. *Go ahead*, she told him in her thoughts, *pretend that everything's under control. We'll show you differently ...*

Fifty

Morrison and Dewez were watching the press conference on an ancient Motorola perched on the bar inside the old hunting lodge. Sheriff Moore was with them, leaning against the edge of a long wooden table taking up half the floor. Along one wall was a massive stone hearth and a tall stack of quartered firewood. Sun beamed through the streaks of dirty windows in the other three walls, throwing a slight glare on the TV screen. When Houril finished his final statement and walked away from the podium bearing his presidential seal, the image on the screen changed to that of a network commentator who was already prepared to analyze the press conference. Moore moved away from the table and muted the sound.

"Look, guys, I gotta be heading out."

"Go ahead and turn it off," Dewez told the sheriff. He and Morrison followed Moore to the door.

"We appreciate you coming by with this," Morrison said, indicating a manila file in his hands. "It's going to be a big help to us, believe me."

"Just holding up my end of the deal," Moore said on his way out.

Out on the grass next to the lodge, ten men in army surplus fatigues were doing push-ups under the supervision of Rowdy Trent. None of them looked to be more than twenty years old, and only two of them were able to keep up with Trent. The others straggled behind, bodies shaking from the workout, sweat already staining their uniforms under the sun's glare.

"Come on, damn it!" Trent howled at the recruits between breaths. "You fuckers won't last ten minutes in the sack if you can find some bitch dumb enough to spread her legs for you. Come on, hump that earth, up and down, up and down!"

"Quite a crop, eh?" Moore chuckled from the lodge porch, watching a couple of the young men collapse on the grass.

"We've whipped worse groups into shape," Dewez said. "Give 'em a few days and they'll be tough."

"Or gone," Moore added. "I doubt that the Brotherhood'll be interested in being protected by a pack of wimps."

Dewez went over to join Rowdy and recruits as Morrison walked with Moore to the sheriff's patrol car. "You'll be sure to mention our offer to your people, won't you?"

"Yeah, I'll bounce it off them, all right." Moore opened the car door but waited to get in, pausing to take in the scenery around the lodge. "I got a feeling they'd like a place like this, if the price was right. Of course, seein' how you folks are going to have to pull stakes, that shouldn't be much of a problem, should it?"

Morrison remained expressionless in the face of Moore's sly grin. "That's something we'll discuss if your people come back with an offer."

"You know, I haven't had a full tour of the whole

ranch," Moore said. "Are you sure you don't have some plans or whatnot I can show them?"

"If they're serious about wanting this place, I'll be glad to meet with them and bring as much documentation as they want," Morrison bartered. "Obviously, we aren't going to put all our cards on the table if the Brotherhood's not interested in making a legitimate offer."

"Sounds like we got a Catch-22 here, doesn't it?"

Morrison shrugged. "We're looking on this as a business transaction. If your people think the same way, there won't be any problem. However, if they think that by peddling themselves as some nonprofit religious organization we're going to be overcome with charity, they're mistaken. We let them come out ahead on that deal with the foodstuffs as a show of good faith."

"Special introductory offer."

"Exactly."

"Well, just don't forget that my services got thrown into the bargain," Moore reminded Morrison, nodding at the file the other man was carrying. "And I plan to keep you posted if anything new comes up."

It was Morrison's turn to offer up a sly grin. "And, of course, we're grateful for your input. You might want to keep in mind that we'll be giving you a ten percent commission if the Brotherhood meets our terms on the ranch."

This was the first time the figure had been mentioned, and the revelation had the impact Morrison hoped it would. Moore was stunned initially, then reverted back to his crafty self. "Now you're talking," he said as he got in behind the wheel of his patrol car. Morrison stood back as Moore drove off. In the background, Dewez took charge of the recruits, freeing Rowdy Trent to walk over to Morrison.

"You wanted to see me?"

Morrison nodded, gestured for Trent to follow him back inside the lodge, where he opened the manila file and began showing the ranch hand a series of teletype printouts and photographs. "The hounds are on the scent," he told Trent. "We need to be ready for them."

Rowdy skimmed the printouts and quickly flipped through the photographs. He stopped, letting his gaze dwell on a picture of Jane Britland.

"This babe looks familiar," he muttered.

"She should," Morrison told him. "She should ..."

Fifty-one

Bismarck was the longtime seat of Burleigh County, and it was in one of the spare rooms at the old courthouse that Jack Demarrest and Dan Carlisle set up the North Dakota headquarters of the special task force. A dozen field agents who had been roaming the state throughout the past month were on hand, most of them standing to leave their supervisors with enough room to pass out updated reports and also to give working room to a pair of phone installers putting in a private line. The room faced southwest, overlooking the Missouri River, but there was no air conditioning and no breeze to relieve the rising temperature, so the men tugged at their collars and fanned themselves with papers as Carlisle laid out the battle plan that would govern their movements for the next week or until extenuating circumstances dictated otherwise.

"Demarrest will stay here with a team covering a fifty-mile radius around Bismarck," the large-eared man explained, back in control of his emotions and once more the dull-faced authoritarian he'd been when Seamus

McTeague had first met him in Chicago. "I'll do the same based out of Jamestown, and Dugas will take Dickinson."

"Your individual assignments are spelled out on the sheets we just gave you," Jack went on. "You might want to jot down our number here..." He glanced at one of the installers, who called out the number.

"Whenever you're working solo," Carlisle said, "you'll be expected to call in to your partners or here, on the hour. Repeat, on the hour. And we expect you to use your best judgment in terms of cover stories, but just remember that it's been our experience that the more complicated you make your cover, the tougher it's going to be to maintain it. Keep it simple. Any questions?"

One of the agents near the window raised a hand, tapped a finger at his handout. "What are we supposed to do if we run into this Jane Britland?"

All eyes turned to Jack. He shifted in his seat, not so much out of nervousness as to relieve some of the pressure on his spine. The airline flight had wreaked havoc on his lower back, and despite a steady diet of aspirin and the application of an ice pack to the area, he was still in great pain. There was no way he was going to own up to it, though. After coming this far, he would see things through even if it meant spending the entire time feeling as if some far-off voodoo doctor was stabbing his doll likeness with hot pins. "Just let her do her job," he told the group, "but call in here with her whereabouts."

"Anything else?" Carlisle asked. When no one raised his hand, he said, "Good. Then let's get out there and teach these sorry shits a thing or two..."

The field agents filed out of the room, breaking off into their assigned teams on the way to the parking lot. Carlisle and Jack remained behind, waiting for the installers to finish their job.

"Supposing she does turn up in this neck of the woods?"

Carlisle speculated. "What kind of trouble do you figure she could get herself into?"

"Don't play naïve," Jack said. "You've dealt with reporters before. I don't care what they say at the *Sentinel*. I'd bet anything she's going to show up here trying to scoop us."

"If she does, it'll be a fucking embarrassment for us, I'll tell you that much." The FBI man got up from his chair, headed for the door. "I'm going down the hall for a Coke. Want anything?"

"Something cold," Jack said.

Less than a minute after Carlisle had left the room, the installers made their final connections and one of the men set a phone on Jack's desk while the other started gathering up tools.

"You're in business."

Jack picked up the phone and put a call through to Washington. By the time he was put in touch with Seamus McTeague he had the room to himself.

"Hey, Jack. Got the gears in motion out there?"

"Pretty much." Jack filled McTeague in on the meeting that had just ended, then asked, "What about you? Any word on Hoummari?"

"Yes and no. Ben White heard from some of his people in Lebanon, and word is she's definitely here in the States, but we haven't had any luck finding her yet. Still trying."

"And Jane?"

"Sorry, Jack," McTeague told him. "She didn't bother to get in touch with her parents, and all she told the gal upstairs from her apartment was that she was going out of town indefinitely and wanted her to take care of the mail and house plants for her."

"She's here, I know it," Jack said. They traded a few more words. Then Jack hung up. Carlisle came back in with two cans of Coke. Jack took one of them and said he was going for a walk. Leaving the courthouse, he went out to the river's edge and stood with the cold can pressed against his lower back. The Missouri was running high this time of year, wide and brown, churning up small waves. He remembered a few months back when he and Jane walked along the Des Plaines River outside Chicago, throwing snowballs at half-submerged trees and eventually getting caught up in a lively battle with some students from the nearby college. They'd ended up straying too close to the embankment and slipping into the icy waters. It had taken a good hour of lovemaking in front of a raging fire back at his brother's place before the chill had been chased from their bones. There was no snow here in Bismarck, however, and he found himself alone, missing Jane, worried that she was somewhere in the vicinity, trying to become involved in a battle where the enemy fought with weapons more deadly than snowballs, where the losers would need more than the warmth of a fireplace to recover from their fate.

Fifty-two

Under her assumed name, Jane had reservations at the Bismarck Holiday Inn, where two members of the special task force also had rooms. Had the briefing at the county courthouse ended ten minutes earlier, those two agents would have run into Jane in the hotel lobby. As it turned out, however, by the time they had returned, Jane was already a block away, looking over the lunch menu at the El Coyote Cantina. Jane had skipped the meal offered on her plane ride to North Dakota and had taken a nap and shower after checking into the hotel, so she was now famished, deciding on an order of huevos rancheros with sides of toast and bacon to go with the pot of coffee she drank in hopes of neutralizing jet lag so she could get to work immediately.

But where to begin?

Prior to her departure from Washington, she and Pierce had discussed several approaches, all of them requiring her to steer clear of other reporters and any members of the task force for fear that her disguise would prove woefully inadequate to those aware that she might be in the area. The safest course seemed to be for her to deal directly with the people of North Dakota, asking questions as a reporter and hoping that she might unearth some key witness who had been thus far overlooked by the authorities. As she sat before her empty plate, mulling over one last cup of coffee, this plan now seemed ridiculously farfetched, a needle-in-the-haystack strategy that was more apt to consume her time in the pursuit of dead ends than to produce results. So close was she on the heels of the euphoric anticipation that had brought her here that the intrusion of grim realities was oppressive and dispiriting. Where had she come off thinking she could just fly out here, with only the most negligible of journalistic experience to her credit, and singlehandedly outwit several hundred — if not several thousand — experienced reporters and intelligence agents? She wasn't sure who was the bigger fool — she or J. V. Pierce, for having proposed this quixotic quest in the first place. With a loathsome dread she was already beginning to visualize the sort of story she'd end up filing, some pathetic first-person account of her failed mission, padded with enough inside information to play off her memoir excerpts and justify publication. What a joke. What a cruel, miserable joke.

Then she saw the newspaper.

It was a morning edition of the *Bismarck Gazette*, left behind on the table next to her. There were four front-page stories and two large photos, all of them dealing with the brutal murders that had taken place during the warehouse robbery in Minot. Her pulse began to gallop as she read over the articles, which treated the whole incident as a purely local story, some grim and grisly tale destined to become part of the area's folklore for years to come. Jane, however, saw the robbery as a critical piece of a much bigger picture, the needle in her haystack.

"Top you off, honey?"

It was Marge, the buxom waitress with the beehive, hovering next to Jane with a pot full of fresh coffee.

"No, thanks," Jane told her, barely glancing up from the paper. "Just my check, please."

Taking out a small notebook from her purse, she hastily jotted down a series of notes while referring to the front-page stories, then left a tip and asked the cashier for directions to the police station while she charged lunch to the *Sentinel.* The station was within walking distance of the restaurant, so she didn't bother backtracking to the Holiday Inn, where she'd left her rental Accord.

His office door was open, and while Jane was talking to a sergeant at the front desk, Sheriff Moore watched her thoughtfully. Damn, she looked familiar.

The desk sergeant, a beefy man in his early sixties, trudged back to Moore's office, stuck his head in the doorway. "'Nother skirt reporter. Some rag in Washington. You want I should give her the boot?" He waved Jane's bogus press card in the air as an afterthought.

"Washington," Moore mumbled. Of course. He shook his head. "Nah, why don't you give me that card and send her in?"

"If you say so."

"I do."

The sergeant handed Moore the press card and retreated to his post. Moore stayed in his chair as he read the card over and smirked to himself. *Holly Armstead, my ass.* When Jane walked in, he sat upright and held the card out to her, gestured to a chair with his other hand.

"Have a seat, Ms. Armstead," he told her cordially. "What brings you here all the way from Washington?"

"We got the story about those warehouse murders over the UPI wires last night and it raised my boss's eyebrows," Jane ad-libbed. "There's a few questions we'd like to ask."

Moore frowned, pretended to be puzzled. "You realize

that happened up in Minot. That's Ward County, not Burleigh. Out of my jurisdiction, I'm afraid."

"The robbery was in Minot," Jane corrected, referring to her notes, "but the second two murders happened on a country road just this side of the Burleigh County line. You were mentioned on the wires as heading up that part of the investigation."

Moore smiled indulgently, eased back in his seat. "So I am," he confessed. "Well, if you read the wire reports, you're pretty much up to date, Ms. Armstead. There's nothing new on the case, but of course we're still investigating. A semi as big as that with its front end crunched in is bound to turn up soon."

Through Pierce and Tracy Comstock, Jane had gotten hold of photos of Jake Morrison, Hal Dewez, and Koura Hoummari. She took the shots from her purse and passed them across the desk to Sheriff Moore. "Do you recognize any of these three people?"

Moore looked over the pictures, stroked his chin, blank-faced. "Nope." He gave the photos back. "Should I?"

"We figure there might be a link between this warehouse robbery and the terrorist activity we've been having recently in the States."

Moore chuckled skeptically. "Can't say as I follow you on that one, ma'am. How do you figure?"

Jane was unswayed by the sheriff's convincing display of cynicism. "It's common knowledge that certain fringe elements in the survivalist movement advocate an overthrow of our present form of government," she theorized. "This robbery could be easily linked with such a group, don't you think?"

Sheriff Moore reached for his cigarettes, still playing devil's advocate. "I thought everybody was saying it was Ay-rabs pulling all that terrorist stuff."

"They could be in collusion with the survivalists," Jane speculated. "Especially if these two men in the photographs are involved as middlemen. They're former CIA agents with some background in foreign service."

"Hmm." Moore lit a cigarette, raised an eyebrow. "Well, hell's bells, I suppose anything's possible, right?"

"Exactly."

Moore got up from his chair, reached for the holster dangling from a coat hook behind his desk. As he strapped the holder on and patted the stock of his service revolver, he told Jane, "Tell you what. I was planning to go out and talk to the guy who owns that warehouse this afternoon. He lives just outside of town here. If you want, I can go now and take you with me, give you a chance to bounce your theory off him. Who knows? Maybe you're on to something."

"You think so?" Jane said hopefully, stuffing the photos and her notes back into her purse.

"Considering what's at stake here," the sheriff said, "it sure seems worth looking into. C'mon, we'll go in my cruiser."

Jane followed Moore out of his office and past the desk sergeant. "I can't thank you enough, Sheriff."

Moore told the older man he'd probably be gone the rest of the afternoon, then went and held the front door open for Jane. As she preceded him outside, he told her, "Just doing my job, ma'am . . ."

Fifty-three

Jake Morrison paid only passing notice to the federal investigators prowling the shoulder of the country road where two men had been shot and left for dead in a nearby ditch two nights before. He knew that Sheriff Moore had already combed the area thoroughly, turning up no clues and obscuring as much potential evidence as possible — driving over truck tracks, stepping on footprints. Besides, it wasn't curiosity that brought him out to this remote section of the county. He was merely on his way to Highway 83, Bismarck's main link with Minot and a handful of smaller towns located in between. One such town, Washburn, was his destination. Like Bismarck, Washburn sat near the Missouri River, and the church Morrison sought was just down the road from a bridge spanning the river's bend. The church was old, dating back to the turn of the century, but the cemetery next to it was even older. Among the weather-worn tombstones speckling the burial grounds was a small but significant marker indicating where a member of the Lewis and Clark expedition had been laid to rest in 1805. A row of stately elms bordered the cemetery like sentinels guarding the dead from intrusion by river spirits. The trees were tall, their upper limbs entwined, leaving the cemetery in a gloom of shadow.

Morrison parked on a patch of dirt between the church and burial ground. As he stepped out of his car, the church door opened and a frail man emerged from the vestibule, a white clerical collar contrasting with the blackness of his floor-length robe. For a man obviously well into his seventies, his hair — what there was of it around his ears — was strangely but yet naturally dark, void of so much as a single gray strand. His eyebrows were similarly dark, thick and arched above mirthless, pale eyes. He had a funereal pallor, looking as if he never left the shadows that covered the church and cemetery.

"You are Mr. Morrison, I presume," the priest said in a thin, strained voice, offering his visitor a gaunt, bony hand to shake. "I am Pastor Lewbeck."

"A pleasure, Pastor."

"I take it Sheriff Moore conveyed our interest in your property."

Morrison nodded. "I spoke to him earlier this morning."

"Then I also take it he told you we wanted full details of what you have to offer." The pastor's gaze was as direct as his words.

Morrison nodded again. "And I told *him* we wanted proof that your interest is more than casual."

"You have my word," Pastor Lewbeck said. "That is sufficient."

Morrison looked at the man, decided he was telling the truth. Opening the trunk of his car, he removed a rolled set of blueprints and a packet of photographs and architectural renderings. "I can't leave these with you, you realize."

"I have an excellent memory, Mr. Morrison." Lewbeck pointed toward the cemetery. "Come, there's a table this way. I have a helper at the church who I'd rather not know about this."

"Of course."

The table was made of stone, resting in a landscaped alcove in front of a family crypt. Morrison set down his materials and stepped back as Pastor Lewbeck began to go through them methodically, piece by piece, donning a pair of bifocals and peering intently through them. To Morrison he looked almost comic, like the foil in an old silent film. And yet he knew that Lewbeck headed up one of the most wealthy extremist organizations in the upper Midwest, and did so by virtue of a charismatic persuasiveness he was deliberately withholding from Morrison for the time being. More than twenty minutes passed with neither man speaking. Lewbeck concentrated exclusively on those articles laid out on the stone table. Morrison's attention strayed to the cemetery, its chiseled crucifixes and sculpted angels, the smell of decay. A mound of fresh dirt was piled high next to a newly dug grave twenty feet away. A pot of flowers lay on its side at the base of the mound. Off in the direction of the church Morrison could hear the muffled sound of a pipe organ. Mournful music. He turned back to Lewbeck, joined the pastor at the table.

"I can guarantee that you'll be able to modify the place to suit your needs for a fraction of what it'd cost you to build from scratch, Pastor."

"Sheriff Moore speaks highly of it, I'll grant you that. And it seems suitable from what I see here." The elderly man removed his bifocals and carefully folded them before setting them in a pocket of his black robe. "Of course, the rest of the board members would have to join me in an on-site tour."

"That can be arranged," Morrison said. "I suggest you

make it soon, because I can't guarantee there won't be other offers."

"I understand."

Morrison gathered up the materials and carried them back to his car. Lewbeck kept up alongside him, seeming to grow stronger by the minute. "Why are you selling this place, Mr. Morrison?"

"Simple economics," Morrison said as he put his things back in the trunk. "We make as much off the survivalist courses as we do off the dairy. By moving our operations south to Arizona we won't have to shut down the school during winter."

"Ah, yes, that was the reason." Both men knew that he was being facetious, but neither pressed the issue. They shook hands again. Lewbeck said, "I'll contact the others and get back to you as soon as possible."

"Fine."

Morrison got back in his car and pulled away from the church. Lewbeck turned and headed back toward the cemetery. Morrison reached the main road, clearing the shadows cast by the giant elms. The warmth of the sun never felt so inviting.

Fifty-four

Bismarck wasn't so small a town that all its citizens were privy to one another's doings, and those who were tapped into the community grapevine by and large were distrustful of strangers asking too many questions. Like most of the other field agents working the Dakotas and other states in the task force's search area, Jack learned quickly that his only hope of securing any cooperation was to be straightforward, showing his credentials and casually mentioning the six-figure reward being offered for usable information about any of the targeted figures in their investigation. Even this strategy, employed during more than two hours of walking the city streets, had yielded no more than a mild confirmation of what he and his colleagues already suspected — that Jake Morrison and Hal Dewez were somewhere in this part of the state. Unfortunately, those reward-hungry townsfolk who claimed to have seen Morrison and Dewez in Bismarck periodically over the past two years had different, unsubstantiated theories as to the reasons for their presence. Zach Holm-

stead cut Jake Morrison's hair every month and swore
that they had had numerous conversations about the coming of doomsday as predicted in the New Testament.
According to Zach, Morrison had a place south of town,
a pig farm he ran with a wife and three kids. Postmaster
Owen Peterson had waited on both men from time to
time, sending parcels to post office boxes in Maryland
and Virginia. No, he couldn't recall any return address
on the packages, and the men always paid cash, but he
seemed to remember Dewez mentioning that he lived
across the river, out near Little Heart Butte on Route
6. At Bismarck Building Supplies, owner Abby Shayne
acknowledged selling a small fortune in materials to the
men, supposedly for a housing development they were
erecting some thirty miles east of town, out near Long
Lake. Neither Jack nor any of the other field agents had
yet stumbled across anyone familiar with the survivalist
school or Darwin's Den.

The walking had further aggravated Jack's tender back,
and he was grateful for the chance to get off his feet
when he joined his temporary partner for a prearranged
late lunch at the local Howard Johnson's. Chris Osborne
was in his late twenties, one of the youngest men on the
task force. He'd been covering another part of town, with
even less success. However, the two people who had recognized Osborne's pictures of Morrison and Dewez both
agreed that they were somehow involved in the dairy business and had usually come to town for meetings at a
distributorship across town.

"Sounds like our best bet," Jack said, nodding gratefully
at a waitress who had brought him a Ziploc bag filled
with crushed ice. He placed the bag against his lower
back and sighed with relief at the numbing chill, ignoring
Osborne's concerned look. He checked the distributor's
address on a map of Bismarck unfolded across the table.

"That's out where I figured to be heading after lunch," he told Osborne. "Mind if I check it out?"

"No problem," Osborne said. "They say you can't miss the place. Has a plastic cow on the roof big as a billboard. You sure you want to do a lot more pounding the pavement with your back acting up like that?"

"I'll live," Jack promised.

When their food came, the men exchanged small talk for a few minutes, then ate silently. Jack knew that as head of the government's investigation in Bismarck he not only could get away with staying at the courthouse, but he might serve his function better there. But there was something about being cooped up in an office that bothered him. Most likely it was his fear of being relegated to a permanent desk job, an unpleasant option that had caused him more than several sleepless nights during his convalescence. He thought the problem over more while he finished eating, finally deciding he'd see through the day on foot, then try staying at the courthouse the following day to see if he could cope with the confinement of four walls without going stir-crazy.

Osborne brought up the topic of the so-called Warehouse Murders that had been monopolizing the local media spotlight, suggesting a possible link to their own investigation. Jack conceded that he'd been thinking along the same lines, and when he called in to the courthouse to check for messages, he left word to have a few calls placed to federal agents working the area around Minot to see if they'd come up with any solid connection. Before returning to his table, Jack placed another call to the county sheriff, only to be told that Moore was out on business and wasn't expected until later. Jack left his name and asked that Moore get in touch with him tomorrow at the courthouse.

Done eating, Jack and Osborne paid their bill and left

the restaurant, heading off in separate directions. Rather than trying to get in touch with each other in an hour, they agreed to put their update calls through to the main office at the courthouse.

Jack was halfway to the dairy distributorship, its landmark cow already visible in the distance, when he passed a mini-mall where his casual glance happened to catch the small sign for Dawin's Den. On a hunch he crossed the small asphalt parking lot, saw a Closed sign posted in the shop's window. It was dark inside and the door was locked when he tried it.

A grizzly faced man in a polyester suit was busy in front of his antiques shop next door, loading stock onto an old red wagon. He was either preoccupied with his work or else ignoring Jack, who finally had to cough to get the man's attention.

"Excuse me."

"Closin' up, fella," the other man said gruffly. "Can't help ya."

"It's about this shop next to you."

"Don't own that," Grizzly snapped. "Ain't my concern." He was about to wheel a load of antique gumball machines into his store when Jack stepped into the doorway, blocking his way. He took out his identification and held it out at the shop owner's eye level.

"I just want to know how long they've been closed."

Grizzly's left cheek puffed out, filled with a chaw of chewing tobacco. He turned his head and spat a brown flow onto the sidewalk, then looked back at Jack. "They closed this time yesterday and didn't open up today. That good enough for you?"

"Any reason why they didn't open?"

"Who knows? Maybe they got sick of beef jerky. Like I said, ain't my concern. Now, will you get your butt outta my way so *I* can close?"

Jack stepped aside. The owner pulled his antiques inside

and slammed the door behind him. Jack went back to Darwin's Den, leaned close to the front window for a better look inside. The place looked sparsely stocked, messy. Some loose cans on the floor.

A Jeep pulled to a stop in the parking lot behind him. Jack turned around, saw Rowdy Trent get out of the vehicle and head for the front door.

"No one here," Jack told him.

Trent caught himself before knocking on the door. He looked at Jack. "You sure?"

"I think so. Guy next door says they were closed all day today."

"That's odd," Trent said. He seemed genuinely perplexed. "Guess they musta got caught up with gettin' things ready at the ranch."

"Ranch?" Jack said, trying to sound calmly curious. He felt he was on to something, had to play it out cautiously.

Trent eyed him with equal suspicion. "You signed up for the survivalist class, too?"

Jack paused a moment, then nodded. "Yeah."

"Well, they told me if the place was closed to just head out to the ranch."

Jack played out his bluff. "My secretary made my arrangements," he told Trent. "She didn't say anything about the ranch. Just to come here. I took the bus."

Rowdy started back toward his Jeep, told Jack, "You want a ride, hop in."

Jack hesitated, wondering if he should stall long enough to call the courthouse. Trent got in the Jeep, started the engine. Jack joined him up front, deciding not to push his luck by having Trent take him to a phone.

"Thanks," he told the driver. "I appreciate it."

Rowdy Trent smiled. "Guys like us gotta stick together, right?"

Fifty-five

It was dusk in the forest. Owls hooted in the elms, ready for a night of foraging. A chill carried through the trees, rustled last fall's leaves on the ground. The young recruits shivered in the same breeze as they crouched near the edge of a small pond, drenched and miserable, faces muddied and scratched. Hal Dewez was with them, dry, unperturbed, a stopwatch in his hand as he gazed out into the middle of the pond. A small water strider danced along the pond's surface, leaving delicate ripples in its wake. Then, without warning, the small blackish pool churned with a violent frenzy and one of the young men burst upward from the depths, arms flailing as his tortured lungs expelled air in a loud cry of pain. Half blinded, he staggered toward the embankment, struggling for his footing. He managed a few steps, coughing and sputtering for breath, then pitched sideways and sank. Two of his fellow recruits slipped down the steep pitch of the embankment and waded out, helping him back to the surface and dragging him ashore.

"Nice try, sweetheart," Dewez said, checking his stop-watch. "But you're way shy of the mark."

Bent over in agony as he lay in the mud, the recruit began to weep. "F-f-uck it!" he managed to stammer between sobs.

Dewez rose from his crouch and walked over, looming above the younger man, laughing down at him. "Hey, don't give up. Shit! You get to rest at least another five minutes before you have to try it again."

Tears began streaming down the trainee's face. He shook his head fitfully, eyes closed, trying to shut out the world around him. "No!" he wailed. "Nooooooo!"

"That's no attitude," Dewez scolded, clucking his tongue with disapproval.

The man on the ground opened his eyes, stared at Dewez with hatred. He was crying uncontrollably now. "Fuck you, asshole!"

"Oh, trying to butter me up with flattery, is that it?"

When the recruit lashed out feebly with one foot, trying to kick his tormentor, Dewez grabbed him by the boot, twisted the man's foot until he was screaming. Dewez shifted his grip, jerking the recruit by the collar of his shirt, pulling him to his feet as if he were no more than a rag doll.

"Hey, man, give the guy a break!" another one of the trainees complained.

Dewez shoved the weeping man back into the pond, then swung around, whipping out a long-blade hunting knife from his ankle sheath and holding the gleaming edge close to the throat of the man who'd stood up for his comrade.

"You maybe want to join him, shit-for-brains?" Dewez asked.

The dissenter glanced down at the knife, eased himself away from it, falling in with the other men. A few yards away, the recruit in the water could be heard thrashing his way back to shore. Dewez took a step back, putting away the knife. He looked at the recruits, disgusted. "You fucking Girl Scouts came here figuring you were gonna leave like soldiers, but all I've heard outta you is nonstop whining. A couple of you already packed it in and went home crying because you couldn't cut it.

"Tell you what. Anyone else wants out, fine. Mommy's waiting at home to change your diapers and tuck you in with a bedtime story. Just do it now so I don't have to put up with you anymore, okay?"

Dewez looked the men over. Most of them avoided his gaze, although a few stared back, trying to make a good impression. The trainee in the pond collapsed halfway up the embankment, leaving his legs in the water as he held on to a small boulder for support and tried to muffle his sobs.

Dewez heard a car horn and glanced over his shoulder. Up on a nearby ridge overlooking the pond, Sheriff Moore stood next to his patrol car, which was barely visible in the tall grass and brush. Moore waved for Dewez to join him.

"Take five," he told the recruits. "When I get back, you've got another hour to go before you crash."

The sun was down now, and there was little twilight to guide Dewez's way up the winding slope to where Moore was waiting. He turned his ankle stepping in a gopher hole and gritted his teeth, suppressing a grimace of pain. Linking up with a footpath, he cleared the rest of the way more easily, though his ankle still throbbed.

"What's the problem?" he demanded.

"No problem." Moore leisurely finished his cigarette and cast it aside. "I got a little something for you, that's all."

"What?"

"See for yourself."

Moore turned slightly, directing Dewez's attention to

the inside of his patrol car. There, bound and gagged in the back seat, was a woman. It was too dark for Dewez to make out who it was until he opened the front door and took a good look at her under the dim glow of the dome light. Almost immediately his mood brightened. "Well, well, now," he chortled. "What do we have here...?"

Fifty-six

There were countless figures on Capitol Hill who felt that it was in the country's best interests for President Houril to cancel his scheduled weekend summit with representatives from Saudi Arabia. There had been days of fierce lobbying, backed by scattered demonstrations, both in Washington and in other major cities, but Houril was equally passionate in his commitment to carry on the duties of his office without kowtowing to the threat of terrorism. Subsequently, the already stringent precautions that had been taken were supplemented by even more drastic precautions. Sand-filled dump trucks were parked across access routes to both the White House and Capitol Building, left as a second line of defense since there were already antitruck barriers in place below the ground, ready to spring up by hydraulic pressure when triggered by the approach of unauthorized vehicles. Elsewhere throughout the city, smaller vehicles were used in conjunction with pylons and sawhorses to block strategic side streets. Police rerouted traffic away from the perimeter of Capitol Hill and the adjacent mall area. This late at night the disruption was nowhere near as severe as it would be the following day, when those tourists undaunted by the threat of violence would descend upon the city streets and sidewalks. There had been a marked decrease in tourist traffic already, what with a veritable army of sharpshooters stationed on rooftops and other locations, lending support to ground troops who were hard-pressed to stay clear of the public eye. It was estimated that millions of dollars were lost every hour that Washington was subjected to such drastic security measures.

No one felt the tension gripping the city more than Seamus McTeague, who was one of a handful of key people in charge of choreographing the intricacies of protecting an entire populace as well as the President. Nerves on edge, body aching for the comforts of a soft bed and the recuperative powers of sleep, he forged on with his fellow members of the task force, constantly monitoring the situation and making whatever adjustments seemed necessary. They'd moved to a larger office, equipped with a bank of phones and other communication equipment, scattered desks, walls lined with maps of Washington, outlying areas, and the rest of the United States. They were patched into a direct line with the Pentagon, White House, Saudi Embassy, and United Nations. If worse came to worst, things would be happening so fast that it would be imperative that concerned parties be kept apprised of the latest developments. McTeague hoped to hell it didn't come to that, because that "worst possible" scenario took into account the release of the contents of all three nerve gas canisters, and against the likes of that even the most sophisticated and mighty force of arms was useless.

"Okay, McTeague, you're spelled for two hours," Quinton Daniels told Seamus as he entered the noise-filled room.

"What's that?" McTeague raised his voice to be heard.

"Go on, get some shuteye," the CIA officer told him. "They've set up cots in the office next door. We're going to start working in shifts until this is all over. Four hours on, four off. Only way we'll make it."

McTeague's first instinct was to resist the order and stay on the job, but he knew Daniels had a point. With a reluctant sigh he pushed himself away from the desk he'd been sitting at for the past four hours. Daniels slid into the seat and grabbed the phone when it rang. McTeague was almost out the door when Daniels cupped his hand over the mouthpiece and swung around in the chair, calling the Secret Service agent back.

"It's Bismarck," Daniels reported. "Demarrest is missing."

Jack concocted a fictional biography to go with the fictional name he'd used when he introduced himself to Trent. He kept as close to real facts as possible, but as far as Rowdy was concerned, he was Jack Wentworth, an insurance salesman from Fargo coming back from a boating accident and wanting to see what kind of shape he was in. Thinking ahead, Jack already foresaw problems in trying to explain the fresh scars from his bullet wounds and surgery. But he'd thrown himself behind this, the most promising lead to have turned up during the whole investigation, and he had no choice but to see where it took him. It was already getting dark, and he figured more than two hours had passed since they'd left Bismarck. He wasn't sure where they were now, but he know that he was long overdue to report back to the courthouse. If he ran into trouble, he could only hope that Osborne would retrace Jack's intended itinerary after they had left the Howard Johnson's. Once it was determined that he'd never shown up at the dairy distributorship, the trail would then lead down the street he'd been walking along when he'd stumbled upon Darwin's Den. That might be all they'd need to deduce his whereabouts. A run-in with the proprietor of the antiques shop might help matters, but he couldn't count on it.

"This is taking longer than I thought," Jack commented, keeping an eye on the scenery for landmarks he could commit to memory. Now they were passing a dairy farm, with a forest off in the distance.

"Well, the waiting's over," Trent announced, turning off the road and idling the Jeep while the gate to the ranch was opened. He waved a greeting to the ranch hands as he drove onto the property and circled around the old barn.

"Nice spread here," Jack said. "Hardly looks like a survivalist compound."

"That's the idea." Trent slowed down a second time before the wooden gates built into the raised knoll. When they parted, revealing their steel counterparts, the driver went on: "They don't take a liking to other people nosing around in their business, if you know what I mean."

Inside the large underground chamber there was a bustling of activity. One crew of workers was taking goods out of a large semi and stacking them along one of the walls. A second group guided a large four-wheel cart in from one of the underground tunnels reaching out from the main room. On the cart were file cabinets, several computers, and a small cache of weapons. Jack felt eyes on him as the Jeep pulled to a stop near the semi.

"Here we are," Rowdy said, killing the ignition. "End of the line."

Jack looked over at Trent, saw a gun aimed at his midsection. "What's going on?" he asked.

"Jig's up, G-man," Trent told him. "Get out. Slowly."

Jack balked, sizing up the situation. Behind him, the steel gates were still open. The Jeep's keys were still in the ignition. Jack didn't like the odds, but he also didn't like the idea of staying here, waiting for sure death.

"Okay, okay," he said casually, starting to get out of the Jeep. Then he suddenly veered around, lunging into Rowdy and knocking the man to the floor. Slipping into the driver's seat, Jack started up the Jeep and shifted into reverse. Four ranch hands were on him before he could escape, however. He fought as best he could, lashing out with his fists, pressing one foot on the accelerator so that the Jeep lurched backward. The vehicle jerked a few yards. Then Jack's foot was dragged off the clutch and the engine jolted to a stop. One of the men crawling over him had a wrench, and he used it against Jack's skull. The fight went out of him, and Jack slumped across the seat, lost in a void of blackness.

Fifty-seven

Jack awoke tied to a chair in a darkened room. His hands were also bound behind his back, his ankles secured to the chair's legs. His back sent sharp pains running the length of his spine, far surpassing the intensity of his other assorted bruises and wounds combined. He had no idea how long he'd been unconscious, but there was a sliver of illumination creeping beneath the bottom of the door he was facing, and after several minutes of staring he decided it had to be daylight.

Thinking back to the night before, he recalled the underground chamber, the ranch hands working around the semi. He suspected that an evacuation was in progress, no doubt triggered by a combination of what had happened with Cal Winslow and word that the dragnet was closing in on this part of the state. True, he hadn't seen Hal Dewez or Jake Morrison yet, but he felt certain it would be only a matter of time before that happened.

He was right.

Half an hour later there were footsteps outside the door, then the scraping of a key. The door swung inward, blinding Jack momentarily as the room filled with sunlight. Rowdy Trent stood in the doorway, a silhouette, gun in hand.

"Sleep well?"

"I've had better nights." As his eyes adjusted to the change in light, Jack recognized Trent, who was untying his feet and torso from the chair.

"Got somebody wants to talk to you." Trent pulled Jack to his feet, stuck the gun against his ribs. "Let's go."

Jack's hands were still tied behind his back. Each step sent a fresh pulse of pain rushing through him. They walked down a carpeted hallway lined with paneled walls and windows providing a view of the woods he'd seen upon his arrival the night before. He guessed he was in the main house.

Jake Morrison was reading the morning paper when Jack was brought into the living room and shoved into another chair. "Morning, Mr. Demarrest," Morrison said as he set the paper aside. "Nice of you to come visit."

"Such cheap rates, how could I resist?"

Morrison laughed lightly, noticed Jack looking into the adjacent kitchen, where Brady stood before a stove watching bacon sizzle in a skillet. "We'll have some breakfast shortly, but first let's chat."

"Chat?"

Morrison picked up a cup of coffee, cradled it in his hands. "We have a lot in common, you and I. I thought we could compare notes, fill in some of the missing gaps on both sides."

"Dream on," Jack told him, shifting slightly in his chair, trying to reduce the pain. Trent pointed a gun at his face.

"Keep still." Jack stopped shifting.

Morrison said. "I'll go first, okay?"

"Suit yourself."

"Cal Winslow was a valuable conduit for us," Morrison explained, refilling his cup and adding cream as he talked. "We have other contacts on the inside, but it takes time to work them up the ranks."

"Who's Eckland?" Jack asked.

"A movie star, isn't she? British, I think."

"Comedy's not your strong suit," Jack told Morrison. "Winslow had a replacement lined up. Code name Eckland."

Morrison smiled. "Must be frustrating, being that close and then running into a wall, hmm?"

"Oh, I don't know. Seems to me if this Eckland was as well placed as you want me to think, we wouldn't be having this conversation. I'd be the same place Tony Bex ended up."

"Ah, so you knew Mr. Bex?"

"He's dead, isn't he?"

Morrison nodded, feigning sadness. "Such a stiff price to pay for uncooperation."

"You can bury me next to him if you want," Jack said. "I'm not talking."

"You're sure about that?"

Jack fell silent and bowed his head, stared at his knee-caps. Trent wanted to intervene, grab Jack by the neck and give him a little encouragement, but Morrison called him off. He got up from his chair and took Trent's gun, sent the ranch hand out of the room.

"Now, then," Morrison went on, moving before Jack. "If you're so eager to meet your Maker, we'll be glad to oblige you. Matter of fact, we can even see to it that you go with a guest."

Rowdy returned to the living room, dragging Jane along

with him. She was still blindfolded and, like Jack, had her hands tied behind her back. Jack glanced up, trembled inwardly at the sight of her.

"Jane!"

"Jack?" Jane's voice was fearful, whispery. She tried to take a step forward, but Rowdy reached out and held her back. Morrison likewise had to jab at Jack with the revolver to keep him in his chair.

"She's been blindfolded since we brought her here," Morrison told Jack. "That leaves us with the option of letting her go once we're ready to move from here. It's all up to you, of course."

"Don't give in to them, Jack!" Jane cried out.

Jack sat still in the chair. His decision wasn't quite so clear-cut anymore.

Fifty-eight

Destiny.

This was the day Koura Hoummari had been waiting for, her day of glory. Let the American pigs try to defend themselves. She had fought in the raging streets of Beirut, in the countryside outside Damascus, in countless hell-holes throughout the Middle East. It would take more than the presence of a militia to deter her from her destiny. Today she would serve up far more than steamed egg rolls from her vending van. She would serve up death to the infidels, strike a blow against the heathen empire they might never recover from.

They approached the capital circuitously from George-town, taking Massachusetts Avenue instead of Pennsyl-vania, avoiding the roadblocks and detours, yet still arriv-ing at their favored location, a quiet side street just north of the Children's Emergency Home. There was an avail-able curb space and Hoummari parked in it, then left the van, wearing her tinted glasses and a large straw hat.

She crossed the street, camera dangling from her neck by a shoulder strap. At the corner she raised the camera, peering through the viewfinder. She took pictures, but only for the benefit of any passers-by who might be observing her. Her real purpose was to double-check the heights of the taller buildings surrounding the van, making sure the rocket launcher would be able to clear them when the missiles were fired. She was pleased at what she saw. The men had been generous in their estimates of the heights; the buildings were all somewhat shorter than she expected, all the better for giving them leeway in regard to the trajectory of the missiles. A good sign indeed. Allah was smiling on their efforts.

But wait.

She was about to cross the street when she saw a police car cruise past her and slow to a stop halfway down the block. Two officers got out of the vehicle and went to the nearest van, asking someone inside to show an operator's licence and some personal identification. Hoummari retreated from the curb and sat down on a bus bench, pretending to look for a loose stone inside her shoe. She cast a sidelong glance at the policemen as they proceeded to her van, confronting the two men in the front seat. Hoummari knew that all the necessary forged papers were clipped to the visor on the driver's side of the van, but she was nonetheless concerned. Even as the Lebanese man in the driver's seat handed the police those selfsame papers, Hoummari put one hand in her purse, seeking out the automatic pistol secreted there. She would gun down the officers if need be, hoping that there would still be enough time to execute their attack before government reinforcements could intervene.

Apparently satisfied with what they saw, the two cops gave the papers back to the men in the van and crossed the street to query yet another vendor. Hoummari rose from the bench and joined a group of pedestrians heading toward her van, taking care to turn her head away from the officers as she passed by them.

"Hey! You openin' today or what?" An irate tourist was badgering the man in the front passenger's seat of the van. "I wanna egg roll already."

Hoummari stepped between the customer and the van, offering a patronizing smile. "I'm sorry, sir, but everything we serve is cooked fresh, and we haven't even started our burners yet. It'll still be a few minutes, I'm afraid."

"I can't wait," the tourist complained. "I'll just have to take my business elsewhere."

"As you wish."

Hoummari watched the angry man storm off toward the next van. Then she quickly diverted her gaze as the police car rolled past her. She pretended to glance over the menu posted on the side of the van until the police had rounded the corner and vanished from view. Then she circled around to the back of the van, using a key to let herself in. Her four comrades eyed her expectantly. *It's time,* her look told them.

"You're trying our patience, Mr. Demarrest."

Jack stared past Morrison's gun, saw Jane still in the hands of Rowdy Trent. Past them, in the kitchen, Brady turned the bacon one last time and turned down the flame, then took a stack of plates from a cupboard and let himself out onto the patio, where he began to set the table, his back turned to the house. Jack drew in a long, slow breath, subtly tensing himself in the chair.

"All right," he said wearily, looking up at Morrison. "I'll talk."

"Don't, Jack!" Jane shouted from across the room.

"Stay out of this," Jack told her. He swallowed hard, leaning slightly forward, shifting his weight toward the balls of his feet. "The task force is made up of Secretary of State Kopp, Quinton Daniels from the CIA —"

"Don't bother with the roster," Morrison told him. "We already know who's involved. We want details about the actual operations of —"

The clanging of a phone two feet away interrupted Morrison. He reached for it without taking either his eyes or his gun's aim off Jack. "Hello?" His face brightened visibly at the sound of his caller's voice. "Ah, Pastor Lewbeck . . ."

Jack waited for a lapse in Morrison's vigilance, the first sign that the man's attention was significantly diverted by his conversation on the phone. It didn't take long. After hearing what Lewbeck had to say to him, Morrison grinned happily, shifting the focus of his gaze to a faraway look, concentrating on the offer the pastor was making.

"Jane, your left!" Jack shouted as he plunged forward, leaving the chair and ducking his head to one side so that he collided with Morrison shoulder first, taking the older man down. His hands restricted, Jack relied on his legs and head as he wrestled with Morrison, who'd dropped both his gun and the phone when he was tackled.

On Jack's cue, Jane leaned sharply to her left. From the way Trent was holding her, she had a good sense of his position, and when she brought up her knee with a sharp jab, she came close enough to her captor's groin to double him over. Still blindfolded, she shoved Trent, knocking him off balance and falling with him to the floor.

Across the room, Jack risked rolling away from Morrison to give himself space enough to lash out with a quick series of karate kicks. He clipped Morrison's skull with the first swipe and connected more solidly with the second. The man in the suit dropped limply to the carpet. Pastor Lewbeck's tiny voice spilled out of the nearby phone, falling on Morrison's deaf ears.

Jack crawled across the floor to Morrison's gun, controlling himself to get a grip on it with his hands still tied behind his back. Lying sideways on the carpet, he took an awkward aim at Trent, who had pushed clear of Jane and was on his feet, reaching for his own gun as he kicked the woman in the ribs. Jack fired two shots in quick succession. Trent reeled away from Jane, bleeding from wounds in his thigh and chest. He leaned against the wall for support, slowly raising his gun, pointing it at Jane's blindfolded face. Another shot rang out, again from Jack's pistol. When the bullet flattened itself into the wall behind Trent, it was already misshapen, having passed through the man's skull. Rowdy dropped loudly through the kitchen doorway, landing on Spanish tiles.

With great difficulty, Jack was able to pull his arms out under his bent legs so that he had his hands in front of him by the time Brady rushed back inside, alerted by the shots. Brady managed to fire an errant shot at Jack before three bullets punctured his chest, ripping through flesh and bone as they sought out his heart, shut it down. He landed a few yards away from Rowdy Trent.

Rushing to Jane's side, Jack pulled off her blindfold and unbound her wrists. She embraced him quickly, met his lips with passion. They parted, looked at each other.

"Get my hands loose and let's get out of here," he told her.

She fumbled with the knots securing Jack's wrists. Despite her fear, she was able to smile. "It's good to see you, too."

Jack grinned back at her. "I've got a few things to say to you, Jane Britland, but it's going to have to wait." Once his hands were free, he handed Jane the gun he'd been using and grabbed Trent's fallen weapon on their way to the sliding glass door leading out to the patio.

Another of the ranch hands had just dismounted from a horse near the barbecue. Spotting Jack and Jane, he unslung a rifle from his saddle.

"Put it down!" Jack warned the man, gunning him

down when the order was ignored. As they ran toward the tethered horse, Jack asked Jane, "You think it'll hold both of us?"

"Let's find out," Jane suggested, unhitching the beast as Jack climbed up into the saddle. He reached out to Jane, pulled her up. She sat behind him, sharing the saddle, arms around him as he tugged the reins, urged the horse away from the house and across the wide clearing that led to the woods.

Hal Dewez leaned across the hood of his Jeep, smoking lazily, tossing stones into the nearby pond. Twenty yards away, the recruits lay on the hard ground around a smoldering campfire, sleeping off their exhaustion, most of them still wet from the previous day's exercises.

When the dispatch radio mounted under the Jeep's dashboard crackled to life with a familiar voice, Dewez flicked his cigarette into the pond and leaned over the windshield to get at the radio mike.

"Yeah?"

"That Secret Service agent and the woman are heading your way on horseback," Morrison told him.

"What?" Dewez was incredulous. "This is a joke, right?"

"Hardly."

"What the fuck happened?"

"I don't have time to explain!" Morrison's voice was thick with rage. "Just make sure they don't get away. Kill them if you have to."

"Christ!" Dewez muttered. He signed off and slammed the microphone back into place. Several of the recruits stirred in place as he kicked the hood angrily and jumped to the ground, circling to the back of the Jeep and unlocking a large footlocker. Inside were a dozen Kalashnikov rifles, polished and gleaming. Dewez took one of them out and clipped a black, banana-shaped ammo cartridge into its stock as he cried out to dozing recruits, "All right, girls. Get your asses up and over here!"

The men awoke reluctantly, moving slowly, their bodies stiff, sore.

"Got a little war game we're gonna play this morning." Dewez tossed one of the rifles at the man closest to him. The recruit caught it clumsily. As he started passing out similar weapons to the others, Dewez continued: "Here's the scenario. A pair of Commie spies — man and woman on a horse — is making for the border with government secrets. It's World War Three unless we stop 'em. That simple enough for you?"

One of the trainees glanced down at the rifle he was carrying. "Is this loaded?"

"Blanks, sweetheart," Dewez told him. "It's a game, remember? Now, let's head out and get to it. Winners get the afternoon off. Whaddaya think of that?"

Inspired, the recruits let out war whoops and followed Dewez away from the campsite, a trigger-happy posse. They started down a well-trod path winding through the forest. Then Dewez waved for the men to fan out into the foliage. He put a finger to his lips, ordering them to fall silent, the better to stalk their quarry.

Jack and Jane rode headlong into the woods, more than a hundred yards ahead of two horsemen who had taken up the chase after a general alarm had been sounded at the ranch. There was little time or opportunity for them to talk, and aside from a few brief words shouted above the clopping of hooves, each telling the other how they'd wound up being captured, they kept their minds on more immediate concerns. Jack had spent a few summers on horseback in his college years, retaining enough familiarity with the reins to get the horse to do their bidding, breaking from the main path and cutting a zigzag swath across the forest floor until they reached a clearing the size of a football field, filled with tall grass and the yellow glow of goldenrod swaying in the sun.

"I think that way's north," he said, pointing across the clearing after a quick glance up at the morning sky. "There should be a road somewhere past the trees."

Behind them, both Jack and Jane could hear thrashing in the woods. Jack dug his heels into the horse's flanks, coaxing it across the clearing. Jane could feel the sting of the high grass and goldenrod against her bare ankles. Up ahead, she saw the stump of a fallen tree rising up from the ground, half hidden by the overgrowth. Before she could shout a warning, Jack saw the obstacle as well and jerked sharply on the reins. The horse veered hard to one side, losing its footing as its front hooves failed to clear the stump's raised and gnarled roots. Throwing its riders, the beast went down hard, landing on its side, stunned momentarily. Jane was also shaken up, but not so much so that she couldn't rise to her feet and rush through the grass, trying to reach the horse before it pulled itself up.

"Stay there, lady," she cooed, holding one arm out before her, fingers closing in on the reins. The horse was spooked, however, and neighed loudly as it hurtled off across the clearing. Jane chased after it a few steps, then gave up and headed back to Jack. He was lying face-down in the grass, not moving.

"Jack!"

She knelt beside him, turned him over. He was breathing, and soon his eyes blinked open. It took him a moment to get over his disorientation. Then he tried to sit up. He couldn't.

"Jack, what's the matter?"

"My legs," he muttered, looking down at his uncooperative limbs. They were as still as the two long branches lying in the grass beside him. He was paralyzed below the waist again.

There was no time for brooding. Off in the woods they could hear activity, drawing closer. "I'll try to find where our guns fell," Jane whispered, willing herself not to panic. Crouched over, she began to search the ground, pushing aside the thick grass, the tall stalks of goldenrod. No sign of either weapon. She suddenly dropped low in the grass, glanced back at Jack, signaling for him to be quiet. Forty yards away, two men in combat fatigues had wandered into the clearing, each of them carrying an automatic rifle. Jane froze, watched them scan the meadow without breaking stride. Interminable seconds dragged by. Then the men were back in the forest. Jane crept back to Jack's side, taking his hand.

"We'll get through this," she said, trying to inject a sense of conviction into her words.

Only Koura Hoummari and her short-haired compatriot remained in the van. The others were outside, stationed at three separate locations on the same block, ready to create a diversion if necessary to allow for the master plan to be at long last carried out.

The second woman had already assembled the rocket launcher and she was now securing it with makeshift braces to the van's serving counter. Pointing through the gap where customers paid for their orders, the launcher would be ready for firing the moment that Hoummari went outside and pulled open the swing panels that presently allowed them to work unseen by anyone outside the van.

Hoummari carefully unfastened the false top to the soft-drink canister containing the first missile. She reached into the cylinder, slowly withdrew the sleek projectile. It had been a nearly impossible task transferring the nerve gas from its original container to the rocket, but now the weapon was ready, put together in such a way that the gas wouldn't be released until after impact.

Both women cautiously fit the missile into the loading chamber of the mounted launcher. It fit snugly, clicked into place. They smiled at each other. Moments from now, they would fire the first missile at the White House. If they succeeded in getting off the shot without being detected, they would swing the van around and launch a second rocket at Capitol Hill.

Suddenly there was an explosion outside the vehicle, rocking it slightly from side to side. Before either woman could react, the rear doors swung open and two gas-masked figures rushed inside, aiming M-16s at the women.

"No!" Hoummari screamed defiantly.

The short-haired woman grabbed for the trigger of the rocket launcher, but the concussive force of high-powered gunfire propelled her backward, away from the weapon. She crumpled distortedly against the soft-drink dispenser, wide-eyed but unseeing.

One of the soldiers reached Hoummari before she could get to the launcher. She fought back fiercely, knocking the man off balance so that they both fell sharply against the counter. Jarred loose, the launcher teetered to one side, began to fall. The second soldier raced past his cohort and Hoummari, righting the weapon and holding it in place as the Lebanese woman was roughly escorted from the van, struggling all the way.

Outside, Hoummari saw that the area around the van had been cordoned off. Her other accomplices were in custody across the street, handcuffed by the same police officer who had earlier confronted the men for identification. In all, there were more than two dozen armed men swarming the block, most of them wearing gas masks.

Seamus McTeague walked away from a group of soldiers and approached Hoummari. "Sorry to spoil the party, Koura," he told her calmly. "You should have waited a while longer before going to the van. We might not have recognized you."

Hoummari strained to get free of the man holding her, without success. "Bastards! Jackals!"

"Save your breath, Koura," McTeague told her. "You'll need to to answer a few questions..."

Hal Dewez brushed aside a wasit-high fern, swatted at a mosquito buzzing near his face, cursed under his breath. He was hiking along the edge of a narrow creek meandering through the woods. Mud tugged at his boots with every step, making loud sucking sounds. He finally rose to higher ground, all the while keeping his eyes trained on the wooded area around him. Sunlight poured down through the treetops, creating innumerable deceiving shadows. Bugs flitted in the bright shafts of light.

When he heard the unmistakable sound of hoofbeats, Dewez quickly ducked behind the nearest tree, a tilted elm with thick moss growing up its north facing. He tightened his grip on the Kalashnikov. The horse was coming his way, heading down a wide, leaf-strewn path. When he felt the time was right, Dewez bolted clear of the tree and swung the rifle up into firing position. Instead of firing, though, he let loose with a volley of profanity, realizing there was no one in the saddle. The horse reared momentarily, then charged off in the other direction. Dewez made a fist and buried his knuckles in the elm's moss, cursing some more. When he heard another sound of thrashing in the brush, he looked and saw one of the recruits straggling through a clump of briers. In his frustration, it was all Dewez could do to keep from emptying a cartridge into the other man.

Using the branches, Jack tried to pull himself up onto his feet, but with no sensation in his legs it was a hopeless venture. He tossed the tree limbs aside and slumped into the grass.

"You can crawl," Jane suggested, still crouched beside him.

He shook his head angrily. "I'd only slow you down."

"Jack . . ."

"Listen," he told her firmly, "your best chance is to leave me and try to make it to the highway on your own. If you can reach help, you'll know where to find me."

"I won't leave you!" she whispered back at him.

"Why not?" he demanded. "I was the one who left you to come here, remember?"

"Let's not get into that."

"If you had listened to me, you wouldn't be stuck with me here," Jack told her.

"This is where I want to be, damn you!" she retorted. "Now shut up before you —"

Jack raised a hand to her mouth, closing her lips as he looked off toward the woods. She heard it, too. Someone entering the clearing again, looking their way. She saw his rifle first, his face second. She knew who he was and ducked low once more, mouthing Hal Dewez's name to Jack.

Dewez waded into the meadow, eyes on the wake of bent grass and goldenrod left by the horse. An easy trail to follow. He bent slightly, lowering himself to the same height as the surrounding grass. Wading forward, he stopped once, veering to pick up a revolver tangled in the weeds. He looked the weapon over, smiled at its familiarity before proceeding, clutching the gun in his left hand.

Fifty yards away he came upon Jack Demarrest, lying at an odd angle on the grass, apparently unconscious

Dewez took another step forward, jostled Jack's leg with his toe, aimed his rifle at the agent's head.

Startled by a blur of motion off to his right, Dewez turned and saw Jane running away from him, arms held high at her sides so they wouldn't catch in the grass and slow her down.

"Stop!" Dewez shouted, taking aim at her.

Jack twisted abruptly in the grass, lashing out forcefully with one of the tree limbs. He caught Dewez behind the knees, knocked him down, and fell on him, ignoring his deadened legs and fighting for control of the gun Dewez had managed to keep hold of. Half paralyzed, Jack was at a clear disadvantage and Dewez was about to overpower him when Jane stole up behind him, snatching up the fallen rifle and swinging the barrel sharply against the back of Dewez's skull. The man squeezed off a shot into the dirt before dropping his gun and keeling over onto his back, no longer in the fight. Jack made sure his foe was unconscious, then took the gun and smiled up at Jane.

"Nice teamwork, lady."

"Thanks."

The celebration was short-lived, however. Within moments, a Jeep rolled out from the woods and idled in the clearing. Morrison was behind the wheel. One of his ranch hands was standing up in back with a shotgun in his hands. He spotted Jack and Jane, pointed them out to Morrison. Morrison leaned on the Jeep's horn, drawing the attention of the recruits, who found their way to the meadow, approaching it from several different directions. When the two horsemen from the ranch rode into the clearing as well, Jack and Jane saw that they were vastly outnumbered and surrounded.

"Well, it was a nice try," Jack muttered, using Jane for support as he sat up. She squatted down beside him.

"The way I see it, we can either go peacefully and let them kill us, or we can take a few of them with us. Either way, this is it."

Jack and Jane looked at each other, shutting out the world around them for the moment it took them to clasp each other's hands. Jack leaned his head forward, kissed Jane's fingers.

"I love you, Jack," she told him.

They set down their weapons and drew closer together, bracing against the inevitable. It sounded as if the Jeep was coming toward them, but when they looked they saw that the vehicle hadn't moved. The sound persisted, grew louder. Jack and Jane glanced up.

First one, then a second and third helicopter swept into view above the treeline and began circling around the meadow. There were stenciled stars on the sides of the choppers, along with large black letters proclaiming the capacity in which they served. A man in one of the aircraft leaned near his doorway, shouting a command through a bullhorn that could be heard above the combined drone of rotors.

"This is the Highway Patrol! Put down your weapons!"

"I don't believe it!" Jane exclaimed, putting a hand to her brow to block the sun while she took a closer look, seeing police sharpshooters crouched near openings in all three copters.

"Put down your weapons!" the voice from on high repeated.

The recruits, not sure what was happening, decided to play it safe and lowered their rifles, let them drop into the grass. The two horsemen did the same. Overhead, the choppers slowly descended, turning the meadow into a turbulent sea of swaying grass and goldenrod.

Jake Morrison wasn't prepared to surrender. He grabbed the shotgun from his underling and fired a blast at the closest helicopter, ripping out a section of the craft's siding, forcing it to dip wildly before the pilot brought it back under control. Shifting into reverse, Morrison accelerated the Jeep, trying to back into the protection of the woods. One of the other copters swooped across the meadow, getting close enough for the sharpshooter inside to fire three quick shots. The Jeep's windshield shattered and Morrison pitched to one side, losing control of the vehicle, which crashed to a jarring halt into an elm tree at the forest's edge. Morrison's flunky limped clear of the wreckage, hands in the air. Morrison lay dead across the front seat.

Huddled together in the midst of the commotion, Jack and Jane watched the choppers land, then turned their gazes back to each other. Neither of them spoke. There was nothing to say.

Epilogue

"Hoummari told us their location," McTeague explained. "She had a score to settle with them, thank God."

"It couldn't have gone down much closer to the wire," Jack agreed.

They were in a private room at Bismarck General Hospital. Jack was sitting on the edge of his bed in a hospital gown, while McTeague stood before him, glancing down at his friend's legs. "Good news there, too, I understand."

Jack looked down, wriggled his toes. "Just a trauma reaction from the fall and all that abuse I put myself through," he told McTeague. "They say a couple days' rest and I'll be able to pick up where I left off."

"That's great to hear," Dan Carlisle said, having just entered the room. He joined the other two men and handed Jack a newspaper. "Here, hot off the press ... well, actually, it's the morning edition."

Jack opened up the paper, smiled at the sight of Jane's by-line on the front page, under the main story relating what had happened in Bismarck.

"Damned fine piece of writing, too," McTeague assured Jack. "She sends her love, says she'll be by after she wires in the follow-up."

Jack skimmed the first few lines of the article, grin widening by the second. He finally looked up at the others and set the paper aside, pushing off from the bed and standing weakly on his feet. He took a pair of crutches and used them for support as he took a few tentative steps across the room. McTeague and Carlisle watched him worriedly, but he told them, "Hey, I'm just practicing, okay? Have to get myself in shape for a walk down the aisle, you know ..."

BESTSELLING SELF-HELP TITLES

from

PaperJacks

_____ **THE FOOD SENSITIVITY DIET** — Doug A. Kaufmann with Racquel Skolnik 7701-04711/$3.95
How to eat for your health.

_____ **THE FORGOTTEN CHILDREN** — R. Margaret Cork
7701-03650/$3.50
Provides insight and understanding of the effects of alcoholism on the youngest members of the family.

_____ **MIND TRICKS FOR PARENTS** — Helene Hoffman with Janet Rosenstock 7701-02271/$2.95
Useful ideas for enjoying and coping with your children.

_____ **READIOACTIVE: HOW TO GET KIDS READING FOR PLEASURE** — Joe Meagher 7701-03693/$3.95
A guide for Parents and Teachers.

Prices subject to change without notice

📭 BOOKS BY MAIL

320 Steelcase Rd. E.	210 5th Ave., 7th Floor
Markham, Ont., L3R 2M1	New York, N.Y. 10010

Please send me the books I have checked above. I am enclosing a total of $_____ (Please add 1.00 for one book and 50 cents for each additional book.) My cheque or money order is enclosed. (No cash or C.O.D.'s please.)

Name _____

Address _____ Apt. _____

City _____

Prov./State _____ P.C./Zip _____

(SH/3)

FREE!!
BOOKS BY MAIL
CATALOGUE

BOOKS BY MAIL will share with you our current bestselling books as well as hard to find specialty titles in areas that will match your interests. You will be updated on what's new in books at no cost to you. Just fill in the coupon below and discover the convenience of having books delivered to your home.

PLEASE ADD $1.00 TO COVER THE COST OF POSTAGE & HANDLING.

- -

BOOKS BY MAIL

320 Steelcase Road E.,
Markham, Ontario L3R 2M1

210 5th Ave., 7th Floor
New York, N.Y., 10010

Please send Books By Mail catalogue to:

Name _____
(please print)

Address _____

City _____

Prov./State _____ P.C./Zip _____

(BBM1)

WAYNE D. OVERHOLSER

WESTERNS

JOHN BALL
AUTHOR OF **IN THE HEAT OF THE NIGHT** INTRODUCING, **POLICE CHIEF JACK TALLON** IN THESE EXCITING, FAST-PACED MYSTERIES.